TRIAL AND RETRIBUTION

LYNDA LA PLANTE was born in Liverpool in 1946. She trained for the stage at RADA, and her work with the National Theatre and RSC led to a career as a television actress. She turned to writing – and made her breakthrough with the phenomenally successful TV series *Widows*. Her five subsequent novels, *The Legacy*, *Bella Mafia*, *Entwined*, *Cold Shoulder*, and *Cold Blood*, were all international bestsellers and her original script for the much acclaimed *Prime Suspect* won a BAFTA award, British Broadcasting award, Royal Television Society Writers award and the 1993 Edgar Allan Poe Writers award. Lynda La Plante also received the Contribution to the Media award by Women in Film, a BAFTA award and Emmy for the drama serial *Prime Suspect 3*, and most recently she has been made an honorary fellow of the British Film Institute. She is currently writing a sequel to *Cold Blood*, and with her production company is developing film and television work in Britain and America.

LYNDA LA PLANTE

TRIAL &
RETRIBUTION

PAN BOOKS

First published 1997 by Pan Books
an imprint of Macmillan Publishers Ltd
25 Eccleston Place, London SW1W 9NF
and Basingstoke

Associated companies throughout the world

ISBN 0 330 35297 0

1 3 5 7 9 8 6 4 2

A CIP catalogue record for this book is available from
the British Library.

Typeset by SetSystems Ltd, Saffron Walden, Essex
Printed and bound in Great Britain by
Mackays of Chatham plc, Chatham, Kent

This book is dedicated to Norman Black and all the members of the organization Support After Murder & Manslaughter (SAMM), who work so tirelessly to support those bereaved by violent crime. In sharing their experiences, knowledge and sometimes humour, they help others to survive their tragic loss.

ACKNOWLEDGEMENTS

I WOULD like to sincerely thank the following for all their generosity and assistance:

Jackie Malton, David Martin-Sperry, Jeffrey McCann, Liz Justice, Dr Roger Berrett, Dr Liz Wilson and Detective Sergeant Ron Turnbull at the Forensic Science Service, Dr Iain West and Dr Ian Hill at Guy's Hospital, Bob Greenwell at Fulham Mortuary, Manuel Pereira, Chris Rank and Deline Richards at Westminster Mortuary, Detective Superintendent Richard Bell, Detective Sergeant Geoff Sinnott, Detective Constable Rod Austin, Detective Sergeant Andy James, Inspectors Douglas and Skinner at Kilburn ID Suite, Sergeant Adrian Elgstrand, and Inspector Stan Tullett from TSG, Marc Berners at Essex Police, Peter Kemp of Westminster Health Authority, Mike Cobb from the Metropolitan Police Press Office, Jo Scarratt, Dr Prance at the Forensic Science Service in Huntingdon.

There isn't an actor in *Trial and Retribution* who didn't give a performance of the highest quality. Special thanks must go to David Hayman, Kate Buffery, Helen McCrory, Anastasia Hille, Rhys Ifans, Lee Ross, Colin Welland and Corin Redgrave.

The talented cast and crew were led by a wonderful director, and friend, Aisling Walsh, supported by the peerless skills of executive producer Steve Lanning. I thank all the cast and crew equally for their dedication and hard work. Thanks to Howard Baker and the editing staff Terry Warwick, Rosie Dowson, Adrian Bleasdale, and Nigel Parkin at YTV in Leeds, Howard Lanning and all the post-production team. To Clare Forbes, Susie Tullett, and Georgina Weatherill and all at JAC.

Sincere thanks to Vaughan Kinghan for all her hard work and her awesome legal mind.

To Nick Elliott, Jenny Reeks and Marcus Plantin at the ITV Network Centre for making it all possible. Keith Richardson at Yorkshire Television.

Thanks to my literary agent Gill Coleridge, and to Ian Chapman, Suzanne Baboneau and Philippa McEwan at Macmillan.

Many thanks to Sue Rodgers and Duncan Heath at ICM, my agents and friends.

To my own team for all their hard work, Liz Thorburn, associate producer, Alice Asquith, researcher, Ciara McIlvenny and Lucy Richer, script editors.

I would like to give my sincere thanks to the talented writer Robin Blake for his care and skill in adapting the film of *Trial and Retribution*.

CHAPTER 1

I T HAD rained in the night, just as the television said it would, and water lay around in pools and puddles, making the asphalt of the estate's roads, walkways and playground shine. It was the only time the place looked halfway clean, just after a shower. Even better when the sun was out – nothing like a few rays on the wet ground to give a bit of sparkle. But even on a cloudy day, like today, the view from the sixth floor looked better in the eyes of Enid Marsh. The weeks of the summer heatwave, trapped in her flat, had seemed endless.

'Flat? Prison cell more like,' she muttered to herself, wiping the kitchen surfaces down.

Had she wiped them already? Couldn't remember. Anyway, soon Mrs Wald would be here with her meals on wheels. Got to lay the table.

She shuffled painfully into the lounge and stood for a moment in the middle of the room. The television murmured in its corner – something about a by-election. Her eyes slid past the screen on which a reporter was talking earnestly in front of a polling booth. Politics. Life's too short – and that's one thing the politicians will never tell you.

Enid blanked out the reporter's voice and looked

1

towards the window. The plate glass was rattling as a plane circled somewhere near. Noisy beggars. More and more, she noticed everything: planes, police sirens, heat and cold, close air, buzzing bluebottles in her room. There was nothing much to keep her mind off all that annoying background noise. Most people go through life hardly thinking about them, but Enid heard every crying child and barking dog, every thump the woman next door got from her chap and every swearword that they hurled at each other.

Enid was not a profane person. But she'd lived through the war, been bombed out, helped dig out her own dead sister from under the rubble even. You used to hear plenty of language and rough stuff then, just like you did living here. Had to take it in your stride.

She grasped at her zimmer frame. Stride! That was good.

An ambulance siren wailed. One day that would be for her. What was hard was not being able to put the noises into the background and forget them. It was like a pain you couldn't put away from you, a nagging tooth, or this beggar the arthritis. A little bit of deafness would be a mercy, she sometimes thought.

It was all on account of the arthritis. She could hardly move some days. It was a life sentence – her and the walking frame. Next time they took her out it would be in a stretcher or a box . . .

She clicked her tongue to snap out of this. It had rained now, and you had to be thankful for half a cup of anything. The damp wasn't much good for her joints, but pleasure's got to be paid for.

'Ryan! Ryan! Come on, it's half-past twelve! Ryan!'

The voice rose from the playground down below.

There'd be the usual gang of little ones down there now and a few mums having a gossip. There usually was, dinnertime.

Enid started to move towards the wide plate-glass window, her slippered feet never out of contact with the carpet. Like someone learning to skate, she always thought. She arrived at the door of her balcony, hobbled outside and leaned over her parapet. She could see half the playground from here, surrounded by its cage of wire mesh. A couple of eight-year-olds were on the round-about, pushing it on the run then skipping on and off it, squealing at the danger they could create for themselves. A slightly younger boy was taking penalty kicks with a stone against the concrete wall. If he should kick too high and a bit to the left he'd smash the glass in that stairway door.

And who would care? His mum, standing with a small group of women on the far side of the playground, certainly wouldn't and Enid could understand why. Half the doors and windows in sight were boarded with plywood and most of the rest had been splintered and starred by flying missiles. Enid had seen the TV newsfilm from Sarajevo during the fighting there. This place didn't look that much different, not to her. And they wouldn't be fixing any of it. The whole lot was coming down, so they told her.

'*Julie! Don't you go in that puddle, you hear me?*'

That would be the mother of the little blonde-haired one in the red anorak, calling down from her balcony. Four months gone with her fourth. They lived below Enid. What a pet she was, that Julie, not like her brother on the roundabout. He was a holy terror but she was a proper little angel. Goldilocks, Enid called her in her

3

mind. There she was, standing on the edge of a great lake of a puddle that had collected around a blocked-up drain, splashing the water with a stick.

'*Jason! Watch your sister! You got ten minutes ... did you hear me? Ten minutes and it's dinner.*'

Enid kept her eyes on little Julie, watching how the ripples she was making in the black and silver puddle twisted the scarlet reflection of her jacket this way and that. She leaned out and looked until she got tired. Then she began the long trek back inside. Where *was* Mrs Wald? Hardly ever late, that woman. Set your watch by her as a rule. And what was that TV programme last night? Enid had been dying to tell Mrs Wald about that. She knew she'd be interested. Oh yes, the cookery thing where you had to make a meal in fifteen minutes. Must get Mrs Wald to stay for a cuppa so she could tell her. Enid prided herself on her memory. Unlike a lot of pensioners she'd known, she was as sharp as a hatpin when it came to remembering certain things.

'Roll on next week and the start of term, that's all I'm waiting for,' said Anita Harris to her boyfriend Peter who was stretched out, legs splayed, under the kitchen sink. 'Those war toys of Jason's are all over his bedroom and I specially told him to tidy them away before he went out. Sometimes I could cheerfully kill that boy.'

'And he's *your* flesh and blood. Just think what *I'd* like to do to him. He needs unblocking, that kid, like this bleedin' pipe. Got a bucket?'

Peter was struggling with a heavy wrench, tugging the locking nut on the S-bend section. Anita looked down at him from the kitchen table, where she was mashing potatoes, pumping the masher down strongly into the pan of spuds. She straightened up and sighed.

'If only he was like Julie.'

'He's a boy, 'Nita! Can't be like Julie.'

'No, I mean, if only he was good – well, better anyway. How are you doing? I want to use that sink soon.'

'Don't know. Reckon I'm going to have to unscrew the whole S-bend. Because I've tightened everything up and it's still leaking.'

He raised his head to see where the copious leak was coming from. A drip of greasy water splashed into his eye.

'Shit!'

Anita laughed. 'I told you. You want to ask whatsit – you know, from the newsagent. Got his card in the window. Plumber.'

She stepped over Peter to get to the cooker, where a pound of sausages whispered and spat on the gas. By the window near the cooker little Tony sat in his high chair. He'd got a teaspoon and was busy cramming it between his toothless gums, most of his hand following it. Anita prised his mouth open and extracted the spoon.

'Tony, don't eat this.'

She picked up a plastic toy of Jason's, some kind of caterpillar-wheel space buggy which had somehow got on to Tony's table. Inside was a plastic helmeted khaki figure with a backpack and automatic weapon raised in the firing position. She never looked at one of these things without thinking of Jason's dad. Not to mention the entire bloody British army.

'I wouldn't trust 'em,' called Peter, his voice muffled.

'Who?'

'Those cards in the newsagents. They're cowboys.'

'You should try putting one in there yourself then.'

5

Peter craned his head out. He was laughing. 'Har-har. bitch.'

'Can you get the kids up for me? It's dinner.'

'Yeah, in a minute. I can't do everything at once.'

As she stepped back across his recumbent body, Peter's hand shot out and up Anita's miniskirt, his finger and thumb cowbiting the inside of her thigh. Anita laughed and flipped on the cold-water tap. The sound of water splattering over Peter's head and shoulders was covered by his howl of surprise.

'I'm sorry, Pete. Did you say you wanted a bucket?'

Peter slid out, flicking the waterdrops from his hair and eyes. 'Bit bloody late for that. Look at the state of me.' He clutched at Anita, mock-biting her neck and she melted into him for a proper kiss. He let her go and turned to the child.

'Here, Tony! What you laughing at? Want a tickle from your dad?'

Tony threw his head back and gurgled in ecstasy as Peter's hands found his ribcage.

Despite laying just for one, Enid took more than ten minutes to arrange the table for dinner. It may be only a meal on wheels but she insisted on everything being properly served, with the appropriate tableware neatly set out beforehand. It was hard to do it and manipulate the Zimmer but at last she had it laid out entirely to her satisfaction.

But *where* was Mrs Wald? She moved painfully back to the balcony. No sign of Mrs Wald's white van. The parents had gone in to cook lunch in those microwave ovens they all had now.

She looked around. There was nobody, except – yes, little Goldilocks, backing into view from the other half of the playground. Shouldn't she be in for her lunch? Enid saw her throw back her head, laughing. Then the child lifted her hands to her face. With fingers interlaced she covered her eyes and peeked through them. *Peek-a-boo*. Who was with her? Must be playing with brother Jason.

Beyond the play area, a white van rolled into sight, negotiating the estate's speedbumps with care. And about time, thought Enid. I was starting to get hungry. She gathered herself to turn – turning was one of the most difficult manoeuvres for her – but as she did so she saw Goldilocks drop her hands. Another hand came out from the dead ground that was blocked from her view by the side of the building. This hand took one of the child's hands. It was an adult's hand, attached to an adult's arm, and its owner was leaning down. He was wearing an adult's long dark coat. And just before Enid started back inside she saw Julie's companion straighten up and begin to walk away, skirting the roundabout and the playtrain. The little girl went too, trotting contentedly along with him.

Going to get their lunch too, thought Enid. Hungry, like me.

Carrying her meal trays stacked, Mrs Wald pressed the circular stainless steel lift-call button and waited. A remote sound of clanking and whirring came down the lift shaft but the door did not slide open. She had five clients in this tower. Two of them were robust enough old folk, able to get down to the pub or the day centre. But she worried about Mrs Marsh – housebound, abandoned by her family, hardly ever saw anyone except the meals on wheels service.

The trays had begun to feel heavy as she waited. To distract herself she read the bold marker pen inscription on the steel door: SKANK CITY FC: TICKET-HOLDERS ONLY. She did not understand what it meant. Again she pressed the button, on which the same pen had drawn an A in a circle. She sighed when there was still no response. She would have to take the stairs.

She swivelled and then stared in surprise as a man plunged down the flight of concrete stairs she was about to climb – a youngish fellow, late twenties, shoulder-length hair and wearing a long dark coat. No doubt a perfectly nice-looking young chap, except that his dirty, greasy long hair practically hid his face. Bet it didn't get washed more than once a fortnight, if it was lucky. As is the way with chance encounters in the hallways of London's more desolate council tower blocks, their eyes didn't meet and no words were exchanged. The man simply hurried past, crashing through the swing doors that led to the outside.

When at last she reached Enid's, her final call in this block, it was almost half-past one, by which time the poor thing's meal must be practically cold.

'I'm late, love, I know. Sorry. But I can't stop.'

Enid was standing there expectantly, with a small metal teapot in her hand. Mrs Wald swept past her and into the kitchen.

'Better just pop this in the oven, warm it through, eh? Give it ten or fifteen minutes before you take it out. Don't burn yourself. Oh dear, I've been late all round today. It's way after one now – in fact it's . . . What is it?' She looked at her watch, squinting and tilting her glasses to focus on the impractically small watchface. 'Dear, dear, it's one-thirty.'

Enid hovered anxiously, gripping her tea pot, attending to Mrs Wald with all the concentration of a coarse-fisherman watching her float.

'Got to be getting along, love,' said Mrs Wald, briskly returning to the flat's front door. 'Have a cuppa tea tomorrow, shall we? OK? Don't you worry, let myself out! Enjoy your dinner. Tarra!'

The door's clunk as she shut it behind her had a very precise finality about it. Enid stood looking at it for a moment, then zimmered over and lifted the safety chain back into its groove, running it along to the end with a suddenly impatient flick of her arthritic fingers.

In her van, Mrs Wald depressed the clutch and turned the ignition key. The engine clicked and then gave a whirr followed by a dry *whumph*. Nothing more. She did it again, with the same result.

She clicked her tongue, pulled out the choke, pumped the accelerator and the clutch pedals and even, in her frustration, heaved herself backwards and forwards in her seat, rocking the vehicle on its springs. Nothing.

Mrs Wald looked around for someone to ask. She could see no one except an ice-cream van away over by the road. She remembered about flooding the carburettor and, though she had no idea what it meant, she knew you had to wait once it had happened. A man in a long dark coat – he looked like the fellow she'd seen on the stairs – was chatting with the ice-cream man. Then a boy came running up to stand jiggling next to the long-coated man, his face turned up imploringly. He appeared to get short shrift and by the time Mrs Wald turned back to her ignition to try it once more he had peeled off and was pelting towards her, his arms flapping.

Her engine hawked and spat into life at last, just as the boy, whose name (though she didn't know it) was Jason Harris, careered past her towards the tower-block entrance. She could see him in the rear-view mirror, through the puffs of smoke rising from her exhaust.

Jason was hungry now. As he took the stairs two at a time he knew his mum would nag him. And she did.

'I said ten minutes, not an hour and a half.'

She had rewarmed the sausages and mash. Now she put it down in front of him with an impatient flourish.

'And where's Julie? She with Peter?'

'Gone to get a plumber, he says.' Jason looked at his plate dubiously. 'Why can't we have chips?'

'Because we've got mash. Did he say how long he'd be? I wish he'd waited till after his dinner.'

Jason answered with an exaggerated shrug, picked up his fork and harpooned a sausage. What did it have to do with him, anyway?

Still having her appetite, which no one could deny, Enid finished the pudding to the last crumb of apple pie and smear of custard. Out of nowhere, it occurred to her that the chink and scrape of this spoon in this bowl made exactly the same sound as spoons had made on pudding bowls when she was a baby and just learning how to hold a spoon. Funny how the world can be so different from what it used to be – more like another planet, if truth be told – and at the same time stay just the same. You can be watching a programme about microchips and there'd be some sound from outside, didn't matter what, and inside your head you'd go straight back to the days of trams and stays and ocean liners and the Crazy Gang.

It was not much use, knowing that the past never truly went away. But it *was* comforting anyhow.

'Julie! Julie!'

There it was, that voice again, outside on the estate, calling and calling. Enid looked up, tuning in to it. It was a woman's voice. First it had come from below in the playground, but now it was further away, almost distant, carried faintly on the blustering wind that had got up since morning. She remembered her own mum calling her in for her milk and a biscuit.

'Enid! Enid!'

The rattling plastic washing line on Enid's balcony half masked the voice of Julie's mother as she went on calling. Where had that little Goldilocks got to now? Enid chuckled. Hope she's not in trouble with the three bears again.

'Julie! Joo-oolie!'

Enid reached for the TV guide and carefully turned to today's page. *Call My Bluff* was on at two. She looked at her mantel clock, which showed ten past. Pity. She'd missed the start, but never mind, she liked that pro-gramme. She settled in her chair and switched on. There was a burst of laughter from the studio audience and, as it died away, she could still hear the mother's voice coming and going on the wind outside.

'Joo-oolie!'

*

When Peter came in without Julie, Anita simply assumed she'd gone round to her friend Hillary's. She was in a world of her own sometimes, that kid. If she thought of something she just did it and she'd been prattling on about Hillary's new kitten all morning. She'd probably gone over there to see it.

Without a phone it meant walking over. The Collins didn't live in the tower, but in one of the tiny ground-floor flats at the back of the old shopping parade. So Anita took her purse and put Tony in the buggy, thinking she'd collect her daughter at the same time as picking up a few things from Ali's convenience store.

But, of course, when she got there and rang the bell, there was no one at home in the Collins place. Which was quite natural when Anita thought about it. Hillary's mum, Sam, worked, so she had her kids over in the school-holiday playcentre at the church hall during the day.

So where was Julie? For the very first time a seed of dread started to sprout inside Anita. She stood at the Collins' front door, rocking Tony in his buggy to keep him asleep, and looked up and down the curved terrace. Someone might have seen her if she did come over here.

Sam Collins's neighbour on one side was an old bloke she knew by sight. He came to the door in response to her knock wearing slippers and vest.

'What time was that, love? No, sorry, haven't seen no little girl round here, but I wouldn't have, see? Been watching racing on telly. Gone and fallen asleep, haven't I?'

The flat on the other side of the Collins was boarded up and as she walked along the terrace she found only three more places with curtains up to show they were occupied. No one had seen Julie. Anita's heart was beating – not faster exactly, but more heavily, as she suddenly had to accept the fact: it may be only temporary, it may be all over in one minute's time, but at this precise moment she didn't know where her little girl was. Every cell of her body was in revolt against this idea. What good mother couldn't account for the whereabouts of her children? And if she wasn't a good mother, what was she?

Anita turned and hurried back to the tower. Julie would certainly have come home by now. After all, it was *way* past dinnertime and she'd be starving. Had a great appetite, that little girl, when she didn't fill herself up with too many chocolate bars.

But Julie was not at home and it was nearly half-past two. Peter ran out to the shops, see if Ali or the newsagent had seen her, or the attendant in the launderette. Anita questioned Jason. Had he seen Julie with anyone else? When they were in the playground together, did she run off anywhere? And why, why, *why* didn't he keep an eye on her? Christ, he was eight years old now, she was only five. It was *his* responsibility.

Jason said nothing, just shifted from foot to foot, staring at the wall behind his mother's head. And Anita knew what a lie she had told him. It wasn't Jason's responsibility at all, never had been. She was Julie's mother. The responsibility was hers.

She went back out with Tony and the buggy and just walked around, calling Julie's name. She marched three hundred yards along the main road, then doubled back towards the water. Behind the estate was the Royal Albert Dock, a vast basin of deserted, disused water. Someone had once told her that in its heyday it had been capable of docking a ship as big as the *Titanic*. It had been fringed by great warehouses and massive cranes until a few years ago. Now most of the land around the dock had been levelled and was strewn with all the rubble of demolition: broken bricks, shattered concrete piles, haystacks of rusty girders. The waste ground was relieved by the odd building site – the next phase of London's dockland development was due to occur here one day. But, judging by the desolation Anita saw all around her, it was a far-off day indeed.

She approached the edge of the dock. The wind was getting stronger and a few drops of chilly rain spattered her face. Anita scanned the gunmetal-grey water, which was beginning to rise in little peaks under the increasing breeze. She put her hands to her cheeks, scanning the surface for anything red, anything white.

'Oh, dear God,' she prayed. 'Please let her not be here.'

But there was nothing to be seen afloat on that water, just a few sticks, bottles and drink cans.

'Oh, this is such crap,' she told herself. 'Your daughter would never have come here on her own. It's too far, woman. You're imagining things.'

But there was already an edge of desperation in her voice as she pushed Tony back to the tower block, still calling Julie's name. There was a small knot of residents standing near the playground, and they'd heard that Julie was missing. Well, bad news travels quick. Karen Hyam, Ivy Green, Ron Hall and a few others were there when she went up to them. They knew Julie and her blonde curls all right. But none of them had any idea where she was now. Peter ran up as she was talking to them. He'd drawn a blank at the shops.

Exhausted, Anita agreed to go back home while Peter

went on searching. She dragged herself and Tony up to the flat. The moment she was dreading most of all was almost upon them: the moment when they would have to call in the police.

Chapter 2

SKANK CITY FC – TICKET-HOLDERS ONLY

While they waited by the lift Police Constable Simon Phelps read the inscription on the door and wondered if he should make a funny comment. But something about Detective Inspector North's way of doing things made it difficult. She was the most poised woman copper he'd come across during five years in the job. Thirty-five, not by any means a dog, unmarried but living with her boyfriend (so they gathered at the station) and, on top of that, smart as a whip. She was definitely Premier League to his Leyton Orient. Not that Phelps meant to stay Leyton Orient for ever but, even so, the Detective Inspector inhibited him. So he kept stum, allowing Pat North to take the lead. She nodded at the graffiti.

'Got your season ticket then, Simon?'

'Not yet, ma'am.'

'Don't bother. It's hard to see a player in *this* club scoring. Anyway, they'll be on borrowed time. This estate's condemned. Coming down as soon as they can find somewhere to park the people.'

Phelps looked around at the hallway. It was bare and brutal. 'Not a very nice place to lose your kid in.'

'Say that again. And have you ever been here when the bloody lifts have been working? Come on – stairs.'

They began slogging up to the third floor, where she indicated flat number nineteen. Phelps rang the bell.

Jason Harris opened the door and led them to his mother, who stood in her kitchen with two plates of sausages and mash, one in each hand. She was holding them helplessly, as if they were stuck to her and she could not dispose of them. Pat North could see the congealed white fat streaking the outside of the bangers. These meals had been cold for hours but their continued existence was a potent act of denial: the food *would* be eaten by the persons it was intended for, and then everything would be back to normal.

As Pat North did the introductions, Anita deposited the meal plates deliberately on the laminated counter. With the automatically appraising eye that she had long ago learned to use on domestic visits, Pat clocked the kitchen. It was clean and well stocked. The microwave looked fairly new and so did the toaster. Nothing was more than five years past its sell-by. Nothing was out of an Oxfam shop or the local purveyor of house-clearance junk.

'We've searched everywhere,' she said. 'Peter's still round the back, looking over the building site and I've been knocking on everyone's door.'

Her voice betrayed her. She was still in control, just. But she was close to panic, the classic patterns Pat remembered from psychology class: articulating rapidly and unevenly and with an intonation pattern in which the stresses hit unnaturally high notes. Meanwhile genuine, high-decibel hysteria was supplied by the toddler who was sitting in his highchair and beating his skull against the

17

padded headrest. His screams would have doubled for a circular saw getting to work on a tough piece of hardwood. Pat caught Phelps's eye, nodded at the two children, then glanced back into the lounge.

'Is there somewhere else we can talk, Mrs Harris?'

Anita ushered Pat from the kitchen as Phelps bent to pick up a plastic toy space-tank, which he presented to Tony. It went straight up to the child's mouth, efficiently cutting off the screams. Phelps beamed with satisfaction.

'Maybe she's just gone into someone's flat,' Anita said, following the policewoman into her lounge. 'She's ever so friendly.'

She began darting about, picking up toys and cushions and a stray pair of trainers that were strewn about. Pat North could hear Phelps in the kitchen, talking to Jason in what he hoped was the tone of a friendly uncle.

'So, Julie's your little sister, is she? Eh, come on. You're not scared of me, big lad like you?'

'No I ain't. But you give him my Bone-Breaka, you tosser!'

Anita didn't seem to hear any of this. She was pitching a handful of toys into a drawer. Pat sat down on the sofa. She had no children of her own – she could only imagine what Anita was going through.

'Why don't you tell me what happened, Mrs Harris? Just the bare facts. When did you personally last see Julie?'

'Oh, yes. All right.'

Anita stopped moving and pressed her fingertips into her closed eyes, concentrating.

'It was about twelve-thirty. She was there when I looked over the balcony. I remember calling out to her not to get her feet wet.'

'In the playground just below you mean?'

18

'Yes. She was playing by a puddle.'

'Do you know if anyone saw her after twelve-thirty?'

'I sent Peter out to get them. But he said he couldn't find them.'

'Them?'

'Yes. She was with Jason. Julie was. Their— I'd got their dinner on the table for them. I didn't know— I don't know if anyone saw them.'

The front door crashed and a moment later Peter came into the lounge, a glowering, unkempt figure in a tatty long overcoat. Anita ran to him.

'Peter! Haven't you found her?'

Peter looked sullenly at the police officer. She was plain clothes but obviously a copper. Peter didn't like the filth.

'No,' he said. 'I've been all over the estate. Nothing.'

Pat turned to the sideboard, where a large selection of carefully framed family photos were arrayed. She picked one up which was obviously of Julie.

'Mrs Harris?' she asked in a low voice. Having been in this situation a couple of times before, she knew it was the question that really scared the parents. But it had to be asked. This was a missing persons case and, at this stage, nothing more than a missing persons case.

'Mrs Harris, do you have a recent photograph of Julie we can use?'

From the squad car on her way back to Southampton Street, Pat North got on the radio to Sergeant Paul Donaldson at the station. She gave him the bare details of her interview with the Harris family and instructed him to set up an incident room and get a team together smartish.

There was no knowing how long this might take but one thing was clear: the search area was neither small nor perfectly formed.

It was typical of Skipper Donaldson's devotion to efficiency that a dozen faces were already assembled as North walked into the Incident Room at Southampton Street police station.

'Right,' she said, looking around to see who she had to work with. 'We have a missing child on the Howarth, a little girl called Julie Ann Harris, aged five. Photo's being copied now. She was last seen in the playground this morning, in full view of the tower blocks. There were other kids about but, unlike them, Julie Ann never came in for lunch. I don't need to remind you all of the possible implications, just that we want her found, and before dark. OK?'

Donaldson shouldered his way through the doors with a sheaf of stapled notes. The first page of each was a colour copy of Julie Harris's photograph. He began handing the notes round, alert to the change of atmosphere, a sudden sobering, as the officers studied the image of the gap-toothed little girl staring out of the snapshot with such beguiling natural confidence. If Julie was alive, and maybe lying injured from an accident somewhere, to find her quickly was a reasonable prospect. Even if the accident was more serious and she was dead, they should still find her. As for the other possibilities, they all knew them and nobody wanted to think about them – not until they were forced to, anyway.

North was tacking a copy of the photograph on to the board behind her when PC Bavesh Marik cleared his throat.

'We going to get any back-up for the search?'

North knew these uniformed lads were keen and

20

thorough, she had a lot of confidence in them. But she couldn't hope they were numerous enough to cover the ground without assistance. She'd already contacted the Metropolitan Police Territorial Support Group, the reserve of officers kept chiefly for public order duties. TSG could usually be relied on to provide numbers for large-scale searches in London. She might also need POLSA, the specialist search boys. They were nauseatingly gung-ho, most of them ex-military, but they tended to get into places other coppers couldn't reach.

'Yes. TSG are coming in, probably POLSA too. But in the meantime, we get things started. I want a full house to house. It's a big estate and, remember, she's only five years old. Skipper, who've you got?'

Donaldson straightened to attention to call out the names from a clipboard.

'Constables Brown, Phelps, Barridge, Henshaw, Marik and Maudsley. That's all we can spare immediately for the estate.'

'Not bad for a start. And who's doing family liaison?' North looked round. A pleasant-faced, neatly dressed woman of about thirty made a signal with her hand.

'Me. Er, PC Meg Richards.'

North pointed with her handful of notes at Richards.

'Good, I want you to get over to the Howarth Estate straight away. The mother's Anita Harris, aged thirty-four. She's pregnant, by the way – four months gone, she tells me. And there's a toddler, two years old and a boy, Jason, nine.'

Donaldson was frowning over his papers. 'Who's this Peter James?'

'Live-in boyfriend,' said North. 'Aged twenty-seven and unemployed – then again, down there who isn't?'

'Record?'

'We're checking the computer now. I've got a few more details on Anita. She was previously married to a Thomas Harris, divorced three years ago. He's in the army reserves in Ireland.' She looked up. 'Thomas Harris is the little girl's father. We have no reason to suspect he's anywhere but in Ireland as I speak, but we're checking on that too.'

A low buzz of conversation and speculation had begun in the room. North raised her voice.

'She's been missing five hours already, so let's get going.'

The officers began to leave the incident room in twos and threes. North called Sergeant Donaldson over.

'One thing I want to do right away – check on any residents with previous.'

Donaldson gave a sardonic laugh. 'That's half the estate.'

'Specifically sex offenders.'

'That's *still* half the estate – joke . . .' He held up his palms. 'Just a joke! But that place is a nightmare.'

'Don't remind me,' said North grimly. 'I was there less than an hour ago, remember? But at this moment it's Mrs Harris's nightmare and we've got to sort it for her.'

'What d'you make of the family? Flat a tip?'

The DI shook her head. 'No, *not* a tip. Very far from it. She's houseproud. Everything's clean, place smells of furniture polish, all the surfaces are wiped, carpets hoovered, beds made. She's not a slut.'

'Got a job?'

'No, housewife. And she *likes* the Her Indoors bit. But the second thing is – there's money coming in. New appliances, lots of videos and toys, good carpets, children neatly turned out. Boyfriend looks a bit of a scruff but that's just him.'

'Where's it coming from? Chummy's on the dole.'

North shrugged. 'Needn't be more sinister than he's moonlighting. Plus her ex is in the army. He's probably generous with maintenance. It all adds up, and she's careful, no question. But there *is* one thing about that family which doesn't quite fit the Bisto commercial.'

'Oh?'

She strolled across towards the picture of Julie Harris, Blu-Tacked to the laminated board. 'It's the older kid, Jason. He's a tearaway, yeah?'

'What is he, eight?'

'Nine. And the point is, I saw his arms.'

'You saw his arms? Christ, Pat, not needle marks?'

North turned and grimaced at Donaldson. 'No, you berk, *bruises*. And, in my professional opinion, somebody's beating those kids up.'

CHAPTER 3

THE HOWARTH ESTATE was built in the 1960s on the wave of the nation's desire to be shot of old terraced slums and get as fast as possible into modern tower blocks.

The Howarth had two such towers, each of twenty storeys. They were made from prefabricated concrete sections bolted to a Meccano-like steel structure and clad in roughcast and plate-glass framed in aluminium. Their position overlooking the children's playground was deliberate. The architect's fancy was that the towers were two parents, standing guard over their children's play. Beyond the playground was a row of lock-up garages and, alongside these, a parade of shops. The shops, too, were an important part of the original scheme. At one end the local pub had been the pride of the East End's largest brewery chain, designed to serve ploughman's lunches and chicken-in-the-basket along with the beer. The shops, too, had seemed to offer variety – a Co-op food market, fishmonger, Post Office, children's clothes shop, bakery, hardware store, launderette, hairdresser.

But the Howarth Estate represented something more even than that. In the East End of thirty-five years ago, still with brick and slate back-to-backs by the square mile,

24

this was modern and it came packaged with a vision of the new good life, free of poverty, crime and ugliness. In this urban utopia the young could raise their families and the old live on in apple-cheeked sufficiency.

But history played a cruel trick on the Howarth: the vision was shown up as a delusion. In the era of glue sniffing and junk food, of daytime TV, catalogue shopping and snuff horror, it soon fell victim to poverty and human isolation.

Meg Richards noted the signs of degradation all around as she drove with PC Phelps on to the estate. Everywhere the concrete was stained and graffiti-painted, the hallways and stairs smelled of excreta and most of the shops were gone. The Co-op, its windows boarded up, was a low-grade carpet warehouse and all that remained of the others was the heavily fortified launderette, about-to-close Post Office, dodgy betting shop, off-licence and an Indian newsagent with a sideline in video rental. At the pub, if you asked for food, they threw a bag of crisps at you. The two towers, the lock-ups, the shopping parade were all earmarked for demolition. No one could say just when, or how, it had all gone wrong.

The Detective Inspector's instructions to the Family Liaison Officer hadn't been too specific – 'Get over to the estate' – but DC Richards knew what was expected of her. This was to play the sympathetic ear but also to open a line of communication, relay any necessary information to the home and bring back to the station her own assessment of that home. Most serious crimes – assaults, murders – happen within families and it has been known for a result to be gained from the work of the FLO alone.

As she entered the Harris flat she was struck by the essential decency of the place, at such odds with the surrounding environment. Now, as Anita painstakingly poured her a cup of tea, she noted the pristine tea service, the bowl of lump sugar, the milk in a jug.

'I keep going over and over everything,' the mother was saying. 'I keep seeing her in the yard. She's no trouble, never any trouble, not really. And she's friendly, you know? Very friendly.'

She put the tea pot down and dragged a wisp of hair back behind her ear.

'But of course, she knows not to go with strangers. We've told her I don't know how many times.'

The toddler was sitting on the floor screaming and the older boy, Jason, was shouting at him, his mouth right up to his ear: '*Shutup! Shutup! Shutup!*'

Richards sipped her tea, trying to block out the noise. 'And you don't think Julie's gone to the house of a friend or neighbour?'

'I've called round to everyone she knows. Now everyone on the estate's helping look for her. They're all so kind. They *will* find her, won't they? Do *you* think they'll find her? I mean, she could just have crawled into some place, got trapped or something. She's ever so inquisitive. Bit naughty like that, really.'

'Mrs Harris, we have uniformed officers doing house-to-house inquiries right now. In no time they'll have covered every single household on the estate and if we don't find her we'll move on to the surrounding area. We also have a large search team on its way, but there's every chance we'll find her even before they turn up.'

Four floors above the Harris's PCs Brown and Barridge were knocking on the doors of two adjoining flats. Each had a copy of the electoral register but, as far as Howarth Estate was concerned, this seemed to be a largely fictional document. It was Brown who had the quicker response.

'Excuse me, Mrs—?'

'Yes? What's it about?'

'There's a missing child, Julie Ann Harris. Five years old, lives on the third floor.'

'I know her.'

'She was last seen this morning. I—'

'She was last seen by *me*. With my Ryan and some other kids playing on the roundabout.'

'When would that be, exactly?'

'Be about lunchtime.'

'Do you know the *exact* time at all?'

The woman still hadn't opened the door more than a crack. Brown could see that she had not unlatched the safety chain.

'Well, one-ish. I was getting my kids in for their lunch. That good enough for you?'

'And your name, madam?'

'Hyam. Karen Hyam. But you ask Ivy, my next-door neighbour, about that pervert – what's his name? Well, *some* people reckon he's a pervert. She's had words with him before now about him and the kids and that . . .'

But Barridge hadn't needed prompting. He was already prising the information from a mock-reluctant Mrs Green in the doorway of her flat.

'There's this bloke, see?' she was saying. 'Real alkie he is. And he's always messing about with the kids, know what I mean?'

'No. What *do* you mean?'

'I mean he gives them sweets. They go in there, watch his videos. Cartoons apparently.'

'He live locally?'

'Oh, yes.'

Barridge sighed, writing. 'Name and address?'

'Ivy Green, Flat number—'

Barridge held up his hand and coughed discreetly. 'No, I've got yours, Mrs Green. What's *his* name and address?'

'Oh! One of those ground-floor flats, down behind the shops. Howarth Parade, number twelve I think it is. Anyway, his name's Michael Dunn.'

Barridge was still scribbling in his notebook when Ivy Green touched him lightly on the forearm.

'I don't want *my* name mentioned, though. I don't actually *know* anything, know what I mean? I can't make a statement or nothing.'

Barridge nodded sagely. 'I understand, madam, but your help is much appreciated.'

On the next floor down, Brown was having one door slammed in his face whilst Barridge became Enid Marsh's second visitor of the day.

'Good evening, Mrs, er . . .?'

'Yes?'

'I am Constable Barridge, Southampton Street police. We're doing a flat-to-flat inquiry about a little girl missing from number nineteen on the third floor. Julie Ann Harris?'

Like most of the people Barridge had spoken to since he got here, Enid had opened the door with the safety chain in place. She peered anxiously at him through the crack, shaking her head. 'I don't know anybody here.'

Barridge placed a hand reassuringly on the door frame. 'But your balcony looks over the playground, doesn't it? Did you see anything at all today? About lunchtime?'

Enid froze for a moment. She was concentrating. Her memory . . . Then she shook her head, even more vigorously. 'Lunchtime? Mrs Wald was late. Late with my lunch.'

'Could I just have your name?'

'What do you want to know about me for?'

'Just to eliminate you from our inquiries . . .' He noticed the old lady stiffen, as if about to slam the door on him. 'I mean, to note down that we asked you a few questions, that's all. Are you, er . . .?' He squinted at the electoral roll. 'Are you Mrs Edith Shaw?'

'I'm Mrs Enid Marsh. I'm seventy-eight years old and I've lived here for . . .'

'Well, that's all I need, love. Thank you for your cooperation and I'm sorry to bother you. Thanks for your time.'

Brown wandered up to him. 'That's my lot for this floor. Electoral register's crap for this job. I've not got a resident off it yet. Any joy with you?'

Barridge shook his head. 'Nope. All dodging bloody council tax!'

Julie Ann Harris had now been missing for nine hours. The atmosphere in the Incident Room had grown more serious and urgent. Pat North's team were, almost imperceptibly, putting aside the innocent reasons for the child's disappearance and focusing on all the possible criminal explanations.

At nine p.m. Pat North conferred with Donaldson in the incident room.

'Are there any more addresses for uniform to check?'

'There's a few we couldn't get access to. But, by now, everyone up there knows she's missing, so those who don't cooperate can be treated as suspects.'

'I hope not formally,' warned North. 'Please, *please*, don't tell me you want warrants at this time of night.'

'No, don't worry. But telling 'em don't half scare them shitless.'

The DI and her sergeant laughed.

'Anyway, it doesn't really matter,' she said. 'For tonight we're going to assume she's outside somewhere. TSG and POLSA will be arriving on site about now. Might even have started covering the ground. It's pissing down but they're used to that.'

'Well, while we're on the subject of suspects . . .'

North snapped her fingers. 'Oh yes, *suspects*. I can't tell you how much trouble we've had over the father. He started whirling round in my head the minute we knew she hadn't popped round to watch a neighbour's videos.'

'What's been the problem? Wait a minute, don't tell me – army liaison?'

'You've got it. You wouldn't believe how cagey they are. In the end I got someone I know in the RUC to chase him up for me.'

'And?'

'Well, it seems that Thomas Harris – that is this little girl's real father – is in the clear. He's in Ireland with his regiment.'

Donaldson could tell she was disappointed. For Julie Harris to have been kidnapped by a father who loved her, however jealously, was preferable to almost all the other remaining possibilities. He said, 'About Peter James.'

'Oh yes. What you got?'

'He's on probation for – wait for it – handling stolen

bricks. Probably nicked them off that massive building site on the estate. Also he's got two previous and . . .' He paused for effect.

'Well? And what?'

'He was arrested in eighty-nine for indecent assault. Charge dropped.'

North's face tightened. She picked up her bag.

'Go and question Peter James. I'm going down to the search.'

It was Meg Richards who opened the door to Sergeant Donaldson. She had stayed in the flat answering the phone and trying to remain discreetly useful without entirely surrendering her dignity as a member of the Metropolitan Police investigating this serious disappearance. Tony had been very unsettled and she'd eventually picked him up and jiggled him about until he went to sleep. He was still slumped in her arms, his mouth jammed into her shoulder, drooling in his sleep.

'Hi, Meg,' said Donaldson. 'Peter James here?'

'Yes, just come in.'

'I got to have a word.'

'Must you?' whispered Richards. 'He's been trying to help with the search but he's knackered.'

Donaldson looked at her in surprise. 'Yes, I got to. DI North says.'

'Oh, all right. He's in the kitchen.' She stepped aside to let Donaldson move towards the kitchen.

As he did so he whispered, 'Proper little earth mother, you!'

Richards didn't react. She could hear Anita's voice from the lounge.

'Jason, what did I say? Get to *bed*!'

Before Richards could leave the hall the doorbell rang and she opened it again. A dark-haired, comfortable looking woman of about fifty stood there shaking out an umbrella. A small suitcase stood beside her.

'Yes?' enquired Richards.

'Oh, hello!' The woman's voice was hesitant, trembly as she went on. 'Are you one of the neighbours?'

'No, I'm a police officer, DC Richards, Southampton Street. Can I help?'

'Oh, I see. I'm Mrs Hughes – Helen. The little girl's gran?'

'Oh, Mrs Hughes, of course.' Richards stood to one side, swinging back the door. 'Please, come in. Let me take your case.'

Mrs Hughes ignored the hand which Meg had extended to take the case, and parked it in the small hall, propping her dripping umbrella against it.

'I came as quick as I could. Is there any news?'

'None. I'm sorry. We're still looking.'

'Yes, I saw the search party out there. Awful weather they've got, too. How's the boys? I see that one's taken to you. What about Jason?'

'He's asleep, or going to sleep anyway.'

'Those are two very different things to that boy. *Anita*? It's *me*.'

She pattered into the lounge where her daughter was standing alone and in a kind of daze. She turned slowly, her face sparking in recognition as her mother came in. Helen opened her arms and Anita walked gratefully into the hug.

'Oh, Mum. She's going to be all right, isn't she?'

The mother patted her daughter's back. 'Sssh. We've

got to stay calm and think if there's any place, or anyone, she might've gone to.'

Helen moved a step back from the embrace and held Anita by the shoulders, looking intently into her face. It was just what she used to do years before, when she sent Anita off to school. A single hair had come loose and was hanging down over Anita's face. Helen brushed it back with her fingers.

'They got a nice woman looking after Tony, anyway. And Jason – he's asleep?'

Anita made her hands into fists. 'I'd like to wring his bloody neck! It's his fault, Mum. I said to him, Jason, look out for Julie. Never listens to a word you tell him. Never.'

'You're going to make yourself ill, love. Try not to worry.' She nodded at Anita's swollen belly. 'And you don't want to start hurting the baby, now, do you?'

'But Julie, Mum . . . *She's* my baby too. Oh God, please, don't let anything have happened to her! Please!'

There was an efficient tap on the door and Meg came in with a tray. More tea. Anita swung round.

'Where's Peter? He still outside looking?'

Richards smiled and placed the tray on the low coffee table.

'No, he's here. Just talking to Sergeant Donaldson in the kitchen. Mrs Hughes – some tea?'

Helen's mouth was crumpled, a film of tears beginning to form over her eyes. She shook her head, as if she hadn't properly understood the question.

In the kitchen Peter James and Donaldson were facing each other across the small formica tabletop. The Sergeant was stirring three sugars into his mug of tea. He had his notebook open in front of him. Peter was slumped forward on his elbows. His head with its lanky unwashed hair hung down.

'I've said all this,' he mumbled. 'How many times do I have to repeat it?'

Suddenly he jerked his head up and nodded at the window. 'I should be out *there*.'

'Come on, son,' said Donaldson. 'You've been out there all afternoon. Mrs Harris is going to need you here, you know.'

'Why?' demanded the young man. He was agitating his head frantically up and down as his eyes challenged Donaldson. 'Why did you say that, that she's *going to* need me? Do you know something?'

Donaldson shook his head slowly. 'You know we don't. But there's fifty men out there searching already . . .'

'I don't understand why everybody keeps making me go over and over it.'

Donaldson used this as a cue to pick up his notebook and study it.

'Now you said there was an ice-cream van . . .'

'Yes!' Peter was being overtly aggressive now. He didn't like coppers at the best of times. 'I went up to him, asked if he'd seen Julie.' He shut his eyes and jammed the heels of his hands against the closed lids. 'That's another thing. Everybody keeps on calling her Julie Ann. It's not. Ann was her second name. We just call her Julie.'

Donaldson was still staring at the notes he had made. He cleared his throat. 'It's just that we're trying to pinpoint the last time she was seen.'

Peter shook out a cigarette from the packet which lay

in front of him. 'One o'clock. I told you . . .' He leaned back in his chair and was rummaging in his jeans pocket. 'One o'clock,' he said. 'That's . . . *how* long ago is that?'

He pulled a butane lighter from his pocket, flicked the flame and applied it to the cigarette, inhaling viciously. 'What time is it? What time is it *now*?'

Donaldson glanced at his watch. 'Just gone half ten, Peter.'

'Ten hours . . . Nine and a half *fucking hours*!'

In the living room, Helen had switched on the television. There was a comedy on BBC 1, but you couldn't watch that, so she'd switched to the national news on ITV. She sat with her daughter on the sofa and watched it through to the 'and finally' and Trevor MacDonald's goodnight. Neither woman had taken much in but there was relief in the numbness of watching that rapidly moving screen, flipping from one bland political interview about the Berringham by-election to the next, from one remote foreign conflict to another – Chechnya in flames, American presidential candidates on the stump, a football team unexpectedly losing.

During the adverts the telephone rang. It was Thomas Harris, calling from Northern Ireland. Helen took the call. She liked Tom and had never blamed him for the break-up of his marriage to her daughter. He wanted to know what the hell was going on. He wanted to know if they'd found his daughter. He wanted to speak to Anita. But when Helen looked across at Anita she saw her face white and rigid with shock as she stared at the television screen. Helen herself looked at the screen and understood why.

'Tom,' she said as calmly as she could, 'Anita can't talk right now . . . Look, I've got to go. I'll call you back as soon as something . . . Soon as I can . . . All right. Bye.'

She hung up and moved back to the sofa. The programme was the local London news bulletin *London Tonight*. The first story was Julie.

Detective Inspector North was standing on the steps of her police station. You could see the traditional blue police light above her head, artfully placed in shot by the cameraman. A knot of journalists was jostling around her.

She was saying, 'Julie Ann is wearing a green pleated skirt with a blue and red anorak and she has curly blonde shoulder-length hair. She has blue eyes. We are asking anyone who has any information at all to contact either the Incident Room at this station or any police station. The number is . . .'

Anita and her mother looked at each other. Neither spoke for a long time. Then Helen reached for the remote control unit and switched off the set.

'Mum.' Anita's voice was a whisper. 'Mum, she said *is*. Julie *is* five years old, Julie *is* wearing an anorak . . .'

Helen took Anita's hand and carefully stroked the back of it, as you might reassure a frightened cat.

'I know, love. I know she did. Got to hang on to that, right?'

CHAPTER 4

FIVE VANLOADS of TSG officers had arrived, with a catering unit and a pair of motorized telescopic masts mounted with arc lights. Their powerful beams shone down from sixty feet, making the raindrops glitter like tracer bullets. And above these, the area helicopter circled, directing its own searchlights downwards through the sousing cloudburst. Every officer on the ground had a personal radio and a constant traffic of radio signals crackled on the air.

Using the classic method whereby a large stretch of ground is meticulously combed, the area around the Howarth Estate had been subdivided into a grid and seven search parties, with seven officers in each, were formed. Togged up for the driving rain in rubber boots and Gortex jackets and equipped with powerful torches, crowbars, probes and other tools, these parties were now patiently trudging in lines across the ground allotted to them, marking the terrain section by section as they went with plastic yellow tape and a waxy yellow waterproof crayon.

Barridge was with the other locals. They'd been formed into a single search party under PC Phelps and detailed to cover one of several demolition and building sites scattered around the area. In spite of the foul weather conditions, he felt excited. He was like a kid, a Cub Scout taking part in a field game. He hadn't really thought about the purpose of the search or what would happen if and when something was found. Barridge was that kind of officer. Enthusiasm, he had it to spare, but all too often he'd throw himself into an action without looking to see where it might lead or what it meant. As far as he was concerned, policing didn't feel too different from his kiddy days in Scouts – with added fast cars screaming up and down Victoria Dock Road on a Saturday night. Like every young policeman, he loved the fast cars. He also loved the rugby, the martial arts, the swimming galas. The slow, meticulous side of the job was not high on his list of favourite things.

He was paired with PC Marik tonight. They were in a half demolished building when all of a sudden Barridge found the rubble slipping away from under his boots. For a brief moment he was sliding downwards as his footing simply disappeared beneath him.

'Jesus Christ!'

He lurched sideways and immediately his hip and elbow found solidity and he came to rest. But his legs were dangling into empty space.

'There's a bloody great hole here! I nearly fell in.'

Marik shone his torch. Half concealed by a sheet of corrugated iron was an opening in the ground. He could see steps descending below Barridge's feet.

'Some kind of cellar. You all right?'

'Yeah, I reckon.'

Barridge scrambled up and directed his own torch beam into the hole. Stone steps, damp and slippery with lichens, descended into the earth. Gingerly he probed with his feet but realized the aperture was not big enough for him. He came out and both men grasped the corrugated iron and pulled hard. At first the sheet stuck, then slid free. As they tossed it aside, a small avalanche of bricks and rubble bounced into the hole. They heard it plopping and splashing into deep water. Edging down the steps they shone their torches into the now fully revealed cellar.

'Oh, shit,' said Barridge. 'It's flooded.'

It also stank of oil mixed with organic decay. Marik played his torch over the surface of the water, liquorice-black except where a patch of petrol showed up in rainbow colours. A few items of flotsam could be seen – a plastic bottle, a shoe, a shapeless bloated mass of fur which Marik prodded with his toe. It rolled in the water and the remains of a small face turned up to them – empty eye-sockets and grinning, pinlike teeth. Marik gagged.

'Oh, God, it's a dead cat. Get me out of here.'

They hustled back up the steps and out into the clean rain, sucking in air. At this moment Henshaw appeared in the broken doorway of the house.

'Found anything?'

'Cellar, flooded. Could be something in there. We're going to need some equipment. You two stick around and I'll go and ask.'

Barridge stumbled past Henshaw and went in search of Phelps, who was with PC Brown examining the contents of a skip.

Barridge ran up to report. 'We need waterproofs. The cellars are flooded and they stink.'

Phelps had been in the job five years longer than Barridge. The kid was an innocent and Phelps enjoyed winding him up.

'First on the scene were you, Barridge?'

'Cellars? Yeah.'

'Well, finders get wet, son. That's the rule. Go back and stop wasting time.' He snorted. 'Waterproofs indeed!'

Barridge turned and started to trudge back as Brown came round from the other side of the skip.

'Hey, don't be a bastard. Oi, Barridge!'

Barridge turned and Brown pointed in the direction of the distant arc lights. 'There's a TSG van parked on the edge of the estate. They're handing out the gear.'

He saw Barridge change direction with a cheerful wave of his hand. He was a good-natured lad, you could say that for him.

Many of the Howarth residents wished to play some part in the drama that had seized their community, even if only that of idle spectators. So, despite the rain and the late hour, a number had drifted out in their parkas, macs and plastic hats. The TSG's tea van, known to the policemen as Teapot One, proved an irresistible draw and now a knot of locals were standing around chewing on free sandwiches, sipping from styrofoam cups and speculating about the outcome of the search.

Among them were Ron Hall, and the two friends, Ivy Green and Karen Hyam, from the seventh floor.

'We had a kid missing before, remember? About five years back.'

'Oh, yes,' said Karen. 'That MacKenzie girl. But that was different, she was—'

'She's been brought back four times, that one, bloody little tart.'

'Yes, but she was fourteen. This one's only five.'

Ivy was remembering her exchange with that nice-looking constable. 'First place I'd look is that wino's flat.'

'Which wino?'

'You know – on the parade! Disgusting pervert, he is.'

Karen tapped her on the sleeve. 'And you tell me how *he* gets a council house and d'you know, my sister with two kids has been on the waiting list nearly three years.'

'That's terrible,' said Ivy, clicking her tongue. 'Mind you she wouldn't want his place, it's a tip.'

'I told her, I said she should ditch her husband, then she'd get one.'

'S'cuse me, ladies!' Having obtained a sweet tea and a cheese and pickle sandwich from the counter, Sergeant Donaldson was sidling through the group of residents. He spotted Phelps a few yards away, warming his hands on a cup of tomato soup.

'You'd think that lot'd give us a hand,' muttered Phelps. 'All they're doing is cadging drinks and sandwiches.'

'That kind of help's more trouble than it's worth. Should leave it to the professionals.'

Phelps laughed. 'Not short of advice, though, are they? Uh-oh. Here comes another one.'

Ivy Green was approaching, with Karen and Ron in close attendance. She spoke loudly, as if addressing them from a soapbox.

'You checked that corner flat on Howarth Parade? If you ain't, you should. Be the first place I'd look. He's a drunk.'

Brown appeared as Donaldson bent his ear towards Ivy.

'Corner house, Mrs, er—? What number would that be?'

'Twelve, I think. Proper pervert he is in there.'

'Have we checked that one out yet, Skip?' asked Brown.

Donaldson consulted a clipboard. It was covered with a plastic sheet and the rain snapped down on it. He ran his index finger down a list of names and addresses. 'Number twelve. Name of . . . Michael Dunn.'

'That's him,' said Ivy. 'I've told my kids to stay well clear of that animal. He's always messing with them, he is.'

Donaldson glanced at Brown and then back at Ivy. He was interested.

'*Is* he now? And we *haven't* yet checked him out, so it seems.'

Barridge had picked up a rope and some chest-high waders from TSG. When he got back to the cellar, Marik and Henshaw had gone.

He found them placing yellow tape around a stack of sewage pipes to show that they'd been cleared. Henshaw had just finished shining his torch into them. The ground all around was a morass of liquid mud.

'Come on,' said Barridge. 'We have to do that cellar. I got the rope and waders but I need back-up.'

'Leave it,' said Henshaw. 'We looked didn't we? Me and Marik had another shufti after you scarpered. There was nothing.'

'There was a shoe, floating. I saw it.'

'Since when did little Julie Ann take a man's size twelves? Since her fifth birthday?'

'It could still be significant. And anyway we got to look in the water, not just on top of it.'

'Needs a diver. One of them POLSA heroes should do that.'

Barridge started walking back to the cellar. 'What's the matter with you two? Finder gets wet – that's me. All you custard creams got to do is hold my string.'

Minutes later, now wadered up and wearing a rope around his waist which Henshaw and Marik paid out above him, Barridge was again cautiously descending the cellar steps. He reached the water's edge and tested the depth with a scaled wooden pole: three foot six inches. The stairs descended another six steps below the water-line. He planted a foot on the next one down, tested it, then transferred the other foot as well. Now standing in seven inches of water, he shone his torch into the interior of the cellar. Several things back there, which had not been visible from his previous position, now appeared. They were floating, half submerged, one of them looked like a basketball, red – no, red and blue. He took another step down, craning forward to see better. There was also a pop bottle and part of what might be a chair sticking out of the stinking water.

'*Shit!*'

A gush of liquid had flowed into his boot through a gash in the rubber. It was cold and, as he knew, absolutely filthy. He tried to lift his foot clear but, full to the brim, it was unexpectedly heavy. He wobbled.

Had Marik been keeping the safety line taut Barridge might still have been saved but it lay slackly on the cellar steps. Overbalancing with a theatrical wave of his arms, and with his mouth open to yell, he pitched sideways into the flooded cellar. Briefly the water closed over him. He kicked and flapped and surfaced, ejecting the oily, brackish mouthful he'd taken in. Even before he'd found a foothold he was yelling.

'Bloody hell! Give me some light!'

His head bumped painfully into something floating on the water. It was his torch, which had gone out. He grasped it, working the switch. Dead as a kipper.

Meanwhile, somewhere above him in the dark, Marik was shouting, 'You all right?'

'Bloody get me out!'

As he thrashed around he realized Marik and Henshaw were hooting with laughter.

'Got your twenty-five yards badge, Barridge?'

'You been bitten by that dead cat or what?'

'Shut it you two! Just give me some *light*! It's freezing and I think I've swallowed some of this bastard water.'

'You'll definitely be needing a stomach-pump, then,' Henshaw managed to say between fits of laughter. They stopped laughing as they saw the terror in Barridge's face as he lost his footing again and went beneath the water. When his head burst to the surface from the stinking black water, his eyes were stark with terror.

'For fuck's sake, pull me *out*!'

Howarth Parade was where Anita Harris had looked vainly for her daughter at the Collins' place the previous afternoon. Number twelve was one of the same small ground-floor flats that had been built along the back of the parade of shops. Originally, each had had its own mini-patch of garden in front, an area now universally reduced to urban wasteground. The garden in front of Michael Dunn's address had been turned at some unspecified time into a dump for useless motorbike parts. Part of his front window was boarded up.

The flat was in total darkness. Donaldson stood back and watched Phelps hammering on the door. Brown was shining his torch in through the unboarded part of the window.

'Mr Dunn! Mr Dunn!' Phelps called, crouching to shine his torch through the letter slot. The flat remained dark and soundless. Phelps straightened up and looked back at the Skipper.

'It doesn't look as if anyone's at home.'

Donaldson shook his head. Dunn was beginning to interest him.

'That doesn't mean he's not there, does it? But there's nothing we can do if he won't open up. If he's as much of a piss artist as they say he might be sleeping it off. Now I think I'll go over to the Harris's place and see what they know about this Michael Dunn.'

The Harrises didn't know much about Michael Dunn but despite Richards's presence and Sergeant Donaldson's skilful exercise of tact, an atmosphere of untargeted hostility was building up on the third floor.

'Look,' Helen was saying, 'has this Dunn man got our Julie? Is that what you're saying?'

'No,' said Donaldson. 'I was just *asking* if Julie Anne knew him.'

Peter got up and advanced on the policeman. He pushed his face almost into Donaldson's face.

'*Julie*! Her name is *Julie*! Not Julie Anne! And I've had enough. I'm not staying in here, I'm going out. And you can't stop me.'

'No,' said Donaldson simply, 'we can't, Mr James. But it really is better for your wife that you stay here.'

But Peter had already pushed past him. In the hall he swept his coat from a hook. Anita caught her breath, as if hit by a twinge of pain.

'I want to go with him! Peter, wait, I'm coming too.'

Meg stepped forward but as she did so, caught Donaldson's eye. He gave a minute shake of the head and Meg stayed where she was as Anita half ran into the hall. They all stood still as the flat door slammed. There was a pause, followed by a hammering on the door. It was Anita.

'Just get *out* of there! All of you. Leave us alone!'

Paul Donaldson and Meg Richards exchanged another glance as the sergeant picked up his cap.

'I think,' he said quietly, moving towards the door, 'that we're going to have trouble with him.'

Barridge was in the TSG van, peeling off the wet overalls so when she looked in to ask what had happened Pat North found him sitting shivering with a towel around his waist.

'Oh! Sorry, Barridge.'

She looked to see if he was embarrassed but Barridge seemed more exhausted than anything else. So she came in.

'You all right? I hear you had a tumble.'

He nodded as her radio squawked.

'Ma'am? Some of the residents, they're talking about a Michael Dunn. You know?'

'Yes, I heard. Don't worry, he's being checked out.'

She was listening to the radio. Pat North felt tired too. This was a big operation – fifty-strong TSG party, POLSA macho-men running around on the docks in inflatable boats and wet suits, estate residents up in arms. If she screwed up she couldn't expect any sympathy from the Super.

Tactfully she turned her back, occupying herself with her radio as Barridge pulled on some trousers. The Control Van was relaying a message from the chopper about Howarth Parade. Barridge continued.

'It's just that the winos from round here – they either hole up in one of the derelict houses if it's bad weather, or there's a park and like a gent's toilet. They meet up there, just across from the Job Centre.' He pulled on a sweater. 'Anyway, as this is Thursday, they'll have got their Giros, so . . .'

'Was Thursday. It's Friday now.' She spoke into the radio. 'OK . . . On my way. Over.'

She turned back to Barridge. He was decent. She said, 'We've got a crowd forming on Howarth Parade. Better go.'

She left Barridge feeling unsatisfied. He hadn't explained his thinking at all well. What he meant to say was that, if Dunn was really a wino, they should interview a few of the other people he hung around with, and that they'd maybe have taken shelter somewhere in one of the derelict places nearby. TSG had probably turned some of them up already.

Outside number twelve Howarth Parade a small mob had been gathering for some time as a growing number of residents converged on the place. Phelps and Brown stood guard in front of the door. The mood of the residents, as soon as they had begun to connect the scruffy toe-rag

Dunn with the disappearance of the golden-haired child, had turned ugly.

Peter James stood at the front, taunting the grim-faced officers. 'Break down the sodding door! What you waiting for?'

Other shouts were directed at Dunn himself. 'Bleedin' *nonce*. Where's little Julie? What you done with her, you bastard?'

Meanwhile three or four in the middle of the crowd began to chant, '*Break* the door! Smash it *in*! Break the bastard's fucking *chin*!'

They must have been the outflow from the pub: there was a noticeable slur in their voices. Donaldson arrived to the sound of their refrain, noticing that Julie's mother was standing at the back of the pack, weeping. A neighbour – the woman he recalled who'd first mentioned Dunn's name to the police – was trying awkwardly to hug her. A few seconds later Pat North joined her sergeant and together they forced their way to where the two constables were looking increasingly nervous.

A half brick bounced off the wall of the flat. Donaldson took PC Brown's elbow and pointed to Peter James.

'That's the kid's stepfather. Get him out of here, right?'

As Brown went to tackle Peter, Pat North said to the sergeant, 'What we got on Michael Dunn? You checked his sheet?'

'Yeah. Nothing apart from persistent vagrancy.'

She glanced again at the angry residents as another brick hurtled towards the flat. 'Well . . . They're throwing bricks. So that gives us a bloody good reason to check this flat – for damage?'

Donaldson looked at his guvnor and smiled. For once a modicum of public disorder was exactly what the police required. It would mean they could effect an entry to the premises without a warrant.

'Well,' he said, 'it's been over twelve hours now so maybe . . .'

'We're looking for a body, aren't we?'

'Right!'

That added up to two possible pretexts to enter the Dunn house without a warrant. The decision was down to Pat North. She hesitated, weighing up what the Super would say. Again a brick spun through the air and clattered against the plywood screwed to Michael Dunn's window frame.

Donaldson said, gently, 'Well, guv? What do we do?'

Pat snapped her fingers. 'All right, do it. Break down the door.'

It was Phelps who sprinted to the equipment van and collected a sledgehammer. When he returned three blows against the lock sufficed to crash through the door. Pat North led Donaldson into the dark interior, with Phelps bringing up the rear. He still held the hammer, as if believing it may come in useful again.

The hall was littered with bottles, boxes, cans and dirty clothes. Broken glass crunched underfoot.

'God,' said the sergeant, 'the place stinks.'

Moving gingerly forward Pat North called into the darkness: 'Mr Dunn! Michael Dunn! This is the police. Is anybody here?'

She paused, waiting for a reply, listening for movement, snoring, a television set, anything. There was nothing. She looked to her left and right and found a lightswitch. She flipped it down. Nothing happened.

'Electric's off. We're in the dark. Phelps, go and get some torches from TSG and in the meantime lend me yours.'

With a barely suppressed sigh, PC Phelps handed her his standard-issue torch and doubled back for his second visit to the equipment vehicle. Pat North shone the torch ahead. There were four doors leading off the hall. She entered the first on the left.

The dank smell of Dunn's sitting room was enhanced by a mixture of stale beer, vinegary wine and tobacco ash. The torch picked out tattered curtains hanging drunkenly over the boarded-up windows, a broken-springed and lopsided sofa, a television set piled with video tapes, a morass of bottles, cartons and takeaway containers strewn about the filthy carpet.

'Don't touch anything!' warned Pat North as Donaldson, wading into the room, crouched to examine the video titles.

'Hmm. Local rental shop might be missing a few videos. Here we have *Die Hard 1*, *Snow White*, *Die Hard 2* and . . . hello-hello, what's these?'

He peered more closely. '*Aladdin*, *Lion King*, *My Little Pony*, *Child's Play*. *Child's Play!* – oh my God.'

Pat North kicked a Corn Flakes' packet that was lying at her feet.

'Well, we can get him on theft. I doubt he's rented all that lot. And, talking of child's play, what do you make of this?'

She was standing beside the sofa, the beam of her torch directed downwards at a blonde Barbie doll lying on the bare and greasy upholstery. She wore only her underwear and one of her arms was missing.

CHAPTER 5

ANITA GOT up at five. For most of the night she'd lain awake staring at the curtained window. Tomorrow, wash day. No orange juice in the fridge and the milk's off. Got to fit in a supermarket shop. Jason needs new shoes for school. Julie's supposed to have that eye-test the Nursery thought she needs. Better cancel. No way she'll be able to go after staying out all night. That teething gel for Tony she'd been looking for yesterday – be in that other handbag. She had it with her last time the two of them went to Mum's. Random, sluggish thoughts about anything but what happened yesterday.

There were a few lapses into sleep but these had been gashed by intense, violent fits of dreaming. She'd awoken each time hag-ridden, her heart pounding, sweat seeping from her armpits and scalp. The last dream had been of a car crash. The image was still vivid. A screeching tear of metal, a reek of scorched rubber, spattered oil, burning upholstery. And then the car – was it a car, a truck? – rolling over and plunging through a bare landscape of slag heaps towards a lake of still, black water. Bursting into consciousness, she had twisted towards Peter's side of the bed, desperate to hug him like a lifebelt. But Peter wasn't there.

51

She rolled from bed, pattered to the bathroom and sat to empty her bladder. Then, dodging the mirror, she scrubbed her teeth and filled the bath.

For half an hour she lay, listening to the bubbles snapping around her stomach rising above the foam like an island. This was the best way she knew to take her away from herself. Lying in an envelope of hot water, surrounded by steam, hissing taps, the smell of soap and laundered towels, she forgot the problems of a grown-up person and was transported back into the raw sensations of a child.

In general, her own childhood had receded to dimness after she became a mother. Wound up in the lives of her children, for their sakes acting the adult, Anita lost contact with the little girl she had once been. Occasionally she wondered if that little girl had survived anyway, inside her. If so, it was a child held hostage and hidden away. It wasn't coming out to play unless the world became a very different place.

If she was truthful with herself, Anita knew she had put away her child-self even before motherhood. She had done it quite deliberately. Leaving aside the usual things that mark the stages into adolescence – getting spots, smoking ciggies down on the allotment, the start of her periods – there was one day that she would remember as the end of childish things. The head teacher had come into her class in the middle of a lesson. He'd put on a long face especially for the occasion. He asked if Anita would please come out of the room and down to his office. Waiting there were Anita's year tutor, Mrs Morris, and the school nurse, who was hovering around in the secretary's room. The nurse being there was always a sign something dramatic had happened.

'I'm afraid I have some bad news to tell you, Anita,' said Mr Passmore at last, in his thin, precise voice. He had one hand up to his neck, nervously smoothing the wings of his spotted bow-tie. With a sound halfway between a squeak and a cough he forced some phlegm to the top of his throat.

'There is no way in which I can soften it for you, so I'm going to tell you straight out.' He had shot a nervous, uncertain glance at Mrs Morris who nodded encouragement. He continued. 'Your father's been in an accident. I'm sorry to say, he's been killed. Nobody knows yet what happened, but it appears he stepped into the path of a lorry.'

Compassion didn't come easily to Passmore. Disapproval was more in his line: how inconvenient of her father to get killed – worse, to do it in the middle of double maths. That was why he had Anita's year tutor at his elbow. Mrs Morris supplied the necessary; she did compassion brilliantly.

'We're so terribly sorry, Anita, dear. This is a tragedy, a real tragedy.'

There was a moistness about Mrs M's eyes that Anita might have found touching, except that nothing *could* touch her just then. She had just felt cold to her very bones.

Back in her bedroom Anita dressed mechanically and, coming back through the lounge, stepped out on to the balcony. A few spatters of light rain, the remnants of last night's downpour, flew around on the wind. She looked down. In the area below the tower block, the roundabout and climbing frames were deserted and silent. It was where she had last seen her daughter. Further away a few police vehicles – not so many as at the peak last night – could be seen in the dawn light. Julie had not been found, but nor had hope been abandoned. Anita had been told they'd go on searching all day.

'Hey!'

She turned. Peter stood just inside the room, still wearing his long overcoat. He had a look that Anita had never seen on his face before. It was a mixture of exhaustion and fear. Her own face must look just the same.

'Oh, Peter,' she said. 'I had such shitty dreams.'

She went to him and they hugged tightly.

He said, 'I've just come in for a coffee and a wash, then I'm going out again.'

She pulled back and took his face between her palms. 'You'll crack up, Peter. Then where will we be?'

He shook his head and there was a staring intensity in his eyes. 'I got to keep going. Don't see how I can stop at the moment.'

She shook her head and kissed him. 'No. I know.'

Pat North had hardly more sleep than Anita. At six-thirty she was back in the station belling AMIP – the Area Major Investigating Pool – to find out at what point they'd be grabbing the wheel.

Wanting to find out wasn't some chippy thing. North was aware of the score: AMIP was the murder squad. Anyway, she really could do with a hand, because already this inquiry had eaten up close to five hundred man hours and hardly seemed to have advanced since the off. They hadn't found Julie. They hadn't found anyone who'd seen her after twelve-thirty, when the group of mothers at the playground had drifted away to dish up their kids' lunches. They hadn't even managed to find a drunken piece of low-life called Michael Dunn. What was she doing wrong?

Back in the Incident Room she joined Sergeant Donaldson and PCs Brown and Phelps. The two constables had been on shift all night. They'd just come back from an early visit to the Howarth, having interviewed the newsagent as he opened up for the early trade. Yes, he remembered Peter James all right, coming in at about 1.15 the previous day looking for Julie, and then returning in the next half hour, all in a panic, to ask a second time. But, like he'd told Peter James on both occasions, the shopkeeper hadn't seen the little girl at all that day.

'So. Has anything useful come in on the phones, Skip?'

Donaldson waved a sheaf of forms – phone-messages to the incident room and faxes from other police stations around the capital. It was the sum of the general public's responses to last night's television news appeal, and they did not make Christian reading. Every one of the messages assumed that Julie Ann Harris had been abducted by a predatory paedophile. Most accepted that she was already dead. By no means all were phoning or faxing to express their sympathy.

'Just the usual sick bastards,' grunted the sergeant. 'Nothing to follow up as yet.'

'Well, I was just thinking – I've got to talk to the Press Office in a minute. So what about another TV appeal, this time by the family? Do you think they'd do it?'

''Course they will. Wouldn't you?'

North checked her watch. It was 7.10.

'I'll get Meg back up there to speak to the parents about it.'

But Donaldson was remembering Michael Dunn and the spin they'd given his flat in the middle of the night. 'Maybe she should ask them if Julie Ann had a doll with her as well, yeah?'

The DI nodded and, lowering her voice, she said for Donaldson's ears only, 'Not looking good, is it? I've contacted AMIP. They're not keen to come in on this unless and until we've got a body. So I've asked TSG to stay put and do the area all over again this morning. But we'll keep our lads after Dunn. While he's still AWOL he's got to be a suspect. Agreed?'

In the cramped Harris kitchen, Helen was feeding spoonfuls of Weetabix into her youngest grandchild's mouth while Jason drove one of his screeching battery-powered battle machines up and down the kitchen table.

'That's it, my pet, here's another one. Open wide.'

Anita came in, depositing an empty mug in the sink. 'Peter's been out all night, he's exhausted but he says he'll keep on.'

The telephone rang and Anita jumped.

'It's all right, love,' said her mother. 'Meg's here. She'll get it – probably for her anyway.'

Anita came to the table. 'Here, Mum, let me. He does it better for me. Come on, Tony, love. Open your mouth, there's a good boy. Jason! I told you – stop that!'

Jason was adding to the noise of the toy with his own

high-pitched impression of a badly shot gearbox. Anita leaned over and swatted his head.

'Oi, Mum!' Jason stood rubbing his head for a moment, then darted forward, lifted his fist and dealt a painful, knuckly blow to Anita's arm. Something inside his mother snapped.

'Don't you do that to me, you little shit!'

Anita raised her hand again, higher this time. Jason flinched, then dodged out of the kitchen. He cannoned off Meg Richards as she entered.

'You all right, Anita?' asked the policewoman.

Anita sighed and, still standing beside the high chair, shoved another spoonful of milky mush into Tony's mouth. 'Yes, yes. Sometimes he can be a real handful. Misses his dad, of course . . .' She looked at Meg a moment, questioning. 'He phoned but I haven't spoken to him . . . Jason and Julie's dad, I mean. They *will* find her, won't they?'

Meg unslung her bag and sat down at the table.

'Don't lose hope. And why don't you just sit for a minute, eh? There's something I want to ask you.'

Anita slumped in the nearest chair. 'What?'

'Do you know if Julie had any – any kind of toy with her in the playground? A doll maybe?'

Anita stared at Meg. Toys? Dolls? What was the woman talking about? As soon as she thought it she gave up the effort of working out how these coppers' minds worked. She merely shook her head. She couldn't remember, anyway.

Dressed in fresh clothes from the bedroom, Peter appeared. Meg was glad he was here. She wasn't sure Anita was concentrating hard enough to give a considered answer to her next question.

'Peter,' asked Meg gently, 'would you be prepared to do a television appeal?'

Peter looked pleased to have been asked. He didn't pause to consider it. 'Me? Yeah, 'course.'

'Inspector North spoke on the local news last night, but she feels it'd be good to do an appeal. It would be broadcast about the time of day that Julie Ann – Julie – was last seen. And it'd be good if it came from . . . from the family.'

'Fine, Meg. No problem. We'll do whatever you people want – eh, love?'

He leaned over and squeezed Anita's hand.

Arriving in a smart, recently registered hatchback, the Scotland Yard Press Officer met Pat North at the main entrance of the tower block two hours later. Her clothes were maybe a touch flashy, her weight was a pound or three over the optimum, but there was no denying the great hair, the brilliantly applied make-up and the fantastic teeth. They flashed and flashed again as regular as a lighthouse.

'Hi,' she said, pumping North's hand briskly. 'Terrible traffic. This where they live?'

'Yes. Let's go straight up. What time is the press conference?'

'Twelve, at Scotland Yard.'

'Any other press action?'

'We contacted all the radio stations and breakfast TV shows overnight and there's been coverage in their morning bulletins. Also, there'll be a photo in the early editions of the *Standard*. Sadly, it's too late for this week's local rags. What are the family like?'

North gave her the facts as they climbed the stairs.

Later, sitting around the low table in the lounge, Anita and Peter were told what they would have to do.

'It's important that we keep it very simple,' said the Press Officer. 'Your little girl is missing. This is what she looks like. Anyone who knows anything, phone this number. Here, I've written out a possible script, something for you both to say. Would you like to try it?'

She drew a sheet of A4 from a file and passed it across. Anita's face was expressionless as she read it.

An hour later they were on their way to Scotland Yard, leaving Tony and Jason in the care of their grandmother.

'I remember, I remember, the house where I was born . . .'

Midge was trying to remember the rest of the poem. Matted pepper-and-salt hair dragged down to the collar of the man's tweed jacket that she wore over a leather skirt and dirty white cotton tights. A can of Tennants Extra was clutched in one claw-like hand. The other held an unlit roll-up.

According to a now barely legible council sign which stood beside its gate, the scrawny patch of railed-in green across the road from the Job Centre had been officially designated Princess Elizabeth Park. But for as long as anyone could remember this well established haunt of schoolgirls on the game had been universally known as the Scrubbery. The bench Midge sat on was the last not to have been dismantled by unauthorized persons or set on fire.

Amateur prostitution being for hot nights in high summer, and with the weather already growing more realistic, the Scrubbery had become a game reserve for junkies, crack smokers and the local wino fraternity. They congregated here to be near the public convenience, a foul and swampy concrete facility, about as far from convenient as you could get without asphyxiation. The ambience suited them, it suited everybody, because nobody else would think of going into the Scrubbery unless it was to vandalize something or for their dogs to relieve themselves. And not even the dogs would go into the Scrubbery's toilets.

On one side of her sat old Bert and, on the other, young Terry. They too had cans of lager and were listening in a desultory way as Midge strained for the next line.

'Well?' growled Bert aggressively. 'How does it go on?'

Midge screwed up her face. 'Hang on! Hang on and I'll tell you. *I remember, I remember . . .*'

'You said that bit. You remember sod all, missus. And that's a fact. The piss has gone and taken away whatever wit you once had.'

'Do not interrupt,' said Midge in her grandest manner, taking another sip of lager and shutting her eyes. '*I remember, I remember, the house where I was born, The little something-something-something* . . . I'll get it in a mo. Y'know my Grandmama taught it us at the Big House when I was a child. S'where she lived, old dragon and s'where I was born too, matter of fact, s'why I still like that sloppy old poem. Didn' I ever mention she was a Lady and Daddy was an honourable?'

Terry groaned. 'Did you ever? You hardly ever mention anything else. Leeches on the body politic, your mob. "The rich may drink the blood of the people but they cannot sap our will." Leon fucking Trotsky said that.'

A squad car containing PCs Marik and Davies arrived at the end of the street, unseen as yet by the trio of drinkers. An observer might have said it was some sixth sense, or else simply a coincidence, but as soon as the car began nosing down towards Nightingale Park, Terry rose and slipped into the toilets.

Marik eased himself from the car and strolled over to the remaining two derelicts.

'You seen a Michael Dunn?' he said to Bert.

Bert wouldn't meet the policeman's eye. He kept his chin jammed against his chest and shook his head.

'You?' demanded Marik, addressing Midge and looking around to see if there were any others in the area. He saw no one. 'Do any of you know a Michael Dunn?'

Midge met the question with a broken-toothed grin. She raised her beer can in salute and shook her head.

In the Harris flat, the television was droning on about the cost of food or something. Jason was lying on the floor of the lounge. Behind him his gran was on the sofa with Tony in her lap. They were staring at the screen but Jason was preoccupied with a game. So he was surprised when, a few minutes later, he became aware of his mother's voice.

'Please,' she was saying, 'if anyone saw my little girl . . . if anyone knows where she is . . .'

Jason looked up, twisting around on the floor and looked towards the door. He saw no Anita so he turned back to the television and examined the screen. His mum was there. Her face was right in the middle of the picture and it was crying, real tears.

He was puzzled. He concentrated on what she was saying.

'Don't hurt her. If you know where she is, or can help in any way, please telephone. All we want is for her to come home.'

Jason rolled on to his side and curled up so he could see Helen. He thought for a moment. What was Mum talking about? And that was another thing. He hadn't seen Julie today but no one had said where she was. 'Where's Julie gone, Gran?' he asked.

At the very beginning of the day the decision had been taken to search the ground all over again, inch by inch, this time with the help of local volunteers and council workers. Men from the various construction sites had also been given leave to join the hunt. Children had taken the day off school. It was an impressive turn-out.

Patiently, and largely in silence, they moved line abreast across the ground, prodding and peering in and under everything in their way. There was little laughter, few smiles. Everyone knew that it could be a body they were looking for now, or clues as to a body's whereabouts. Inspector North had given them a mass briefing before leaving for the press conference, describing every single item of Julie's clothing. It had a sobering effect.

Barridge had hardly slept. After his ducking in the flooded cellar he'd gone home but, as soon as he'd changed, he walked out of his flat and returned to the station. While that little girl was still out there somewhere the idea of sleep was repulsive to him.

Now – still unshaven and buzzing with physical exhaustion – he was with a group of locals, trying desperately to concentrate on the task underfoot. Suddenly he stopped. A desire for all this to be over washed through him like a wave: he wanted done with it, but he could not be until they found the kid.

He scanned the ground ahead. In his path were sewage pipes, surrounded by a litter of wooden pallets and building supplies, which Barridge remembered had been taped off by Marik and Henshaw the previous night. He trudged forward, bending to pass under the yellow control tape. Then, with his first step inside the taped area, the sole of his booted foot felt something beneath it.

'Hold it!' he called, raising his arm to the others.

Barridge got down on his haunches and, using a gloved finger, hooked a little of the mud away from whatever he had sensed in the ground. Part of a black, shiny object appeared with the edge of some metal attachment also visible. Carefully, he removed another small bit of mud. It clung to his finger and he shook it off. The metal was stainless steel: a buckle. And next to it was the unmistakable rim of the upper of a small shoe. A child's shoe.

Barridge's heart lurched. Reflexively he reached for the shoe but, just in time, remembered not to pick it up. Instead he called out.

'What shoes was she wearing?'

Someone said, 'Black and shiny, wasn't it?'

Another added, 'With a T-strap.'

Barridge carefully gouged out some more mud until he could see the shoe clearly. He shut his eyes and opened them again.

'Well, I've just found one. A black patent leather-type shoe with a T-strap. Looks like a little girl's.'

The volunteers began to cluster round. One or two of them yelled and waved, bringing some officers over at the double. Barridge sat back on his heels and looked around. The shoe was about six yards from the sewage pipes, he tonly nearby place of concealment. But they'd been checked . . .

Then he saw what Marik and Henshaw had missed in the night. These pipes were laid horizontally but two did not lie flush and, in the gap between, recessed so that it would not easily be noticed, lay another pipe of smaller diameter.

He strode over, bending to take a closer look. Something was blocking the smaller pipe. He thought he saw something in there, or was he imagining it? A couple of officers who had followed him to the pipes came nearer.

'I'll do it. I can squeeze through!' shouted Barridge.

Barridge stripped off his Gortex jacket. You couldn't get through by standing upright so, on hands and knees, he began crawling between the pipes, a space no more than two feet wide. Barridge was not a fat man, but he was solidly built and a thinner individual would have done the job better, no doubt. But Barridge was not going to cede this job to anybody. Grunting with effort he forced his body into the dark tunnel, gripping his torch with his right hand, making progress by levering his weight forward with his arms. The points of his elbows glanced off broken bricks and lumps of jagged rubble but he didn't notice.

He reached the small, concealed pipe and shone his torch. 'Jesus!'

'Barridge. See anything? Anything there?'

'Move the pipe, the big pipe. I'll need to get round to the other end.'

The pipe to his right began to roll away so that he could crawl past it. As he did so the face of a TSG sergeant appeared in his line of sight. 'Anything in there, son?'

Barridge paused and looked at the older man. He blinked, then nodded his head. So far he had not seen much – pink skin and a scrap of white cotton. But it was enough.

It was not until he had reached the far end of the pipe and looked inside that it suddenly became real for him. He saw a foot with a white sock, another wearing a black, shiny shoe. Between them rested two hands reaching in front of her. Beyond these in the gloom he could see a tangle of golden hair round about where the knees must be. He froze. He looked but couldn't move. The child was bent double inside a pipe little more than a foot in diameter. One of her hands was stretched out and Barridge could have sworn he saw it twitch.

'Oh, God . . .' he whispered. It was not an exclamation but a prayer.

He tore off his gloves and leaned into the pipe as far as he could to grasp the hands. They were icy cold. Barridge pulled but she was wedged too tight. Afraid to tug hard on the frail wrists, he grasped an ankle, pulling harder. The blood rose to his neck and face with the effort which, as much as anything, came from trying *not* to pull too hard in his desperation to get her out of there.

She moved at first by fractions of an inch and then, as he continued the steady pressure, by inches. She had been three feet into the pipe and he had already dragged her a foot nearer to the open air when some hindrance was suddenly released and she slid forward smoothly, easily and alarmingly. Barridge fell back as the small body, naked but for a pair of cotton pants, fell out of the pipe and flopped on top of him.

Other officers leapt to help, to take the body. But

Barridge was already struggling to his feet, holding on grimly.

'It's all *right*!' he was shouting, cradling the child. 'I've got her. And she's all right. She's alive. She's *alive*!'

The other officers knew otherwise. The child's head dangled from her shoulders like a broken flower. They made a close ring around Barridge, which is instinctive behaviour by police officers. It comes not just from a desire to shield members of the public from the sight of death, but from an almost unconscious sense that this moment – the pivotal moment in any police inquiry, the discovery of a body – was one that belonged to them all. And a body so tiny affected every man deeply. It was something they would never forget.

Barridge had taken one of the hands and was rubbing the back of it against his cheek. He was staring into space, seeing again in his mind the image of that hand as it had reached towards him from the depth of the pipe. He saw that slight pudginess which is in all children's hands. The fingers were slightly bent and the nails were rimmed with dirt. The ink of a faded Biro drawing was clearly visible on the back of it, like blue veins arranged to make a smiling face.

'Put her down, son,' said the TSG skipper softly. 'Just put her down, won't you?'

Barridge reacted badly to the suggestion. He took a step backwards, his eyes staring.

'No!' he yelled. 'No. I just need an ambulance. An *ambulance*, right? She's OK and I've got her . . . I *found* her . . . ! She's alive!'

He hardly seemed to have noticed the blue and red plastic washing line that was wound around the little girl's neck.

CHAPTER 6

How do you tell someone their child is dead? North had been called upon to do it only three times before, and each time she had used the same formula – the usual formula. She made sure the parents were both present, if she could, and made them sit down. Then she said she was sorry, awfully sorry, but she had some bad news to tell them. Some very, very bad news.

That was enough, usually – only the most dense could fail to grasp that a death was involved. It merely remained to establish whose death. Sometimes a short guessing game took place. My mother? My brother, sister? My child? The child was the least thinkable option. It always came up last.

Unless, as in this case, that child was already missing.

Meg Richards was standing at the window when the DI and her sergeant arrived below the tower block on the Howarth Estate. North saw her Family Liaison Officer's face on the third floor, looking out. Richards would deduce why they had come. She would know it couldn't be good news, because that can be conveyed on the telephone.

No word had been spoken in the flat but, by the time

67

the officers reached the Harris front door and were let in by Helen, everybody present shared Richards's knowledge. The atmosphere was one of accumulated tension. Knowing and realizing are not always the same thing, and in these situations reality is suspended until something gets said. Only with the release of words into the air, does the unthinkable become a solid, shared fact.

North walked into the sitting room. All those present were already sitting, except Richards. Anita had an album of family snaps open on her knee. Peter was smoking. A plate of untouched sandwiches lay on the low table between them. Everyone was looking at her, waiting. She glanced at each of them first, a flicking glance.

'It's very bad news, I'm afraid.' Anita's pale face registered nothing, not at first. For a few seconds it remained oddly at rest, tilted to one side and looking nowhere in particular. Then slowly it crumpled and darkened, like cellophane on the fire. The album slipped to the floor.

'No.'

She was hugging herself now, rocking almost imperceptibly back and forth. The surrounds of her eyes tightened and creased.

'No.'

She took a long, sighing breath and gave out a hoarse, unearthly howl.

'*No!*'

In a technical sense, with the finding of a dead body, a missing person case is solved and goes away. But, in reality, it simply grows a new identity. Growing and mutating like a monster in a horror-film, it efficiently metamorphoses into a murder inquiry.

To a police officer, murder is the ultimate. It is *Hamlet*, Wembley, Mount Everest: the point at which your professional life peaks and every tough question you've ever been trained to answer will be asked. Murder is the most demanding and a child murder the least forgiving of all a police officer's enemies, an adversary who will take away your sleep if possible or, failing that, creep into your dreams; an enemy who is always there to spring another surprise, to knock you back, find you out. If, with murder, you get it right you can have the Commissioner's pat on the back and some brief media glory. Screw it up and screw you – straight back to car-pound duties.

From the moment that North called in to report PC Barridge's discovery, the Murder Squad – AMIP – waiting in the wings since late last night, started making their dispositions.

'Team'll be deploying into this station within two hours,' said the Station Superintendent to North. 'Of course they'll want an incident room. We can make some suitable space available, I take it?'

'Yes, sir. Conference Suite. No problem.'

'They're assigning Detective Superintendent Mike Walker to the case. You know him?'

'No, sir.'

'He's a good officer. And he wants to co-opt someone local who's familiar with the inquiry so far. I told him you.'

North must have looked alarmed because the Super leaned forward in his most reassuring manner. 'Your first murder?'

North shook her head. 'Oh no, sir!'

Not that she'd been on very many.

'Well,' the Super continued, 'your first child murder anyway, the worst kind. But you'll be fine. I wouldn't give you to Walker if I thought you couldn't cope.'

'Thanks, sir. I'll go up and see how they're getting on with clearing the Incident Room.'

The Super detained her with a gesture of his hand.

'Before you go, I ought to tell you that they're starting the post-mortem in half an hour. Walker may go straight down to the mortuary from wherever he is now. I expect you to attend. All right?'

'I've been to them before, sir.'

'Good. Off you go, then.'

On the first floor, Donaldson was supervising the removal of files from the local Incident Room to the ground floor. Officers Brown, Phelps, Marik and Henshaw were all on shift but these were far from the usual wisecracking men that North knew. The finding of the body had changed and sobered each of them.

She asked the Skipper what Walker was like.

'Used to work here, in Division.'

He plumped another plastic files' bin on top of the stack near the door. Then he scratched his head. 'I wouldn't call him the absolutely top drawer, if you know what I mean.'

North had the impression that the Skipper had more to impart but, just then, Brown appeared at her elbow proffering a file.

'Ma'am, we've traced a Mrs Wald – she's meals on wheels.'

North remembered that several of the old folk on the estate had mentioned meals on wheels being brought into

70

the Howarth about the time of the child's disappearance. She took the file.

'That's good. Anything else?'

'Well, we've also traced Kenneth Poole – the ice-cream seller on the Howarth Estate.'

Opening the file to scan the details, she saw in the corner of her eye a slim male figure entering the room.

'Mr Poole's got a sheet!' she said to the Skipper. 'He's another one of the dirty mac brigade. It says here he was "concerned in the management of a disorderly house".'

Donaldson shook his head. 'So how, in God's name, does he get a job selling ice-cream to kids?'

North was watching the new arrival, who was looking around uncertainly. He wore a suit and his arms were clasped behind his back. She said, 'Beats me. Is this him? Must have left his mac at home.'

Donaldson swung round to look. He suddenly coughed and cleared his throat. 'Oh, er, Detective Superintendent Walker – right?'

'That's right! And you are . . .?'

'Sergeant Donaldson, sir.'

Suddenly Walker produced a raincoat from behind his back, brandished it and said in a soft Glaswegian accent, 'So where do I put this?'

As Donaldson took the Superintendent's coat, North let out a snort of laughter, covering it with her closed fist. She straightened her face as best she could under Walker's suspicious glance. To have confused him with the dirty mac brigade was a major error of judgement, but she couldn't help but find it funny. He was a lean man of less than medium height but with the most vital grey-blue eyes she had ever seen in an officer of his rank. They darted restlessly about, she thought, like target-finders.

'I've been told I've got one of the best from here to join my team. Any idea where—?'

North stepped forward and held out her hand. 'Er – it's me, sir.'

Walker shook North's hand slowly, looking her hard in the face. Before he could speak again, she said, 'Did you know – they're due to begin the post-mortem in fifteen minutes?'

Walker glanced at his watch and took the coat back from Donaldson. 'You can brief me on the way,' he said.

June was the assistant in the path lab and she had had her car broken into the previous night. Now, preparing the post-mortem area for the examination of the little child's body, she just wanted to vent her frustration on somebody, and who better than a police officer – Detective Sergeant Polk, the area lab liaison officer, who was waiting for the officers on the case.

'I said to them, I *am* insured, I've been insured with this company for ten years. Never made a single claim . . .'

She was rattling surgical instruments as she placed them on the tray – scalpels, clamps. Not for the first time Polk reflected on how the situation would look to anyone unused to it. Lying between them, under a sheet, was the body of a child about four feet long and probably weighing no more than three stone. And here was this woman, with her carefully groomed blonde hair and scarlet nail polish clearly visible through the surgical gloves, going on about *insurance*.

After a few moments the pathologist breezed in, already gowned and booted. This was John Foster, in his fifties, with hollow cheeks, prominent cheekbones and long bony fingers. He had a Walkman-size tape recorder and a mini-microphone clipped to his blue plastic gown. He looked around.

'Who've I got with me today? Ah, the lovely June. Your boy pass his exam?'

'Don't speak to me about that little sod.'

Walker and North were on their way. Gloving up, Foster chatted amiably across the body of Julie Harris. Her extinguished life seemed to mean little more to them than a switched-off light. Soon they would be cutting the body open and delving inside.

A fat, moustached man in a green gown looked in.

'Oh, Foster, Detective Superintendent Walker and that other officer are gowning up. Mind if I look over your shoulder on this one?'

Foster shrugged. Arnold Mallory was not a man you said no to unless you wanted a fight. 'All right by me.' He gestured to him for the benefit of June and Polk. 'This is Arnold Mallory of the forensic service. Apparently—' He grinned theatrically at Mallory. 'Apparently our friends over there are uptight about the police removing her from the site.'

Mallory approached the table where Julie lay. He looked at the sheeted shape, shaking his head. 'Too bloody right we are.'

'Well, I'm glad you're here, Arnold. You can take the stomach contents away with you. Save a bit of time.'

Mallory grunted and at this moment, Walker, North and a police photographer arrived. They took up stations around the table, near enough to see without being in Foster's way. The pathologist reached for the sheet and drew it back slowly. In that moment his manner changed. There was no exaggerated reverence, but he was now serious and committed.

'Well, little one,' he said in a soft, intimate voice which excluded the others present, 'let's find out what happened to you, shall we?'

The photographer's camera flashed and the post-mortem began.

Walker had instructed that the whole team assemble in the new Incident Room at five p.m. The preparation of the space was nearly complete, with phone lines and computers installed, desk space for a dozen officers, cabinets and display boards.

As he spoke to them Walker's body language, North noted, was assertively brisk. He wouldn't suffer fools or be much of a diplomat but, at the same time, she could tell he wasn't personally vain. There was no arrogant expectation that people should bow their heads before his person. He worked hard at his job and expected others to do the same.

'OK, listen up!' he called. The buzz in the room subsided to a hush. 'I have with me DI North and DS Donaldson, CID from this station. They'll be working alongside us together with back-up from uniform. We've just come from the post-mortem. And I should add the body has now been formally identified by the grand-mother as Julie Anne Harris.'

He looked across at a dark-haired man over by a whiteboard, who was writing details of the victim along-side a photograph.

'Over there is DC James, our Office Manager. These two are DCs Soames and Harrolds and over here we've got Smith, Macklin, Morrissey and Grimes.'

The two local detectives nodded their greetings, trying to fix the names in their memories.

'Oh, and this is Detective Sergeant David Satchell, my right hand.'

A handsome, smartly dressed man in his early thirties came forward. He was half smiling, an expression that might almost be called smug. Warily North shook his hand – that 'right hand' of Walker's. Satchell looked as if he might be possessive. He might take a little handling.

'And finally, Reg Cranham, our Exhibits Officer.'

Cranham was black and as sharply dressed as Satchell. North thought they were either allies or rivals.

'OK, now! Tomorrow morning we have a Mrs Wald coming in who's meals on wheels. She *may* be able to help as she seems to be one of the few people who was around the estate after twelve-thirty. We also have an ice-cream seller who was parked up on the estate around lunchtime. Otherwise we are very short of leads. We are looking for a wino – am I right? – name of Michael Dunn?'

North nodded. 'He has a flat on the estate. At the moment he's AWOL.'

'Right. Keep chasing him. We'll know a lot more about time of death, et cetera, when the pathologist comes through with his results. Meanwhile forensics are looking at the shoes, the pants, the rope. But we need the rest of the clothes – that's *our* priority right now. OK? Those not on shift tonight, go home and get a good night's sleep.

It'll be the last you get. This inquiry starts, in earnest, tomorrow. Good night.'

Helen sat at the kitchen table, warming her hands around a mug of tea. Her eyes were shut and there was an odd sensation in her stomach, a flickering alternation of heat and cold. Her grief was like the paralysis of fear, a desire to run away combined with the knowledge that – even if her legs would carry her – this grief could never be given the slip. Anita was in her bedroom, trying to sleep. She'd taken some Valium. Helen knew, with a mother's certain knowledge, that Anita was beginning to feel the same way that she was. But Anita was still insulated by shock, going through the motions of ordinary life.

This afternoon had been Helen's second experience of a coroner's morgue. The first time was when Jim was killed and he'd been so badly damaged by the lorry that hit him, his face appallingly crushed on impact. Some of his workmates, for example, might not at first have recognized him, but she'd known him instantly by a hundred small, familiar things – the shape of his ears, his bitten nails, the liver spots on his hands, the old acne scars. It had seemed like Jim, even though he was horribly disfigured.

When the attendant pulled back the sheet this afternoon Helen had had to force herself to look really hard at Julie's face. It would be the last time she would ever see it. They told her they'd already carried out a post-mortem and Helen tried not to think about what that had involved. Anyway, there was no sign of it on Julie's clean, hardly blemished face. Helen couldn't help thinking that she looked perfect, like the angel on Christmas cards.

Helen had assented with a simple quick nod. Yes, this was my granddaughter Julie. She had held back the tears somehow until this moment, but then they came in an unstoppable surge.

All the way back in the police car, and later sitting in the kitchen with a cup of tea, Helen had thought of the little girl alive. Her high-pitched scream of laughter, her skip as she walked alongside you, the squeeze she always gave when you took her hand, the frown and quick shake of those curls when she didn't care to do something. Who had taken this away? Who could possibly do such a thing?

Suddenly a violent noise exploded from the sitting room, the clang of guitars and the thud of drums. Helen jumped to her feet and almost ran into the lounge. Peter was lying slumped on the settee. He'd done almost nothing but drink beer since the body was discovered. Now he was swinging his head to the rhythm of whatever foul music it was he'd put on. She strode to the hi-fi unit and punched the off button. Peter reacted instantly.

'*Leave that on!*'

'No, I will not,' said Helen, shaking with anger and grief. 'What are people going to think? And if *you* don't care, at least let Anita sleep. Let the kids sleep!'

Peter pouted drunkenly. 'Everybody's running around making sure 'Nita's OK. What about *me*?'

'You? You're not pregnant. And she wasn't even your daughter, Peter.'

Peter looked at her menacingly. 'How long you meaning to stay?'

Helen stiffened. She defied him. 'For as long as I'm needed.'

Peter took a swig from the beer can in his hand. He

gave up the battle, as if it required a concentration he couldn't muster. He lowered his head.

'When they going to let us bury her? When?'

Helen turned away to face the sideboard, where family and school photographs were ranged in frames. Now she was crying again.

'I don't know. I don't know . . .'

The last thing Detective Superintendent Walker did before returning home to his family in Grays, Essex, was give a press conference. BBC News and the *News at Ten* teams were both there. He kept his statement very simple, confirming that, after the police's continued search this morning, the body of the missing child, Julie Ann Harris, had been found close to the Howarth Estate and he was treating the death as suspicious. He was pursuing various lines of inquiry. An information hotline had been set up for any member of the public who might be able to help the police.

As in all cases of child murder, the rat-pack was deeply interested. Walker hoped their fascination would be relatively short-lived, as long as he could make a rapid arrest. He had at first considered issuing a description of Michael Dunn, but discarded the idea. The time wasn't yet ripe. He parried the reporters' questions. Asked, inevitably, if she'd been sexually assaulted, he said he was awaiting the pathologist's report. Asked about the murder method, he declined to give details.

He had good reason for this. Crazies routinely telephone the police claiming to have committed such crimes and it's vital to be able to eliminate them with a few simple, circumstantial questions.

Getting into bed beside Maggie, he asked if she thought the press conference had gone reasonably well on television. She looked up from her book.

'Your tie looked awful. And your bald spot was shining.'

He laughed and rolled over on to his side. She was right to stick a pin in his pretension. At the same time he needed to manage the Press. The last thing he wanted was a series of hysterical stories in the tabloids about families that cowered in fear of a madman stalking the estates of East London.

He was hopeful, all in all. He had the rope, the clothes and a suspect who would surely turn up soon. These factors gave Mike Walker comfort as he closed his eyes to begin his nightly battle with insomnia.

CHAPTER 7

MRS WALD'S HUSBAND was an inspector on the buses. She was not exactly used to the inside of police stations, and certainly not their interview rooms, though she'd seen these places on *Inspector Morse*, naturally. They'd always struck her as disagreeably gloomy and dungeon-like but this room was a surprise. It was rather like the little carpeted cubby-hole where she'd recently seen Mr McKendrick at the bank about her mortgage.

Detective Superintendent Walker took her patiently through Thursday morning's meals round on the estate. It was a little difficult at first. Every day tends to be much like another doing meals on wheels and Thursday had already become tangled up with Wednesday, while bits of Monday, Tuesday and Friday also needed weeding out. The weekly roster of menus helped, of course: Wednesday was chicken and Friday fish fingers. On Thursdays the old folks got Irish stew, apple pie and custard. She concentrated on the smell of the stew and it brought some details back to her.

'I remember when I first arrived a young man came tearing down the stairs. He almost bumped into me. Long hair, long dark coat. I didn't really see his face

– he had no manners, never said a word of hello or anything.'

'Did you see anyone else around the stairs?'

'No, just my old people and they were all in their flats. You don't see many people around the stairs and corridors up there you know.'

'But did you see the young man again?'

'Yes, I think so. You see, I was late. Old Mrs Marsh wanted me to have a cup of tea and a chat with her, but I didn't have time. We're supposed to have the vans back at the depot before quarter to two, you know, they're very strict on that. Anyway I did my last delivery at one-thirty, that was Enid Marsh. I remember checking the time in Mrs Marsh's flat. Then I got back to my van after that . . .'

Walker cleared his throat. 'Yes, but I need to know the time as accurately as possible, Mrs Wald. You made your last delivery at one-thirty. What floor was that?'

'Sixth.'

'So then you went down in the lift—'

'Lift? You are joking, Superintendent. The stairs.'

Walker struck his forehead with the heel of his hand. 'Ah yes, I was forgetting. Stairs. You got to the bottom a minute later, then?'

'Superintendent, I'm not Linford Christie and I was carrying stuff.'

'Two minutes, then?'

She nodded.

'What happened next?'

'I got back to my van and it wouldn't start. I waited a few minutes to let it rest. I looked around in case I needed help and I saw that young man again near the ice-cream seller's van.'

81

'Are you sure it was the same young man you saw earlier when you entered the block?'

'Yes, I think so – he was a young man, long hair, long dark coat. But I can't remember his face.'

'Did you see anyone else in the playground area at that time?'

'No, it was empty.'

'So, the time when you saw him, while you were sitting inside your van, was about what?'

'One thirty-five. Not later than one-forty.'

The ice-cream seller's name was Kenneth Poole, a chain-smoker. Sitting slightly hunched in the interview room, he held his cigarette in a cupped hand, and took rapid, nervous drags. His typed-up statement – a brief paragraph – lay on the table. Walker and Satchell were taking him through it one last time.

'I was parked at my usual pitch at twelve-thirty.'

'You're absolutely sure about that?' asked Walker.

'Yeah, twelve-thirty. There was nobody around except this bloke.'

Walker and Satchell exchanged looks.

'Can you describe him?'

'Long hair, black coat. He came up and asked if I'd seen his little girl. I said I hadn't.'

Poole's eyes were darting around and he seemed anxious to go.

'And you didn't see any children in the playground?'

'Nope. I usually stay on the Howarth Estate until two, two-thirty. You know – get 'em before lunch and after. Then I move on to the pitch near the comprehensive school.'

There was a long pause. Poole looked uncertainly from Walker's face to Satchell's and back again. Walker stood up.

'Thank you, Mr Poole. If you would just sign your statement you can go.'

Poole seemed surprised as he took the pen proffered by Satchell.

'Oh, OK. Thanks. Thanks a lot. Sorry I couldn't be more helpful.'

Walker picked up the signed paper and examined the rapid scrawl of Poole's signature. 'There's just one thing I was wondering, Mr Poole.'

Poole looked up, his eyes wary again. 'Oh, yeah? What?'

'Are your employers aware of your criminal record?'

Poole looked down at his hand. He mumbled. 'Don't know.'

Walker strode to the door and yanked it open. 'Thank you, Mr Poole.'

He waited as Poole almost ran out, then turned to Satchell. 'Dave – get the sheet on Peter James, will you?'

Pat North had had several glimpses already of the ferocious energy that drove Detective Superintendent Walker. In the Incident Room he paced ceaselessly, smoked without stopping, constantly ripping off the filter and occasionally spitting it out as he bit it off. He asked his questions again and again. Where was Michael Dunn? Where were Julie's clothes? Where did she die? *When* did she die?

What was bothering him now was the disparity between the statements of Peter James, Mrs Wald and the ice-cream seller, Poole, about James's movements that lunchtime. James said he went out about one; the meals on wheels woman said she saw a long-haired man, who could have been James, at one-thirty, whilst Poole was talking about some time after twelve-thirty that James came and asked him about the missing girl.

'Did Peter James give a description of what he was wearing when he went out looking for Julie Ann?'

North didn't have the answer. She flannelled. 'It's been tough to question Mr James. He's been under a lot of strain – very volatile.'

Walker was standing at the pin-board with its diagram of the relationships within the victim's family. He tapped it hard. 'Inspector, it may be difficult but let me remind you that in ninety per cent of these cases the offender is a member of the family. Doesn't matter how tough it is, they've got to be checked out in every detail.'

He swivelled round towards Satchell. '*You* question him.'

'Yes, guv.'

'Meanwhile, Inspector North and I will confer with Doctor Foster.'

Satchell's face was wearing a smug grin as he caught North's eye. One-nil to the visitors.

Walker added before he slammed out of the room, 'And most important, find Michael bloody Dunn.'

Foster stood smoking beside a vertical lightbox. On the screen were fixed nine large transparencies showing close-up post-mortem shots of Julie's body. Walker and North stood like an audience, looking and listening.

'She was a well-nourished, healthy young girl of about

84

five years old. As you can see she has bruising and abrasions to her shoulder, upper arm, legs and buttocks. The abrasions on the limbs were sustained when she was pushed into the sewage pipe. But – this is important – there has been bleeding and bruising around the abrasions to the limbs. And look – there are petechial haemorrhages on the face and scalp.'

Another slide displayed small spots on Julie's skin. They appeared like a rash.

'These are minute leakages of blood into the skin.'

North and Walker looked more closely at the slide indicated by the pathologist. He showed with his pointer the discoloured skin.

'Bleeding, bruising – those are all vital signs. Blood flowed into and from the damaged tissue, which means her heart was beating when it happened.'

He paused, as if waiting for them to grasp the implication.

'She was *alive* when she was pushed in the sewage pipe?' said North.

'That's about it.'

'What about the rope around her neck?'

Foster dragged deeply on his cigarette and exhaled quickly. He was an impatient smoker.

'Oh yes, there was a piece of plastic-coated line ligated around the neck, but she didn't actually die from strangulation.'

'So what did she die of?' asked North.

'Suffocation. She'd probably been made unconscious with the ligature then forced into a folded position with her head resting on her knees like so. She was then literally crammed into the pipe which was too tight. Hardly any air. Died approximately two hours later, judging by the colour of the bruising and degree of blood coagulation. Quite a rare blood group, by the way – AB negative.'

'Was she sexually assaulted?' Walker wanted to know.

Foster consulted his typewritten notes – a transcript of the oral commentary he'd made for the tape during his examination.

'She has a ruptured hymen and extensive bruising to her genitals consistent with penetration with a blunt rounded object.'

'Such as?' asked Walker, then he coughed. 'I mean, apart from the obvious.'

'It may not have been the obvious.' He flicked a glance at North and then went on. 'I mean there are no obvious traces of seminal fluid, although there might be minute traces. We'll have to leave that to forensics. Otherwise, it could be something like the neck of a bottle. There was blood on her pants – her own blood. No traces of semen, as I said. Oh, and here's something else you should know . . .'

He pointed to another slide showing a section of Julie's arm.

'Some of the bruises to her body, such as this one here, are yellowish brown and diffuse – see?'

They looked as Foster stubbed out his cigarette on a saucer.

'It means,' he said, 'that, unlike these bruises here which happened on the day she died, these yellower bruises are a couple of weeks old. Quite severe ones, too. Not the normal knocks a kid gets playing around. Now – contents of stomach . . .'

He strolled over to his desk and flipped open a file.

'According to Mallory, our little lady had cereal and

orange juice for breakfast. The stomach also had traces of milk proteins and nuts – could be an ice-cream eaten some time before she died.'

Walker looked over Foster's shoulder, squinting at the report. 'Can't you give us a time of death, or near enough?'

'Death occurred between three and seven on Thursday, that's the best I can do.'

'Any chance of telling us if it definitely was ice-cream?'

Foster lit another cigarette and shook his head. 'You need to talk to forensics. But if she did eat an ice-cream and they had a wrapper or, even better, a stick, there could be some of her DNA on it, couldn't there?'

Barridge had been in turmoil ever since he'd found Julie's body. Flashbacks of her face kept exploding in his mind, and tears were never far away. He'd cried openly when they'd taken the child's body from him.

This afternoon he was with Brown and Phelps on the search for the child's clothing. It was a more dreadful, because less hopeful, task than the search they'd been carrying out yesterday. Now they were back at the row of derelict houses into whose flooded cellars he had got a ducking on the Thursday night.

He was wearing chest-high waders again as he inched his way through the water, examining every disgusting object that floated on the water. There was plenty of clothing. He thought the worst was the knitwear. It seemed to absorb the most stomach-turning smells and when you lifted it from the water it exhaled them into your nose. Or was he imagining this?

His torch started to flicker. He banged it against his

hand and it came on again. He flashed it into a corner of the cellar where a wardrobe was standing drunkenly askew. He saw a piece of air-filled clothing, floating half concealed behind the wardrobe. It looked red. Then his torch went off again.

'Can you bring some more light over here, in this corner?'

Brown and Phelps started to work their way towards him. They shone their torches at the wardrobe.

'What colour was her anorak?' asked Barridge.

'Red.'

Slowly, he began to force his way towards the soggy lump of red material bobbing in the black water.

The rest of Julie's clothing had turned up in the cellar and, with the anorak, it was bagged and sent down to the forensic science laboratory in Lambeth, where the shoes, pants and post-mortem swabs, as well as ground samples taken from the area around the sewage pipes were already undergoing tests.

Driving to the same destination that afternoon, immediately after their meeting with Foster, North was at the wheel with Walker alongside her. He was smoking and staring out of the window and hardly saying a word. The more the traffic on London Bridge impeded their progress the more fiercely he inhaled the smoke. Here was a man heading for a heart attack, thought North. But then, show me a senior police officer who wasn't.

Sweeping into the labs, Walker was told Arnold Mallory had left for the Old Bailey.

'Great. We come all this way and the man we want to talk to is attending court. Bloody great!'

The next most senior scientist working on the Julie Harris case was James Haggard. When he appeared, Walker demanded a report on the deposits on Julie's shoes. He needed to know where she went after the playground, he needed to know where she might have died.

'And what about the rope? Where did it come from? Are there any prints?'

Walker was like an impatient businessman, chivvying a sluggardly supplier for early delivery of an order and this, as it happened, was close to the truth. In these cost-conscious times, the forensic service is operated as a business, a profit centre. Every test carried out by them, every report printed out or appearance by an expert witness, was costed and charged to the account of the investigation – in this case, to Walker. And the Detective Superintendent constantly had to remind himself that the old profligate, scattergun days when an investigating officer simply ordered any test he wanted, were over. Now he had to work within a budget; he needed, in short, value for money.

Patiently, Haggard parried the questions as best he could. 'All in good time, you know, Mr Walker. We're pulling out all the stops.'

'According to Doctor Foster she was sexually assaulted. Can't you even give me anything on that?'

Haggard was a grizzled old scientist, close to retirement. He'd had all this a thousand times before – pushy detectives demanding instant results. He sighed.

'Detective Superintendent, you'll get all we get as soon as we get it. You know Mallory's heading the team. He's so anally retentive, nothing comes out of here before he's satisfied.'

He looked around a shade furtively. It was a cheerfully clinical room, with laminated tables ranged in rows. At one table, two forensic biologists were microscopically examining the clothing for blood and other stains. At another, chemists were analysing mud from the shoes and other environmental samples. Haggard set off for a corner where no one was working, beckoning the police officers to follow. The section of rope, which the detectives had last seen wrapped around Julie Harris's neck, lay flat on an unattended table. The scientist gestured down at it.

'It was wound round her throat twice and pulled. No knot was tied. Just what you see, a loop one end. The free end has been cut. No touching please.'

Going over to a pin-board with a display of photographs of the exhibit, he started fishing in his lab coat pocket. He tapped a close-up of the small loop and began unwrapping the sweet he'd taken from the pocket.

'The loop has traces of paint on the inside – layer structure, brown over green. It's as it would be if the rope had been attached to a post.'

'So? What are you saying?' asked Walker.

'Find the post—'

'And you can match the paint?'

Haggard popped the toffee into his mouth.

'Oh, yes – no problem there.'

Back in the Incident Room, Satchell was having a go at anyone who'd listen about the late finding of the clothes. Catching sight of Pat North he strode up to her.

'Somebody should give your lot a bollocking. That

cellar had been officially searched. We could have had those clothes yesterday. Bloody incompetence!'

Yeah, yeah, thought North. Local yokel plod. This was the type of thing that gave AMIP its name for abrasive elitism. She was just about to react when she heard Reg Cranham's voice, with a note of real urgency in it.

'Guv! Call just came in from a Mrs Enid Marsh – Howarth Estate.'

Walker remembered the name but he couldn't quite place it. 'And?'

'Well, she was questioned the night the victim went missing. Said she didn't know anything then – but now she's seen the TV news and, well—'

'Well, what? What?'

'She said she saw the victim, guv, with a man in the playground. She then described the clothes – exactly Peter James's appearance – long hair, long dark coat . . .'

'What time? Did she give a time?'

Cranham smiled, with a hint of triumph. He didn't like Peter James. 'Yep! Just after one o'clock, so she says.'

There was a momentary pause, then North murmured, 'So – it's the stepfather. Do we bring him in?'

'And call off the search for Michael Dunn?' Walker held up his hand to check the outbreak of chicken-counting. 'No. If we find Michael Dunn we still hold him.'

'On what?'

'Stolen videos. Come on, Inspector, let's go and talk to Enid Marsh.'

The old lady insisted on serving them with tea which, at her speed of movement, could not be done within ten minutes. Impatiently Walker and North sat on the sofa while the wherewithal was assembled on the low table in front of them. At last, Mrs Marsh was ready to tell her tale. And it was better than Walker had dared hope. Not only had she seen the child – she'd seen her with a man.

'The first time I saw her, it was like she was playing a game. You know, covering her eyes and peeping through. She was laughing. That was a quarter to one.'

Walker took a sip from his tea. It was a good cup, he gave her that. 'And did you see her again?'

'Yes, I did. At exactly five past one.'

She levered herself out of her chair and stood before them in something like a pose. Her sitting room had turned, for her, into a stage.

'He was reaching out, like that.'

She let go of her walking frame and demonstrated. Then she turned and began a long shuffle towards the balcony.

'But anyway, you know, I wasn't paying attention. I was looking for Mrs Wald, waiting for my dinner. I was hungry.'

She had reached the door and was leaning on the handle.

'I went outside. From my balcony I've got a view of a bit of the playground. I often look at the kids down there. And I . . .'

She paused and leaned forward with a small jerk. Her voice flipped up to a higher register.

'But look, that's him! That's him, down there.'

She opened the door and started to shuffle outside. Walker and North were beside her.

'Who?'

'The man. The man who was with the little girl!'

Down below the roundabout was revolving. There was not a child in sight, only a man of about twenty-five, with long matted hair and a shin-length coat of dark material. He had got the platform turning and was now standing dangerously on top of it, swaying and singing as loud as he could. In his fist he gripped a can of extra strong lager.

Detective Superintendent Walker moved like lightning, with Detective Sergeant Satchell at his side. Dunn seemed unaware of their presence until Satchell almost ripped his arms out of their sockets as he grabbed the iron rail to stop the roundabout. Dunn fell backwards laughing, the lager spraying from his can. Droplets spattered across Walker's face. He never lifted a hand to wipe them away. He never took his eyes off the drunk's face.

'Michael Dunn, I am arresting you in connection with the theft of videotapes.'

CHAPTER 8

SUNDAY 8 SEPTEMBER

IT BEING SUNDAY made no difference. At half-past five, like most mornings, Pat North left her boyfriend Graham in bed, still wrapped in several layers of sleep and snoring gently. He was unwakeable before seven-thirty – nine at weekends. Even then, he'd take an hour to come to, mooching around the flat like a wounded bear, slurping tea and growling at his post or the paper. It was better to be out of his way. She knew, if ever they should marry and have kids, this would be the most difficult bit for him – getting up in the small hours, the family breakfast, the carefully timed school run.

Night time was when Graham reached his best. The previous evening they'd gone out to the pub and she'd told him about the arrest of Michael Dunn that afternoon, how he'd fallen about and sung 'Bohemian Rhapsody' for hours in the cell. They'd been back at home in time for the news but there was no mention of Dunn's arrest and afterwards Graham was eager to speculate about the murder.

'Is it this Dunn character, though? Sure, he's a drunk and he's disreputable, so all the neighbours point at him. But is he the only suspect?'

Pat remembered the dressing-down Walker had given

in front of the whole unit, reminding her unnecessarily that about fifty per cent of child murders are committed by someone inside the family. She didn't elaborate, just mentioned the possibility of Peter James, Julie Ann's stepfather. Graham asked about the real father, and by now Pat was becoming loath to discuss it further, saying that Thomas Harris was a soldier in Ulster and had already been checked. To her irritation Graham continued to ask what evidence they had against Michael Dunn. It appeared almost as if he was siding with him.

'For God's sake, Graham. This isn't bloody *Cluedo*. A five-year-old girl is dead. She was molested. The man who did it will do it again unless we stop him. It could be Michael Dunn, it might not be. Our job is to find him. Which is why I need to go to sleep. You may not have to, but I'm working tomorrow.'

She'd gone straight upstairs, leaving Graham to his beloved *Match of the Day*. But what she'd said must have had some effect. He brought her a cup of tea, which she didn't really want. He set it down on the bedside table, leaning forward to stroke her head.

'Sorry. Didn't mean to sound like a prat, but you know sometimes it's good to talk about it. It was the only way I knew how to get you to open up. You may not even be aware of it, but since this little girl case started you've been on edge, biting my head off.'

He smiled, missing *Match of the Day*. She sat up and lifted her arms. It was a hug she needed, and caught in his arms she whispered, 'She was so tiny, Graham.' And the tears she would never allow any of the men or women at the station to see now gave her a much needed release.

*

Driving across London from west to east, she focused on the issue that would dominate the rest of her day. They had a suspect but not a crumb of evidence. They needed time for forensics to search his flat minutely, they needed time to question him. For this, a pretext was necessary, and the best they had was the stack of hopefully stolen videos found in Dunn's flat, which lay on the seat alongside her.

She drove on to the Howarth Estate and past the parade of shops until she came to the newsagent. She opened the passenger door and carried the videos inside. It was six-thirty. Mr Shah was organizing the newspaper boys, giving them their loads of Sunday papers. He glanced at the pile of ten video feature films, running his finger down the titles – *Aladdin, My Little Pony, The Terminator, The Lion King, Die Hard, Child's Play* – and checked for his security mark scratched on the plastic casings.

'Yeah, these were all mine.'

'We found them at the flat belonging to a Michael Dunn. You know him?'

'Yes. He—'

'He stole them from you? They *are* stolen, Mr Shah?'

Shah shook his head and smiled, with his eyes wide. 'I always like to help the police, Inspector, but I'm sorry to say these were not stolen.'

North was aghast. 'Not stolen? But you said they were yours.'

'*Were*. Michael Dunn did an occasional paper round for me. I was replacing or running down my stock of videos. Some of them had snowy pictures – *The Terminator*'s very bad. Customers were complaining. So I gave them to Michael Dunn instead of money – for his paper round.'

'Did he say why he wanted the kiddies' films?'

'No.'

'Or the violent ones?'

Shah shook his head. 'People don't generally say anything about the films, you know. They just take them and leave.'

He shrugged and North briskly gathered up the tapes.

'Since they are not at the present moment yours, you won't object if I take these away again – right?'

As she walked into the AMIP Incident Room she could hear Skipper Donaldson giving Barridge a bollocking.

'You cocked up, you know that? Enid Marsh – house to house. Ring any bells? *You* questioned her. Now she's come forward as our identifying witness . . .'

Barridge blinked miserably. 'Sorry, sarge.'

But Donaldson was only just getting into his stride.

'Plus you were doing the search at the cellar. You only missed her clothing. *And* you missed her shoe by the pipes. How come, Barridge? If you'd been more diligent, we might have got to her sooner. You do know that?'

Barridge looked as if he might cry. 'I wasn't the only one there. I—'

'Don't answer me back, son. I'm telling you, you screwed up. She was alive in that sewage pipe for almost two hours.'

Barridge swivelled slightly, looking for support from others in the room. Detective Superintendent Walker was standing just behind him. In his panic, he appealed to the AMIP Superintendent.

'*Is* it Dunn, sir? I mean, Sergeant Donaldson says—'

But the Superintendent appeared not to hear. He was checking some names on a memo, then looked up to see if the constables in question were present. He pointed to Brown and Phelps and then Barridge.

'You two, and you, are on house to house inquiries.'

There was an audible groan from Brown. Walker shot a look at him that would have stalled the Wall Street Crash. He held up an index finger.

'I want you to check every washing line on that estate. *Every* washing line. We're looking for a match to the one found around Julie Ann's neck. It's there on the board, check it out. We want to know about any washing lines or similar plastic-coated rope that may have gone missing.'

He looked hard at PC Barridge. '*Don't* screw up this time – it's the murder weapon we're talking about, got it?'

Barridge's mouth fell open – so the Super had heard Donaldson's tirade.

'It wasn't my *fault*,' he muttered to Phelps. 'I wasn't the only one there. Bloody hell!'

Walker took North by the arm and guided her to one side.

'Dunn's still sleeping it off – Christ, it must have been some binge. Where'd he get the money? Anyway, it gives us more time to find something on him for Julie Ann. You seen the newsagent? Can we charge him for those videos?'

North shook her head. ''Fraid not, guv. They're all ex-rentals.'

'Dunn bought them?'

'No, Dunn did a few paper rounds and he took the videos instead of cash.'

'Shit! There must be something!'

Walker fished out a Marlboro, broke off the filter tip and stuck the ragged end in his mouth.

'Guv, you know how we got those videos, don't you?'

Walker made a face, removed the cigarette and picked a flake of tobacco from his tongue. 'Yeah, yeah. Pretext was checking for damage.' Walker reversed the cigarette and lit it.

'Well, there were a number of toys – kids' toys – there as well. One of them was a doll.'

Walker's eyes sparked. 'Doll? Haven't we followed it up with the family? Haven't we checked if it was the victim's?'

Satchell got up from his desk and joined them. He knew the boss, recognized the signs. Walker was working his way up through the lower storeys of a towering rage.

'Do you realize,' Walker went on, 'we've got Dunn in the cells and he's our best suspect and unless I get more – and I've got bugger all right now – I'm going to have to let the sorry bastard *OUT*?'

'Guv,' said Satchell, 'I've got a suggestion.'

'Glad to hear it, Dave. Shoot.'

'Put him in a parade. See if old Mrs Marsh can pick him out.'

Walker snapped his fingers impatiently. 'Christ's sake, Dave. I'm already working on that! But *you* know how long it'll take to find lookalikes. If we don't find something in the next couple of hours he's going to walk as soon as he wakes.'

He paused and sucked hard on his Marlboro.

'OK, I know what I want. I want a search warrant for Dunn's place. Pat?'

'It's a Sunday, guv.'

Walker found an ashtray and ground out the cigarette.

'Then let's deliver the local magistrate's *Sunday* bloody *Telegraph* for him, shall we?'

The warrant had been a push-over. The JP opened the door hurriedly, dressed for golf, and stood impatiently while Walker explained his business.

'Yes, of course, I've heard of this distressing death,' said the magistrate. 'And you are who, precisely?'

Walker produced his warrant card. 'Officer in charge of the inquiry – Detective Superintendent Michael Walker.'

'And this man whose home you want to search – is he a suspect?'

'That's right, sir.'

'In custody?'

'Yes, sir, but may be released shortly. In which case we are anxious to give his pad a spin – or rather, his flat a *search*, sir – before he can get home to do what he likes with the evidence.'

'You got the papers there?' The old man looked at his watch. 'I'm due to tee off at eight forty-five and you don't miss the chance of a slot at Sunningdale.'

'Of course, sir. It's all prepared. Just needs signing.'

'Come in, then.'

Driving back with the papers in his pocket, Walker laughed in relief.

'Thank Christ for bloody Sunningdale. Speeded things up a bit.'

They arrived at the Dunn flat at eight-forty where Reg

Cranham, the Exhibits Officer, was waiting for them. Before they could go in Barridge arrived on the run.

'Excuse me, sir!'

Walker waited for Barridge to catch his breath. 'What is it, Barridge? Those washing lines?'

'Yes, sir. One tenant said most of the residents use the local launderette. But there's a recently built housing estate across the road. Got gardens so they're more likely to use proper washing lines. Want me to . . .?'

Barridge gestured with his thumb in the direction of the new houses.

'No. Just report it in, lad. Sergeant Satchell will allocate some of my guys to cover the new houses.'

Walker knew that most of the balconies on the tower blocks would have washing lines. Whether these were ever used or not was beside the point – they had to be checked. Young rookies like Barridge were always looking for ways of cutting corners.

Inside the flat enough daylight filtered through the window boards to reveal the full squalor of Michael Dunn's damp and broken-springed home life. North showed Walker the one-armed doll which lay pink and sprawling on the settee. He bent down and looked carefully at it.

'My kid's got one of these.'

'It looks like a Barbie,' said North. 'Actually it's a cheap market-stall rip-off. Only costs about a quid, while a real Barbie costs—'

'Twelve ninety-nine,' said Walker grimly, picturing his daughter's glowing face on her sixth birthday as she tore off the gift wrap. 'And that's before you've bought the wardrobe. *Reg!*'

Cranham came in from the kitchen with a pained expression on his face. 'Breakfast anyone? I found a couple of sausages in the fridge – best before three months ago. Can't see no washing line anywhere.'

Walker pointed at the fake Barbie. 'Bag the doll. Seal, sign and log it and then test it for prints. Now what's the kitchen like?'

'It smells, guv.'

In the kitchen there were lumps of food adhering to the walls. The sink overflowed with unwashed plates. The floor was caked and tacky underfoot. What interested Walker the most was a small pile of waste paper in one corner – empty crisp bags and ice-cream wrappers. One brand of ice-cream in particular caught his eye: Gnutcrunch. He crouched down.

'Forensic said her stomach contents had maybe ice-cream and nuts – yes? Well, look at these.'

In the other room Cranham had been on the radio. He came back into the kitchen.

'Michael Dunn's awake, sir, but he's asked for something to eat. They can spin things out for a while longer.'

Walker straightened. 'Good. But I wish he'd had the decency to sleep through to lunch.'

He pointed to the wrappers. 'I want these listed and bagged.' He turned to North and pointed to the bagged Barbie. 'We'll take the doll to the victim's family.' He noticed her startled look. 'You got a problem with that?'

'No, sir,' said North and instantly Walker was talking to Cranham again.

'I want full documentation on bar codes and I want to know where he got them. Lolly sticks are vital. We'll comb the whole flat for more of them if we have time, but I want these two tested anyway.'

It would take a couple of minutes for Cranham to complete the bagging. Walker dialled a number on his mobile. 'Dave? I want you to go and talk to the newsagent – can you do it now? Check what he said about Peter James. Then find out what brands of ice-cream he sells. I'm partial to one called Gnutcrunch – yes, with a G – and also if he sold any of the horrible stuff to Michael Dunn. See you later.'

He snapped the phone off. 'Come on, let's see if we can find any more lolly sticks.'

Mr Shah the newsagent was checking a toppling pile of newspapers to see that each included a colour supplement.

'I mean I got to be right within five or ten minutes,' he was saying to Satchell. 'It's my busy time, lunchtime. Pete – Peter James – came in twice. Once to ask about a plumber and then, fifteen or twenty minutes later, he came back again.'

Satchell was looking into the freezer chest, noting down the names of the ice-cream brands.

'Did Michael Dunn come into the shop Thursday at all?'

'No – well, to be honest, I've barred him.'

'But he did the odd paper round for you, didn't he?'

'Yeah, but not for a long time. He couldn't be trusted. Last time I found half the bloody newspapers stuffed into litter bins. I never let him do it any more after that.'

'And you paid Dunn in kind?'

'Yeah – with ice-creams and crisps. That's all he wanted.'

'And videos?'

'Yes, and the videos.'

Outside the shop, Satchell switched on his cellphone.

'Guv? Newsagent's got Cornetto, Snickers, Gnutcrunch, Galaxy Dove, Twister, Wall's Chunky Choc Ice ... Crisps? Golden Wonder, loads of flavours – yes, prawn cocktail. And, guv, listen, Dunn used to be paid for this so-called paper round in ice-cream and crisps sometimes, as well as the videos.'

Satchell's findings had been interesting enough to put a spring in Walker's step as he and North strode towards the entrance to the tower block.

'When we get up there we'll make sure Julie Anne didn't have any ice-cream for breakfast. I told Dave to check with the labs, see if they've got any results in yet on the lolly sticks.'

'Bit soon, isn't it?'

Walker smiled thinly. 'I know. Just pawing the starting gates a little. I'm pinning my hopes on that little dolly right now.'

Anita herself came to the door. She was as pale as paper and the skin around her eyes had taken on the shiny, opalescent colours of grief and insomnia. Her pregnant stomach seemed more obvious too, affecting the way she turned and moved her body.

Walker said, 'Hello, Mrs Harris. I'm Detective Super-intendent Walker, I'm the—'

'Yes, I know who you are,' said Anita. She didn't even try to smile. 'I saw you on the box. Come through, won't you?'

Peter James was in the lounge, pacing around like a trapped rodent. 'All right?' he muttered.

Anita placed Walker and North on the settee and sat down self-consciously between them, as if she preferred not to look either of them in the face. The atmosphere in the place was coldly calm.

Walker started by sketching in the progress of the inquiry. He didn't mention Dunn by name – just talked about 'a man we are interested in'.

'How do you mean, interested?' said Peter James.

'I mean, he may be able to help us. He may have given your daughter something to eat. Could you just remind us what she had to eat on Thursday morning?'

Anita bowed her head and shut her eyes, trying to remember as accurately as possible.

'She had cereal, orange juice. That's it. She never ate much at breakfast.'

'You don't know if she had any ice-cream or any nuts?'

'No. Not here, she didn't.'

Walker turned and nodded at Cranham who was standing with his hands behind his back beside the door. The exhibits officer came forward and carefully placed the transparent evidence bag on the low table in front of Anita.

'Mrs Harris,' said Walker, 'I wonder if you could tell me – have you seen this doll before?'

Anita stared at the pink plastic flesh and tangle of yellow hair, the straight, elongated legs, the pert breasts and the hideous empty arm socket. Her eyebrows drew fractionally closer together. She was about to speak when Peter's voice, excited, broke in.

'Yes, that's her doll.'

He was leaning over, pointing. He was animated for the first time. 'It's Julie's, Anita. She always had it with her. Tell him, Anita. That's Julie's doll.'

Anita opened her mouth and at once her lips began to quiver. Slowly she covered her face with her hands. She nodded her head as her frame shook with sobs.

North looked at Walker's face as he skipped down the stairs a couple of minutes later. It wore a look that said, broadly, 'Got him.' It wasn't exactly happiness but, by the length of the Old Kent Road, it was the nearest she'd seen him get to happiness.

'Come on, you guys!' he called out, a flight of stairs in the lead. 'Don't hang about or that Custody Sergeant will be getting it into his head to let Michael Dunn go. And we can't have that, can we?'

Walker arrested Michael Dunn in the hallway of the custody suite just as Sergeant Johns was signing him out. Dunn had looked at him in hungover bemusement. His reaction to the words 'on suspicion of the murder of Julie Ann Harris' was bovine.

'Who? I've never heard of her.'

'You do not have to say anything,' chanted the Detective Superintendent, 'but it may harm your defence if you do not mention, when questioned, something which you later rely on in court.'

'I don't get it. I been here all night.'

'Anything you do or say may be given in evidence.'

Dunn held his arms away from his side, the hands palm upwards. He shrugged until his shoulders almost touched his ears.

'I don't know what the fuck you're talking about, you know.'

The accent was liltingly Welsh. The breath that delivered it smelt overpoweringly of breakfast and nicotine.

*

Barridge had felt in an extraordinary mood all morning, a kind of reverse high. It wasn't happiness, but a wave of inspired misery that he was riding helplessly. Once he saw Walker and Inspector North leaving the search area, he'd asked to be attached to the squad at the newly built houses and had been assigned to cover Ashcroft Close. Some intuition told him this was where the washing line had come from, so this was where he wanted to be.

For some time now, an inner voice had been talking to Barridge, telling him he had a privileged place on this investigation, a place almost of destiny. If he thought about it properly – if he'd been capable at this stage of detached thought – he might have agreed it was his own voice talking, that he was, in fact, just talking to himself. But, in his present state he thought of it as a voice of inspiration, telling him *he had been chosen for this.*

Who found the body? murmured the voice. Who found the anorak? Who first talked to Enid Marsh, the eye-witness? It was you, Colin. Ask yourself why. Never mind what the Skipper's been saying, this is fate. This is *meant.*

These new houses were small – for young couples, singles. Each was identical and each had an identical rectangle of garden bounded by lattice fencework.

He knocked on the door of number four. According to the electoral roll, it was the address of a Miss A. Taylor. Miss Taylor herself opened. She was a bony woman with bashful eyes, eyes that were always being dragged downwards to look at the ground, as if over-whelmed by gravity.

'Excuse me, madam,' said Barridge gently, 'we're inquiring into the murder that occurred over on the Howarth Estate.'

Miss Taylor's eyes glanced at the constable's face and then dropped to consider his boots.

'Oh yes, that poor little girl. How awful that was! I saw about it on the news. I can't believe it happened right here. How can I help?'

'We're just asking around to find out if any thefts have been taking place around here – thefts from gardens.'

Ann Taylor opened her front door wide and ushered Barridge in. 'Come through! I'll show you.'

As they walked through the house, Barridge noticed Miss Taylor's limp. Not bad enough to need a stick, but pronounced nonetheless.

'I wouldn't have come to live here if I'd known,' she said. 'I mean the level of crime is really bad.' Then she laughed, cupping her hand to her mouth and shifting her eyes from side to side. 'But, of course, you're a policeman. You know that!'

The garden was neatly, if unimaginatively, kept: border shrubs lining the perimeter, an oblong of grass in the centre, a creosoted garden shed with a felted roof standing on duty in a far corner.

'But anyway, you can't leave anything out at night. They come from the estate. I've had plants taken and a white urn from round the front. We've got Neighbourhood Watch, but it's not helped.'

Barridge noticed a washing pole, notched at the top. He looked from side to side. There were posts to which a washing line would normally be attached. But there was no clothes-line.

'Where's your washing line, Miss Taylor?' he asked.

CHAPTER 9

SUNDAY 8 SEPTEMBER. 10.30 A.M.

PAT NORTH found Detective Superintendent Walker sitting at his desk in shirtsleeves, his tie loosened and the telephone receiver tucked between his shoulder and ear. He was tearing the filter off another Marlboro as he spoke into the mouthpiece.

'. . . just wondering if you'd got anything on those ice-cream wrappers . . . Yes, I know . . . it's just that I'm about to interview—' Walker held the receiver away from his ear and looked at North with a thin, ironic smile on his face. 'Mallory!' he mouthed.

From the door she could hear most of the earful Walker was getting from his chief forensic scientist.

'You'll have it as soon as I have it, Walker! The way you buggers reckon you'll get anything faster by pestering me is a bloody irritant . . .'

Walker covered the mouthpiece with his palm. 'What does Dunn want?' he asked. 'A lawyer?'

'No, another breakfast,' said North. 'Guv, the Press Office have been on. It's getting about that we're holding someone and they're being inundated with calls. Do you want to put out a blurb – "helping police with inquiries" kind of thing?'

Walker nodded then, still listening to Mallory, he

raised his eyebrows as Satchell walked in. The Sergeant slid a few paperclipped pages of A4 on to the desk.

'Here's as much as we could get from records – three vagrancy charges, unemployed, on housing benefit. Phone cut off, single, no family.'

'Social services?'

'I'm still waiting on them. They've gone all "patient confidentiality" on us. It could be weeks.'

Walker clicked his fingers three times in rapid succession. 'Get the family liaison officer – Meg Whatsit? See if she can dig around for us.'

Suddenly he realized that Mallory's tirade had stopped. A rasping voice could be heard.

'Hello? Hello? Walker?'

Walker addressed himself to the phone again. 'Look, thank you, Doctor Mallory. I'll be waiting to hear from you. OK?'

Walker didn't just hang up, he mashed the receiver on to its slot. Then he rubbed his palms into his face. To be always waiting – waiting for other people to finish their work, for the law to grind, for something to turn up – that was the worst of the policeman's lot as far as Walker was concerned. He dropped his hands and looked hopefully at Dave Satchell, a man who could always be relied on to keep things turning over.

'Maybe we'll get lucky with one of the lolly sticks or the wrappers,' said the Sergeant. 'If she was in Dunn's flat and ate the ice-cream there, maybe we can prove it with DNA.'

'Yes, I know.'

Walker sighed. 'My kid virtually licks the design off. Shit, this is going to cost a fortune! We got ten wrappers, six sticks and half my budget's already gone to that lunatic

Mallory and his bloody shoe casts. Did you know he's had four plaster casts done – that's a couple of hundred quid *each* off my budget!'

He looked at Satchell, squinting. They'd brought Dunn in last night for theft. Now, having rearrested him this morning they'd got until exactly ten-o-five tomorrow morning to hang a charge on him.

'So. How do we stand re Mr Dunn? The bastard sober?'

Satchell laughed. 'He's had ten hours kip and two breakfasts. He's hung-over, certainly, but . . .'

Walker got up and adjusted the knot of his tie. Then he held out his fist.

'OK – you ready? Prepare, engage . . .'

'Account, closure . . .' replied Satchell, knocking the Detective Superintendent's fist with his own. They were reciting the mnemonic formula for the interview of suspects, something learned by all trainee detectives.

'And – evaluation!' capped Walker, pulling on his jacket and jamming the still unlit cigarette at a jaunty angle into his mouth. 'Let's go!'

PACE is the acronym for the Police and Criminal Evidence Act which since 1982 has regulated all the police's dealings with suspects. Designed as much to shield the police from charges of unfair treatment as to protect the public from oppressive police questioning, it has a bad name amongst serving officers for being cumbersome, bureaucratic and over-restrictive. Under the code of practice, Michael Dunn could be held for up to twenty-four hours without being charged. He could have a solicitor if he wanted and the benefit of a single phone call. If he needed medical assistance because of illness or injuries a local GP on the register of police surgeons would be sent for. The arbiter in all these matters is not the arresting officer but the station custody officer, in this case Sergeant Johns, who is God when it comes to the welfare of the suspect.

Dunn's questioning must be audiotaped in duplicate; in more modern stations it would also be videotaped. A copy of the tape should be given him on request. He must also be given a break regularly every three-quarters of an hour and a hot drink every two hours.

When Johns delivered him to the interview room Dunn looked appalling. The whites of his eyes were streaked with blood. His hair hung in rats' tails, his nose was snotty, his hands, face and neck were caked with dirt. Having removed his clothes for forensic testing they had dressed him in a white paper jumpsuit which rattled to the rhythm of his violent shaking. He shuffled through the door, his feet in police-issue plimsolls, two sizes too large and minus the laces. He hardly looked fit for questioning but Johns had seen colossal hangovers before. There was no call, he had judged, for the surgeon.

'Sit down, please, Mr Dunn,' said Walker, turning to the double tape recorder near his elbow and speaking into the mike. 'This interview is being tape recorded and may be given in evidence. I am Detective Superintendent Walker attached to Southampton Street police station, and the other officer present is—' he cocked his head towards Satchell, who was sitting alongside him – 'Detective Sergeant Satchell, Southampton Street.'

Walker went on, 'We are in interview room one at Southampton Street Police Station, and I am interviewing . . .' He looked at Dunn, who had sat down and placed a packet of cigarettes and a lighter on the table in front of him. He selected a cigarette and lit up. 'Say your name now, Mr Dunn.'

The suspect seemed far away. He roused himself and spoke in a croaking voice. 'Michael Dunn.'

'There is no other person present,' continued Walker. 'The time is ten forty-four a.m. and the date is the eighth of September. At the end of this interview I will give you a notice explaining what will happen to the tapes. Now . . .'

Walker relaxed, pressing himself back against the chair and looking closely at Dunn. 'Let me remind you that you are still under caution, and that you are entitled to free legal advice.'

'I don't want any,' said Dunn.

'Could you state your name and address and date of birth?'

'Er, Michael . . . do you want my middle name as well? It's Michael . . . Frederick Dunn and I live at—'

Dunn screwed up his face. He seemed to be trying to visualize the information, like a witness recalling a car number plate.

'Twelve, Howarth Parade . . . and I was born, er, sixteenth March in nineteen . . . sixty-nine.'

'Good. Do you understand why you have been arrested?'

But Dunn had lapsed once more into a state of torpor.

'Will you say yes or no, please?'

Dunn roused himself, aware of a sharper tone in Walker's voice. 'Yes, yes. I understand. It's OK. Ask me anything you like.'

'Where were you last Thursday lunchtime?'

'Well, I would if I could. I don't remember ... Thursday?'

'Thursday,' said Walker.

'Well, now, let's see ... I get my giro Thursday. I go down and collect it personal because it's always getting nicked.'

'So you do remember Thursday. Good.'

'Yes, like I said. I cashed my giro.'

'Where did you cash it?'

'Post Office up by the newsagent.'

'Uh-huh. And which newsagent would that be?'

'One near the estate, near where I live.' He suddenly began to giggle. 'He got a bit nasty with me, the newsagent. Well, he had reasons.'

'Oh yes?'

'Yeah!'

He was fully laughing now, hunching over, his head going down to the table. 'I stuffed most of the papers I was supposed to deliver in the bins. Especially on Thursday. Couldn't be bothered.'

Dunn's mirth had subsided to a snigger.

'What did you do then – last Thursday?'

'Got me money, went round to the off-licence.'

'Which off-licence is that, Mr Dunn?'

'One near the newsagent. Near where I live. Then I went to the park. I go there.'

'And what do you do there?'

'I drink, with me pals. I'd have been there Thursday.'

Dunn had taken off one of the shoes they'd given him and was feeling around inside.

'Can you name any of these pals?'

'Yeah, er, there's Midge, Terry Smith and, um, some other bloke . . .'

'Do you know what time you met up with your mates?'

Dunn sat without answering for a moment, looking without curiosity at the shoe.

Walker repeated the question. 'When on Thursday? You got your giro and then . . .?'

Dunn roused himself. 'After the off-licence opened, must've been.'

'And what time does the off-licence open?'

Dunn raised his head and said, in mock patience, 'After eleven o'clock.'

'So, tell me what you do before you go to the off-licence.'

Dunn shrugged. 'I get up and I wait – for the off-licence to open.'

'And then, do you stay with these pals all afternoon on Thursdays?'

'Yeah, unless we get moved on. Or the kids start hassling us.'

Walker's eyebrows arched. 'Kids?'

'Yeah, off the estate.'

'Any specific kids? How old?'

'Some about eight, some about sixteen. I don't know. All kinds.'

'Do you like kids?'

'Yeah. But not when they mess me about.'

'What do you mean by that?'

'Oh, nick things off me. Break into me flat.'

Walker was interested now and he wanted Dunn to know it. He leaned nearer.

'So kids go into your flat?'

'Yeah.'

'Girls as well as boys?'

'Yes, they're worse than the lads.'

'Oh? But the little ones aren't, are they?'

'No. They're OK.'

Walker shifted on his chair so he was closer still to Dunn.

'Do you like little girls?'

He let the question hang for one, two, three seconds and then, just as Dunn was about to say something, Walker went on.

'Did you ever play peekaboo with them? You know, hide your face behind your fingers. Did you do that last Thursday afternoon? In the playground on the estate.'

The room was hot, the air fouled with sweat and smoke, the walls crawling with condensation. Dunn was still holding his shoe, looking at it. Walker couldn't tell if he was thinking about the question or his mind had wandered off again.

Then Dunn said, 'No, no. I was with me mates.'

'Why have you got kids' toys in your flat?'

'For the kids ... Well, I mean, some of them, are theirs.'

'Which toys specifically belong to the children?'

Pulling a sullen face, Dunn shrugged. 'I don't know what I've got and what I haven't got, do I?'

'Any kids play in your flat last Thursday?'

'I don't know. I wasn't there.'

'You were with your pals, right? In the park?'

'Yes, they'll ... what's the word? Vouch for me, yeah.'

'What do you mean, vouch for you?'

'Well, you want to know where I was Thursday. They'll tell you.'

Walker sighed and looked at Satchell, then pulled out a cigarette, broke off the filter and lit up.

'OK. What do you do when it's not Thursday? Other days?'

'You mean, when I got no money?'

'Exactly.'

'Stay in me flat, play videos . . . Well, I did play videos, till my video got nicked.'

'Oh? How long ago was that?'

Dunn shook his head and examined his fingernails. Each had a sickle-shaped deposit of black dirt beneath.

'I don't know. Months.'

'And did you play videos for the kids?'

'Yeah. I like cartoons. So do they.'

'What about videos like *The Terminator*?'

'Great.'

'And *Child's Play*?'

'Yeah, that's brilliant.'

'And how do those videos – videos like those – affect you?'

Dunn frowned. He was puzzled.

'How d'you mean?'

'How do they make you feel?'

Dunn frowned, staring up at the corner of the room. 'Feel? Oh, well. Sometimes I get angry.'

'And what do you do about that?'

'Drink.'

'In front of the kids? Are you watching these videos with kids?'

Dunn smiled, a droopy movement of the lips. 'Yeah, I did sometimes.'

117

'Were you watching videos on Thursday?'

Dunn straightened his drooping spine. 'No!' he flashed, angrily. 'You're not listening to me. I said I got no video now.'

'OK. But when you *used* to watch videos, did you ever watch them with a little girl called Julie Harris?'

Dunn had lapsed back into his former torpid state. He appeared not to hear.

'Do you know who she is?'

Dunn was fiddling with his Bic lighter, looking at it with interest.

'What about her brother, Jason?' persisted Walker.

'They were just kids to me, off the estate,' Dunn mumbled. 'I don't know their names.'

Beside Walker's chair on the floor was an exhibits bag, a canvas holdall. Now he reached into it and drew out the doll taken from Dunn's flat.

'I am now showing the interviewee exhibit number RC3.'

He held it up and turned it. The artificial flesh showed through the transparent plastic like real skin. 'Do you recognize this, Michael?'

It was the first time Walker had called him by his first name. Dunn raised his head sharply, then looked away.

'Yeah, it's a doll.'

'I know that. But this particular doll, Michael, we got from your flat.'

Dunn gave that momentary glance again before returning to his examination of his feet. 'It's got an arm missing.'

Walker sighed and spoke slowly and deliberately. 'I am investigating the murder of Julie Anne Harris. A little girl. If you fail – or refuse – to account for this doll's having been found in your flat, a proper inference may be drawn in court.'

Dunn raised his eyes and looked at the doll. Walker turned the evidence bag through ninety degrees in front of his eyes which, though not as blank as they had been, remained dull and unresponsive. Perhaps he was considering what to say. Perhaps his sluggish, abused brain was genuinely striving to remember.

'I found it,' he said at last.

'You found this doll?'

'Yes. Up by the derelict houses. I want to go to the toilet.'

Walker's face was intense now. He searched Dunn's face for the lie, for the flicker of fear, that would tell him Michael Dunn was a murderer.

'*When* did you find it?'

'What?'

'When did you find the doll?'

'Thursday. I found it on Thursday. Look, can I—'

'When on Thursday did you find this doll? It's very important that we know, Michael.'

Dunn opened his mouth to speak, then shut it again. The brain was working better now. He looked at Satchell, who thought he saw a moment, just a moment, of shrewd calculation. It was the look of an animal about to back out of a trap. Then Dunn turned to Walker again. His face creased into a smile. He leaned towards them and put a hand to the side of his mouth.

'I lied,' he confided in a whisper. 'I had it for ages.' He erased the smile and straightened up. 'I have to go to the toilet now.'

Walker leaned towards the tape machine. 'Interview

suspended at eleven fifteen a.m. to allow Michael Dunn to use the toilet.'

Outside the interview room, Walker and Satchell were intercepted by Pat North.

'Mallory called. Says the tests on Julie Anne's stomach contents are going to take much longer than anticipated. Ditto Dunn's clothes.'

Walker groaned and shut his eyes. He stayed like that for a moment, then snapped back into action.

'Get him a bloody solicitor,' he told North. 'In the meantime, we check out his so-called alibi.'

'What do you reckon, guv?' asked Satchell. 'Is it Dunn?'

Walker scowled. He looked as if he might spit. 'Yeah. We just don't have enough to charge him.'

North returned to the Incident Room to check the house-to-house reports from Ashcroft Close and the other owner-occupied houses which had been trawled earlier. Barridge's report was long and painfully detailed.

There have been a lot of thefts [she read] *including washing, pegs, lines, plants and pots. Residents have repeatedly complained to the Council, who have promised to raise the height of the garden fences, but so far there has been no action. A Neighbourhood Watch scheme has not proved effective in stemming the level of crime and residents are critical of the police . . .*

Christ – he'd written a dissertation. She skimmed through the visit reports until one caught her attention.

Number 17 Ashcroft Close: corner house. Owner occupier, Miss A. Taylor, reports that her washing line has recently been stolen. Post to which line was attached had also been recently painted.

Sergeant Satchell came bustling in. 'We've got a Belinda Sinclair, in reception. Duty solicitor for Michael Dunn.'

North frowned, trying to place the name. 'Sinclair?'

'Sergeant Johns says she's only been on the scheme a few months – correction, three weeks. She's fresh as a daisy!'

North held Barridge's report before his eyes. 'I'll take her through to him. Check this, it's Barridge's door-to-door report.' She laid the report against his chest in such a way as to give him no choice but to take it or let it fall. 'Seventeen Ashcroft Close. Get a Scene of Crime Officer on to the post, will you?'

Satchell looked nonplussed. 'What post?'

'Miss Taylor's post – Ashcroft Close.'

'And? What's it all in aid of?'

North had begun to move. She stopped and turned. 'The rope around the victim's neck had traces of paint. It's all in the MG dockets, Sarge, if you would only make time to read them!'

Belinda Sinclair was young and she was a rookie, which Walker knew before he met her. He'd provisionally marked her down as a pushover, but two things changed his mind when he saw her. Firstly, she looked him smack in the eye and the look had ambition written right through it like a stick of rock. Secondly, she was beautiful.

If Ms Sinclair really knew how to handle herself, the beauty would be an asset every bit as useful as a doctorate in law or a father on the Bench.

She'd been escorted into the interview room by North and was reading the casework file. She wanted to master the brief before facing her client. Walker, who'd followed her in, stood by the window, smoking, glancing at his watch, wishing this well-dressed woman would speed up.

'So the twelve videos turned out to be Mr Dunn's own property?' she said, coolly.

'Yes,' said Walker, flicking his ash.

'So you then arrested him in connection with the murder of the little girl, Julie Anne Harris?'

'Yes.'

'But you really have no other evidence . . .' Walker was about to speak but she forestalled him by holding up her hand. She turned the page. '. . . apart from a statement by this Mrs Enid Marsh.'

'Who identified Dunn as the man last seen with Julie Anne Harris. Mrs Harris also identified a doll found in Dunn's flat. It belonged to her daughter.'

'But you haven't placed my client on an identification parade?'

Walker let out a single ironic laugh. 'You haven't seen him yet. It's not so easy.'

She shut the file and smiled at him glacially. 'Well, Detective Superintendent Walker, I suggest you get a parade arranged. If you have a witness, it *would* seem the logical next step – wouldn't it?'

Walker had an urge to tell her what to do with her suggestion, but repressed it.

'I'd like to see my client now. And I'd like access to

the recorded interview *and* a copy of the custody report, which does not seem to be here.'

Walker preceded her to the door and theatrically opened it for her. 'Right away, Ms Sinclair,' he said, barely concealing the sarcasm.

CHAPTER 10

MAKING THE beds Anita was thinking about the word tragedy and she couldn't find any meaning in it. She'd been told her father's death was a tragedy and now they were throwing the word around about Julie. But papers also talked about a footballer breaking his leg as a tragedy, or a pensioner's missing budgie. Anita shuddered convulsively. You couldn't begin to think about who might have done those deliberate, spiteful things to her daughter. Just to call it a tragedy was too automatic, a way of forgetting it – and they must never, ever forget.

She heard the doorbell in the hallway ring once. Suddenly she hated the outside world, the way it came in and interfered and took things. A sudden wave of hatred battered her. There was a bitter taste to it that had seized her from time to time in the last few days. She put up with it. She was still awaiting the sweet release of pure grief.

Entering the lounge a couple of minutes later, Anita gasped and put a hand to her mouth. The tall man standing by the sideboard, with his short hair and impeccable turn-out, was Thomas Harris, her ex-husband. He turned round and she saw in his hand one of the framed photographs of his daughter – the one in which she was wearing a spotted dress and sat astride a blue playground cow.

She looked directly into his eyes, saw their icy clarity. His voice was low, subdued.

'They let me have compassionate leave. Flew in last night. All right, are you?'

Anita remembered Thomas's rages. The worst had been when she'd told him she could no longer bear the bitchy life in army married quarters and was leaving. The anger had always started with Thomas speaking very low, quiet, controlled, before building up to an intensity that was terrifying. He never hit or even touched her. He would simply turn into a different person. It scared her then and, she realized, it still did.

'I swear to God, Thomas,' she said, her voice trembly, 'she was only out playing ten minutes. Jason was with her.'

Thomas returned the photograph to the sideboard. 'I don't know what to say. I can't take it in. She was my baby.'

He bowed his head. At this moment, Peter came in from the kitchen. He looked at Thomas in a way that was at the same time aggressive and guarded. He said, 'They got someone, you know. That pervert, the one from the estate . . .'

Thomas shook his head from side to side. 'Well, I'd like to have ten minutes with him, that's all.'

Pushing past Peter, Helen appeared. As soon as she realized that Thomas had come, she started to weep. Thomas went to her, wrapping his arms around her.

'Hello, Mum. I couldn't get here sooner. Eventually they gave me compassionate leave.'

Finally, Jason came hurtling in and threw himself at his father.

'Dad! Dad!' Jason was so excited to see him; his body trembled and he was close to tears.

Thomas stooped and gathered his son up. Jason clung to him as if afraid to let him go, showing in that moment more affection to his real father than he ever had for Peter James.

Helen watched them hugging and said to Peter, 'Maybe you should leave them alone.'

It was her way of pointing up the difference between Thomas and Peter. Helen had never wavered in believing that Anita and the kids belonged with Thomas. If only they'd stayed with him, how different things might have been!

Peter swung towards her, snarling. 'And maybe you should shut up! Just keep your nose out!'

'Eh!' said Thomas, putting Jason down. 'Don't you speak to Mum like that. You hear me?'

'Oh, this is your house, is it? You pay the bills, do you?'

Thomas raised a finger, real menace in his eyes. 'Julie was *my* daughter. So leave it *out*.'

Peter's lip curled. 'Prick!'

Standing aside, as if accidentally detached, Jason watched the adults. He didn't understand exactly what was going on, but he appreciated his dad telling Peter to get knotted. Peter slunk out of the room then, and his gran and his mum both started crying. His dad wrapped his arms around his mum and hugged her, swinging her from side to side. She pushed her face into his dad's shoulder and just sobbed and sobbed. Jason wanted to be a part of that embrace. He was jealous of her. He wanted to still be held by his dad. He knew that Julie was gone, which wasn't *his* fault. But having his beloved dad back was all right.

Belinda Sinclair and Michael Dunn made quite a contrast – he, in his white paper overall, unshaven for several days, filthy fingernails, matted hair; she, in a dove-grey designer suit and apricot silk shirt, her lips glistening with perfectly applied scarlet lipstick, her blonde hair catching the light from the mundane striplight and turning it to pure gold. She sat upright in her chair with a legal pad on the table in front of her and an expensive ballpoint in her hand.

'You must concentrate, Michael. This is very serious,' she was saying. She could see he had not taken very much of his situation in. He wasn't frightened, but listless, detached.

'You have given two different versions of how you got the doll. An inference can be drawn from that in court, you know.'

Dunn, already sitting bent forward on his chair, slumped against the table, covering his face with his hands. 'I want to get out of here. I want to go home. I need a drink.'

'Michael.' Belinda's voice was coaxing, almost seductive. 'You do realize I am your solicitor. I am not a police officer.'

Dunn raised his head. The red-rimmed eyes looked feverish and hunted. 'Why am I here?'

In frustration, Belinda dropped the pen onto the pad. There was a tap on the door and Dunn, startled, shambled to his feet. It was Satchell. .

'You ready yet, ma'am?'

Belinda Sinclair's response was frosty. 'No, but I will inform you when I am.'

Satchell hung for a moment in the doorway, made as if to speak and then changed his mind. He raised his hand and left.

'Now, Michael, please sit down. We need to talk about this doll. And then there is a small matter of an identification parade . . .'

PCs Phelps and Brown had been detailed to pay a visit to the Scrubbery and pick up any winos in sight – and in particular the one known as Midge. They found her sitting in her customary place, singing 'Somewhere Over the Rainbow'. She said she'd be delighted to accompany Phelps to Southampton Street nick, or to any other destination he might care to name.

'I'd go anywhere with you, darling,' she told him as he assisted her towards the squad car. 'Lovely looking boy like you. Who's a lovely boy then?'

She leaned into Phelps's shoulder and slid her cheek along until her forehead clashed with the line of his jaw.

'Oops! 'Scuse me. Give us a kiss, then – go on. Give us a kiss, handsome.'

Meanwhile Brown had got hold of Bert O'Farrell, who was proving less cooperative.

'I'll bloody kill you! Cart me off in your meat wagon, would you, you bastards!'

'Please, Mr O'Farrell,' said Brown, as his cap flew off. He gestured to Phelps for assistance. 'Look, we only want to talk to you.'

'Slaughter me? I'll bloody slaughter the pair of *you*. Come on, then, come on. Try me. Put up your fists, you pair of fairies.'

Midge Parker-Brown sat in the back seat of the car, watching the tussling men benignly. A fragment of distant memory had entered her brain – a Parker-Brown limousine standing on a gravel drive with her, aged ten, sitting demurely in the back. The engine was purring, ready to whisk her off for a birthday visit to the cinema.

At last Phelps and Brown bundled Bert O'Farrell into the car beside her. As they drove away Midge began to sing.

'*We're off to see the Wizard, the wunnerful Wizard of Oz, because, because, because, becauuuuuse . . .*'

At the station, Phelps got Midge sitting down in the waiting area as a WPC walked past. She took one look at Midge and stopped.

'Hello, Midge. What they bringing you in for this time?'

'You know her?' said Phelps. He guided his colleague out of Midge's earshot. 'That AMIP Sergeant Satchell's going to question her about the Harris suspect. Dunn's named her for his alibi. Trouble is she's pissed as a fart.'

'Nothing new there. Same story on Thursday when I last saw the old bat.'

Phelps did a double take. 'Thursday? Where'd you see her?'

'St John's hospital casualty. Took her there in the morning, about ten, ten-thirty.'

'What happened?'

'She fell down some steps. Suspected concussion.'

'How long did they keep her?'

129

'Don't know. I left her there. I'll look in my notes and give you a firm time. And you can always phone St John's.'

Twenty minutes later Phelps gave Sergeant Satchell the good news.

'Dunn's alibi just blew away, Sarge. Hospital says the Triage Nurse assessed Midge Parker-Brown at ten-thirty and they didn't release her until six at night. Apparently they thought she might have brain damage. That's a laugh. Anyway, she can't have been with Dunn at all on Thursday, can she? Unless they had a liquid breakfast together.'

'No,' said Satchell. 'Dunn didn't leave his house till eleven, as far as we can tell. What about the other bloke you pulled – what's his name, O'Farrell?'

Phelps made a face and shook his head. 'Got a bad case of uniformitis. Thinks he's Mike Tyson at the moment but I doubt we'll ever get anything out of him.'

Satchell smiled. 'Good. About Midge, put it in writing for me, will you, Phelps? And let her go. I'll give the glad tidings to Mr Walker.'

Walker sat at his desk, thinking through the chain of evidence he was constructing against Michael Dunn, link by link. Dunn had been suspected by the residents on the estate. He'd given an alibi, of course, but even though it hadn't stuck, the residents' suspicions would be dismissed by a jury as pure prejudice, except for one thing. Enid Marsh had seen a man with the missing child and he fitted Dunn's description. She was a dotty old lady, which wasn't exactly to her credit as a witness. But it helped in another way because Enid was a recluse and not exactly

130

tuned in to the prejudices of the estate. So she probably didn't know Dunn for the 'pervert' that the residents had tagged him as.

It all hinged on identification: would old Enid recognize Dunn as the long-haired man in the long dark coat who she'd seen in the playground. You never knew with old people. One minute they could name every Grand National winner since 1936 and the next they'd forgotten how to make toast.

But one thing was for certain. Either he'd have to let Dunn go or put Enid's colander mind to the test, and soon. That meant lashing together an identification parade before the end of the day and that wasn't even half as easy as it looked in cop films. They'd have to assemble eight men, each with a superficial resemblance to Michael Dunn, and keep them in one place while the old dear was trundled from the Howarth Estate all the way to the Met's ID Suite at Kilburn.

Walker dared not think what was going to happen to his budget by the time this investigation was over. It was already in shreds. He sighed, flipped open the notebook he used to keep track of costs and began rummaging in a drawer for his calculator.

By three o'clock, eight men who were like, but not too like, Michael Dunn had been found at Kilburn and kitted out in various styles of long coat. The lights in the Identification Suite were down and they stood in semi-darkness, talking in low tones as they awaited the star of the show.

Michael Dunn, now in prison-issue clothes and a long dark coat similar to his own, sauntered in between two officers. He seemed unconcerned.

'Which position do you want?' asked the escorting officer.

Dunn looked at him in foggy puzzlement. 'Eh?'

'In the parade.' He jerked his thumb at the dark-glass window on the wall opposite the line of men. 'This is an Identification Suite. You'll be eyeballed from in there. So where do you want to stand?'

Dunn glanced up and down, scratching his head, then stepped into a place, the other men shuffling to make room. Cards with printed numbers were fixed above their heads. Struck by solemnity in the presence of a possible murderer, they listened to their instructions. They were to remember their numbers and keep their expressions neutral. Dunn's was number three.

'Any questions?'

Nobody had any questions.

The ID Suite at Kilburn is, in the correct marketing jargon, a state of the art facility, with a viewing room behind one-way glass, remote control lighting and talk-back. Enid Marsh entered the viewing room in a wheel-chair, followed by a small retinue of officers, one of them pushing, another carrying her walking frame and hand-bag. Belinda Sinclair was the last to enter. She stood quietly by the door watching Enid closely. The old woman was fidgeting impatiently.

'You can stay in your chair, Mrs Marsh, if you like,' said the Identification Officer.

'No, no. I *can* stand, you know. I don't even have a chair of my own at home. It's just this arthritis.'

She gripped the arms of the chair and heaved herself

on to her feet. She stood for a moment with knees and back braced and slightly bent. Then she straightened, almost triumphantly. 'See?' Looking from face to face, as if expecting a round of applause, she was smiling broadly.

The officer touched a button and the room behind the glass burst into light. The halogen brightness made the men look uniformly pale and unhealthy. Enid scanned them eagerly. She felt rejuvenated, important.

'You want me to pick him out now?'

The Identification Officer cleared his throat and raised a clipboard. He frowned at the witness.

'On September the fifth, at about one p.m., you saw a man take a little girl by the hand in the playground beneath your window. That man may—'

He looked severely at Enid. She was nodding at him like someone keeping time to music.

' – or may *not* be on this identification parade today, but I would ask you not to make any decision as to whether you can identify him before you have looked twice at each member of the parade.'

Enid swallowed. She mustn't rush, that's what he was saying to her, though why he had to read it out like that she didn't know.

'Could they stand up?' she asked.

She examined the man on the end of the line, position number nine. Never seen him before. Number eight, same. And number seven. Where did they get these chaps from? Number six, number five, number four – never clapped eyes on them, though five looked like that nice lad in the fish shop. Number three . . .

'Just take your time,' said the policeman.

Enid's heart quickened. Number three! That was him.

Since she knew about the murder she'd kept an image of what she'd seen from her window fresh in her mind. Same shape of head, same hair, same coat. It was him.

She turned to the policeman. 'Number three,' she said, firmly. 'That's the man.'

Belinda tore out of the ID Suite, keying the office number on her mobile. She had been trying to contain her excitement, but this was news she had to tell someone. She got Jeremy Oxley, one of the solicitors she shared her office with.

'Jeremy? Guess what! . . . No, you berk. My client's just been picked out of a parade. I've got myself a murderer! What was that?' She giggled. 'Of course, I meant an *alleged* murderer. He's called Michael Frederick Dunn.'

Walker was still juggling the overtime figures when Satchell came in with the news that another link in the chain had been forged.

'We going to charge the bastard now, guv?'

Walker sighed and shook his head. 'This is identification, Dave. Too many cases that hinged on the dodgy memory of a witness have gone down the toilet. I need something more, or the CPS won't be playing ball.'

And, to satisfy the Crown Prosecution Service, he knew what he needed was forensic evidence. But did he have the money? He looked despairingly at the column of figures in front of him. If only this wasn't Sunday. On bloody Sunday everything cost double – or was it triple? Oh well, the fuck to it.

'Get on to Sergeant Polk,' he said wearily. 'I want forensics down at Dunn's flat – yes, again! The whole team. I want the floors up. I want every piece of bedbug shit turned over. I want something that'll stick to Dunn like superglue and I want it today or, at the latest, tomorrow. We've got till ten a.m. or this investigation has gone to buggery.'

CHAPTER 11

'HEY, BARRIDGE! What's this? Mine was ham and cheese.'

Barridge swivelled back to the Superintendent's desk, where he'd just deposited a coffee and a bagged sandwich. 'Sorry, sir. I—'

Walker held up the paper bag. 'This is cheese and pickle.'

Barridge looked at the cardboard tray he carried. He picked up another sandwich and gave it to the Detective Superintendent. 'Sorry, sir. Sorry. Got mixed up.'

Walker softened. He'd seen the look of panic on the constable's face. 'Look. It's no big deal, OK? Just I don't like pickle.'

He tossed the unwanted package back to Barridge and opened the second bag. Barridge hovered, waiting to be sent on his way.

'You all right, son?' Walker asked in a low voice as he extracted the replacement sandwich. 'I know it was you that found her. Living with you, is it?'

Barridge tried to stand as upright as possible. 'I'm all right, sir.'

'If ever you want to talk about it, you can go to occupational health. That's what they're there for. I've been there, son.'

Barridge, who didn't think the Detective Superintendent had ever in his life so much as breathed the same air as an occupational health therapist, said, 'Really, I'm—'

'*Don't* bottle it up. Which reminds me – Cranham!'

'Yes, guv?'

The Exhibits Officer came over and helped himself to a sandwich pack from Barridge's tray.

'I want those empty bottles collected from Dunn's place and sent over to Mallory.'

Cranham nodded as he tore open the sandwich. 'I'll sort it, guv. I'm on my way over now.'

'Take PC Barridge with you. Dunn had a bit of a problem with recycling so you'll need some extra muscle.'

An hour later, with Belinda Sinclair beside him, the suspect was back in the interview room facing Walker and Satchell across a table on which there were two brands of cigarette, a lighter, full ashtray, disposable cups. On the wall was a water cooler. The recording machine whirred.

The police were like fishermen moving up and down a riverbank, casting for a rise, but so far the fish stayed locked to the bottom. After more than an hour of questioning, there had been no bites – nothing to enable Walker to charge Dunn.

'This doll . . .' Walker held up the nude plastic doll in its polythene evidence bag. 'Julie Ann had this with her when she left home. She was subsequently found dead. Now, I am asking you again Mr Dunn: why was this doll found in your flat?'

Belinda turned her eyes on Dunn. *Be careful*. But Dunn seemed hardly to be attending.

'My flat? I don't know, do I? I mean, it used to be quite nice when I moved in, like. But me pals wrecked it, and the kids . . .'

He was shivering in rhythm with the throbbing of his head. The white paper suit that he again wore rustled slightly in the hollow room. All sensation, but especially the perception of sound and light, seemed swollen and bruised to him. He reached for the white cup of water and gulped. It felt good except there was no sting of alcohol in his throat.

'You haven't answered the question, Michael.'

Trying to stub his cigarette out against the inside of the cup, Dunn was burning a hole in the styrofoam. 'I found it.'

'When did you find it?'

Still intent on extinguishing his butt, Dunn produced a tentative, truncated shrug. 'About a year ago.'

Walker leaned forward. '*Where* did you find it?'

Dunn had by now poked the cigarette all the way through the cup. He peered at the protruding tip in surprise. An acrid smell permeated the room.

'Will you please answer the question?'

'On the building site – that building site on the estate.'

'Are you sure about that, Mr Dunn?'

Dunn glanced sideways at his brief, who smiled encouragingly. 'Yes.'

Now he was applying the tip of the cigarette tentatively to the white paper of his overall.

'Do you like ice-cream?' asked Walker.

'No.'

'But you have a lot of ice-cream wrappers in your flat. Where do they come from?'

'I don't know. Lots of people, like, come and go.' Suddenly he was shouting and waggling his head. 'Ice-cream van – *Ding-dong, ding dong* . . .'

By now he'd burned a series of holes in his sleeve so that the pale, goose-pimply skin could be seen. Walker shook out a Marlboro and snapped off the filter.

'Did you see Julie Ann Harris last Thursday afternoon?'

'No. I was with my friends, see? Like I told you.'

'Yes – you have stated that you were with—' Walker put the unlit cigarette in his mouth and lifted up his notes. 'Terry Smith, another man you were unable to name, and a woman named Midge.'

'Yes, I was.'

Walker lit the little bush of tobacco that stuck out of the end of his cigarette. 'Well, I'm afraid, Michael, that Midge Parker-Brown was *not* with you last Thursday. We have established that. We know where she was, and it was nowhere near you.'

He studied Dunn intently. He was an angler again, scrutinizing the broken surface of the river. 'What do you have to say about that?'

Dunn was now mashing his cigarette into his arm, to stub it out once and for all. 'I don't know,' he mumbled. 'Must have been mistaken.'

'Mistaken? Can I just go back over that, Michael. You say you were mistaken. About *what* exactly?'

Dunn looked up from his sleeve, which had begun to smoulder. 'What? Sorry, what was the question?'

Walker opened his mouth to repeat the question but he was forestalled. A pale blue flame had appeared on the suspect's sleeve, rimming one of the worn holes he'd made with his cigarette. Then, abruptly, the fire took hold, turning yellow as it licked at the folds of the suspect's sleeve. Dunn was on fire. He leapt up, screeching and pawing at the flame, his chair clattering to the floor behind him. In the same instant Satchell reached for his own water cup, leaned across and threw it over Dunn. With a truncated fizzle, the fire died.

For a few beats, no one spoke. Satchell couldn't, he was trying to control himself – Belinda Sinclair's face could have put a fire out. Most of the water had gone over her anyway. She ran a hand through her hair and cleared her throat.

'Superintendent Walker, I am suggesting a bathroom break.'

She smiled thinly at the interrogators. 'If my client doesn't require one, I most certainly do.'

'Right,' snapped Walker. Then, for the tape: 'Interview suspended at seven-oh-two p.m., to allow Miss Sinclair to take a leak.'

At the Forensic Laboratory, a junior scientific officer rubbed his eyes under his plastic protective spectacles. Sometimes he got called in on Sunday, but not usually for a long shift. Police couldn't afford it. Today, it seemed, was different and he could have done without it. Saturday's rugger match, the party in the evening at Notting Hill and his night with that girl from Streatham – what was her name? – had taken its toll and he was shattered. Still, Sunday overtime was something else on this job.

He reached a latex-gloved hand, holding a pair of laboratory tongs, into the black dustbin bag which stood beside his test-bench, drawing out a crushed and soggy cereal packet. He carefully prized it open to see if anything had been pushed inside. Sometimes at parties he described himself for effect as a Garbologist. Other people's rubbish may be one of the least pleasant, but it was potentially the most revealing, of the stuff that came in for lab examination.

He dined out on the story of when he'd found a set of false eyelashes in the bin of an international opening batsman and DNA testing proved that the cricketer had worn them himself. It actually had nothing to do with the case, but he had never been able to watch the guy play in a Test Match since then without wondering if he wore them on the field.

The cereal packet was empty. He placed it with a pile of discarded packaging and recorded it on his inventory, then tonged out a lump of cheese with a rich crop of furry grey mould growing all over it. Seven to eight weeks' worth, he estimated. He made a note of it and fished again.

The tongs connected with something which at first slipped from their jaws. He took a firmer grip and pulled again. The thing was mixed up with other refuse and he had to tug it free. When it came loose he could see what it was – a tangle of red and blue washing line. One end had a loop. The other looked cut.

He flipped back the pages on his clipboard to the case report, just to make sure: 'A piece of plastic-coated line ligated around the neck, resembling a clothes-line. Colour, red and blue.'

He left the desk and went looking for Arnold Mallory.

'I don't know about any rope!'

They'd been just about to resume questioning the

suspect when North had clattered down the stairs. She virtually ran at Walker and Satchell, who'd been about to follow Dunn and his brief into the interview room.

'Guv, hold it a second! Lab's found something . . .'

When she told him, his face tightened and he grabbed her shoulders, planting a kiss on her cheek. 'Yes!'

Back in the interview room, he told Dunn what he had found, then listened as the man tried pathetically to deny all knowledge.

'I don't know how it got in my bin! I don't!' he bleated.

Walker interrupted him, placing both palms flat on the tabletop and leaning forward to make sure he was clearly understood.

'Michael Frederick Dunn,' he said, 'I am now charging you with the murder of Julie Ann Harris . . .'

CHAPTER 12

A T LEAST an hour of Walker's insomnia that night had been occupied with the magistrate's impending decision on bail. It would complicate things badly if Dunn was released. Walker still needed unfettered access to his flat – with the unused section of washing line found there, more evidence had to be forthcoming. *Had* to be. But if Dunn was out and about – living in the flat, because for sure he had nowhere else to go – that would badly screw up the forensic effort.

It was deep within Walker's nature to lie awake envying his wife's snores and worrying about tomorrow, but in this case it was all unnecessary. Next morning, Belinda Sinclair put in a noticeably half-hearted submission, probably preferring to have her client in the Scrubs where she could always find him and he couldn't drink. Knew what she was doing, that girl, Walker had to admit it. The magistrate duly ignored her trite remarks about her client's good intentions and summarily denied bail. Sinclair didn't even appear disappointed; Dunn didn't look as if he knew the time of day.

A dark fog of bewilderment swirled through the accused's head as he sat in the cells beneath the Magistrate's Court.

Fresh as spring in her expensively labelled clothes, Miss Sinclair sat opposite him, pushing a small sheaf of forms and a Biro across the table.

'Some more forms for you to put your signature to, Michael. This one's the final Legal Aid document. That's so that we can be paid for defending you.'

Dunn stared gravely at the paper and picked up the pen. But he did nothing. Belinda got up and looked at the Prison Officer standing guard by the door.

'I just need to show him where to sign – all right?'

The screw nodded and she moved to Dunn's shoulder. He could smell the mix of different perfumes as she leaned nearer – shampoo in her hair, a scented soap maybe and who knows what else? It stirred him out of his lethargy and he aimed the pen towards the dotted line, where her varnished fingernail gleamed.

'Sign here – see?'

Dunn looked up and down the document. 'It's a blank form.'

'Yes – we'll fill it out later. Just sign.'

Dunn wrote his signature in a shaky, childish script.

'And here and here and finally here.'

Dunn kept signing until she was satisfied. She took the pen from his hand and moved back to her seat, opening a thick notepad. Dunn looked at her, squinting. He was not used to looking at beauty. It seemed to make his situation even more confusing.

'OK, Michael. Let's start with your parents' name and address.'

'I don't have any – parents.'

Belinda scribbled a note and said, 'So, where were you brought up?'

'Foster homes. I don't know if I can remember them all.'

She tapped the Biro against her perfectly white teeth and began to speak, but Dunn cut in.

'I don't want to talk about them.' He lit a cigarette. He was edgy, looking away into a corner of the room. 'I don't, er, remember a lot of things. They said it was me blanking it all out.'

Belinda waited, staring at her client. She gave him a few seconds, then said, gently, 'Blanking out what, Michael?'

Dunn's attention was still fixed in the room's corner. He seemed not to hear her.

'Blanking out *what*, Michael?'

Three dull blows on the door echoed around the cell. The Prison Officer turned and looked through the spyhole.

'That's the transportation. Sorry, Miss, we can't wait any longer.'

With a sigh, Belinda closed her notebook. Dunn looked at her. He was quite good-looking really, under all that crud. But he also looked touchingly lost and alone.

'Where are they taking me?' he asked, looking at her now. He had the eyes of an abandoned puppy.

'You'll go to Wormwood Scrubs, Michael.'

'Prison?'

'The Magistrate has denied your bail. You'll stay there until the trial.'

'What d'you mean? What am I going to do? What's it going to be like?'

Sinclair may be a rookie, but she knew something about what it was going to be like. It was going to be hell in a box. Persecution without end, bawled at day and night, cut up in the showers, your food spat into. Nobody had a

145

worse time inside than a man who might have killed a child – except for a man who actually had.

She stood up and said as softly as she could. 'You'll have to be very, very patient, Michael. Do what they say, and don't cause trouble. Will you do that?'

The Prison Officer swung the door open and moved to stand behind the prisoner. He hooked his hand under Dunn's arm and drew him to his feet.

Going through the day like a robot, Anita had spent a lot of time waiting for the television news. There had been a bulletin on BBC1 at eleven and, still in her dressing gown, she watched it with close attention. The case wasn't even mentioned and she felt bitterly disappointed. Was this what it all amounted to? Her little girl's life worth a couple of days' media attention, and then nothing?

After the news was over, she didn't move, just flicked the picture over to ITV, a morning chat show. She knew there was another news in an hour so she sat on, watching the image on the screen whisk from face to face. She couldn't have told you what they were saying.

Peter was sitting with a pile of music CDs on his knee, sorting through them. He wanted to play something loud and violent. He certainly didn't want to watch a bunch of lottery winners and minor TV stars talking about their philosophy of life.

'There wasn't anything about her on the news,' said Anita.

Peter grunted.

She went on, 'Maybe there will be on the later one.'

Peter tossed a CD down and picked up another one.

'Great,' he said. 'Go on. You just sit there and wait for it. Whole place needs hoovering, but don't worry. You sit there. Nothing *else* to do, is there?'

Anita closed her eyes and rocked forward slightly across her folded arms. 'Oh, stop it, Pete. Just stop it.'

But Peter was just starting. 'There's no reason for your mother to stay either. I'm sick and tired of her bunking up in here.'

He put on a mimicking falsetto. 'Thomas this, Thomas that. You ask me, she fancies Thomas herself. And hasn't *he* been a pain in the arse? I'm glad he's gone back.'

'Maybe I need Mum.'

'And what about me? You don't need *me*?'

Anita looked at him. She seemed drugged, out of it. 'I didn't say that.'

'Feels like it.'

He crashed the heap of CDs on to the coffee table, picked up another from the floor and began impatiently dealing them down on to the table like a pack of cards. When he spoke again, she heard the sing-song of self-pity in his voice.

'I touch you and you, like, cringe away. Sleep as far from me in bed as you can. Don't cook any more. You bloody do nothing but sit in front of the TV, waiting for the news!'

She slid back against the chair, her body going limp. 'I'm sorry. I—'

'So am I.'

When Helen came in seconds later she found the two sitting in silence. She carried a tray which she placed on a low table. There were two mugs of tea on it.

'Here you are, love.'

She handed Anita a tea then took the other one and

subsided with a sigh into the vacant armchair. Peter looked at her murderously. Then, with a sweep of his arm, he knocked the CDs off the table, clattering them across the carpet. One or two hit the wall and bounced back. He jumped up, glared at the two women for a moment and slammed out of the room. A few seconds later they heard the flat's front door cannon against its frame.

Helen took an audible sip of tea, staring fixedly at the wall. 'Good riddance,' she observed.

Anita switched off the television and touched her mother on the arm. 'Mum. Maybe, you know, it's a small flat and I do appreciate you being here. I don't know what I'd have done without you, really. But . . .'

Helen looked. Her eyes and mouth were tight. 'My God,' she said quietly, through closed teeth, '*you* don't want me here for the funeral.'

It was a statement, not a question. Anita said, 'I just don't know when they'll let me bury her. It's all, it's all . . .'

'But that's not it, is it, 'Nita? You let *him* run your life. Why you ever broke up with Thomas is beyond me.'

Anita started to speak but her mother held up a hand.

'I'm warning you! I kept my mouth shut, I never said a word about it, but there comes a time—'

'A word about what, Mum? What are you saying?'

'About why Jason wasn't at school that Thursday – remember? About why you had to take Julie to the hospital, Christmas.'

Helen was staring hard at her daughter, challenging her. All she could see in response was exhaustion.

Anita shook her head slowly. 'For God's sake, Mum. Stop it, just stop it.'

A scream came from the kitchen. It was Tony, in his high chair. He hated being left alone. Helen got up.

'You'll have to be in court,' she said. 'So will Peter. But, well, if you don't need me, fine. I'll go.'

She went to attend to Tony. Anita folded her hands more tightly over her stomach and rocked in her chair. Never had she felt so alone. Now it was just her and the baby inside. Everything else was just a side show, a nothing.

Helen came storming back from the kitchen, pulling Jason behind her. 'He's just dragged Tony out of his chair again! Here, you talk to him.'

She hurried back to the kitchen. 'Jason,' warned his mother gently. 'I told you not to play around with him. He's just a baby.'

Jason pouted.

Anita got up and, wrapping her dressing gown around her, went into the kitchen. Helen was rocking Tony in the crook of her arm. She showed Anita a Gnutcrunch ice-cream, from the freezer.

'Can I give him one of these?'

'I'll do it, Mum. Give him me.'

Back in the lounge, Jason looked round to see if anybody was watching. Then he slipped across to the sideboard and selected one of the framed pictures of his dead sister. He looked at it closely, his eyes about four inches from the glass. He ran his finger over the image of Julie's face. Then he jerked his arm and threw the picture on to the floor. Then he began jumping on it, mashing the glass under his heel.

*

Walker returned from the remand hearing determined to get the budget sorted. He could never remember if the Forensic Lab charged a flat rate for a black sack of refuse, or whether they levied a fee for each article they pulled out. He'd already worked out a sheet based on £500 for a sack, but when he looked again at the faxed inventory of Dunn's rubbish, he thought they might be going to sting him for something like £25 an item – and there were thirty-four items on the list. He groaned. He'd have to recalculate.

The phone rang at his elbow.

'Walker? Mallory!'

'Oh, yes, sir. Anything new?'

Mallory spoke deliberately, in his usual pompous manner. 'On the matter of the material recovered from the dustbin of the suspect in the Harris case.'

'Accused.'

'I'm sorry?'

'The accused, sir. He's been charged. He's on remand.'

'I see. Well, I hope that's not solely on the basis of what I have in front of me.'

Walker sat up in his chair, his eyes wary. 'What have you in front of you, sir?'

'I have in front of me, Walker, one blue and red washing line. And yes, it is the same type of rope or washing line as was tied around the little lady's neck. But it is not *the* rope. I think you'd better come and see me.'

Walker all but slumped forward across the budgetary calculations on his desk. *Not the rope?*

PC Barridge was in the Incident Room when Walker burst from his office and shouted to DI North.

'Pat! I've just been talking to Mallory. It's not the rope! Come on, let's go!'

Not the rope? Barridge walked across to the pin-board, where a picture of the ligature used on Julie was displayed. Looking at it always hurt but he forced himself to do it.

At the lab, Mallory showed both lengths of line to Walker and North. They looked identical and Walker said so.

'Yes,' said Mallory, taking the cut end of the murder rope in one hand and the end of the sample found in Dunn's bin in the other. 'As I said, they're the same type of rope but—'

Slowly and theatrically, he brought his two hands together until the cut ends of the lengths of line met.

'These ends don't match.'

Walker tried hard to control himself. 'So – what *have* you got from the flat?'

'We're working on Dunn's clothes. But so far, I regret, there's nothing for you. We've taken up almost all the carpet but the problem here is, it's hard to find an area without stains. There's more than three hundred of them.'

'You're going to test them all?'

'We've done most of them already.'

He consulted the file, which lay open on his desk. 'Semen, blood, soup, alcohol, chocolate, tea, coffee – you want one?'

The police officers looked blank.

Mallory said, 'A coffee?'

Walker shook his head. 'No, thanks. What about the bottles I sent in? Foster said she might have been penetrated by . . .'

'We've got numerous prints from the bottles, mostly Dunn's, which is not surprising. Nothing to connect them to the victim, though. Now, what else? Oh, yes . . .'

He went to the door and called out, '*Jimmy!* Shoe casts!'

Haggard joined them, dressed in a lab coat, wearing a mask and latex gloves and carrying a muddy, down-at-heel shoe. He looked from Walker to North.

'Oh, ah! Hello, Superintendent, Inspector. You heard about the rope, that it's not—'

'Yes, we heard,' said Walker crisply.

Haggard removed his mask. 'Right, well. Shoe casts. We've cleared the backlog on the shoe casts. Eliminated twenty-four as officers' footwear but this . . .' He held up the shabby shoe. 'This was taken off the suspect, right?'

Walker nodded.

'Well, a good selection of ground deposits similar to the terrain we are interested in – brick dust, soil, cement dust – turned up on it. Plus, the ground near where the victim was hidden in the sewage pipes contained a high percentage of clay, so any footwear with all four samples matching means we can be pretty certain he was by those pipes. It's just that we have no shoeprint in that ground for this particular shoe.'

Walker nudged North and put on his coat. They turned to leave but Mallory called after them.

'Hang on, Walker, it's your lucky day after all.'

Walker turned round, his lip curled. He looked as if he might say something he would later find regrettable, but he curbed the impulse. Mallory was holding up the rope used in the murder.

'You haven't let me finish,' he said, mock-wounded. 'The section of line around the little girl's neck *can* be matched to something after all. In fact, I know exactly where it came from – from a Miss Taylor's back garden or, to be more specific, the post she used to hang her washing line from. Is that any help to you?'

It wasn't until they were in the car and on the way to Miss Taylor's that he remembered he'd forgotten to ask Mallory about the cost of tests on the refuse sack.

At the Harris's place, Jason was playing. He lay on the floor, as near as he could to the action he was creating with the small plastic-moulded figures. His mouth made the explosive noises he imagined would come from their weapons as they fired. It was a dangerous ambush, led by his dad's platoon against an attacking enemy force, riding in on their tank. Jason was so absorbed he never noticed Peter coming in.

'Jason! How many times have you been told not to mess around with Tony?'

Jason exploded the attackers' battle tank. The enemy assault party went flying in every direction. It was satisfying.

'You *hearing* me?'

Jason pulled himself up on his elbow and scowled at Peter.

'You're not my dad. And you're not Julie's dad either.'

Peter was standing with one hand behind his back. He kicked at the plastic tank, which skidded over the carpet and smacked the wall.

'I know I'm not. Because I'd never produce a snotty little bastard like you.'

He produced his concealed hand. It held the smashed photograph.

'Did you break this? *Did you?*

153

Jason cowered. He knew what was coming next.

'*Get up!*'

'No! I bloody won't. You can't make me.'

Quickly he began to wriggle under his bed. Peter tossed the broken picture on to the bed, grabbed and missed. He crouched, trying to fish the child out from the narrow space. His hand cast around but he couldn't reach far enough in to get a fistful.

'I know you did it. I know!'

'Stay away from me! You bastard!'

Jason was crying now, snivelling and crooning, like a trapped animal. 'I hate you. Julie hates you too!'

Peter got up. He stood for a moment over the bed. His voice suddenly became calm and cold. 'You got this room all to yourself now, Jason. And you're going to stay in it today, all day. And all night, too. *You hear me?*'

Jason crammed back into the furthest, darkest corner. He felt something digging into his back but so long as Peter didn't start pulling out the heavy bunkbed, he reckoned he was safe. Then he knew he was, at least for the moment, because he heard Peter slam out of the room. He twisted round and got a hand to whatever it was he had felt. He pulled it out and put it in front of his eyes – Julie's bloody Barbie doll. Yeuch!

He pushed the doll back into the darkest corner under the bed, slid carefully out into the room and began reassembling the enemy force. There was be a renewed assault and no mercy on either side.

CHAPTER 13

ANN TAYLOR was a surprise to Pat North. The disabled parking space outside her house on the new brick-built housing development next to the estate, the spinsterish 'Miss' on Barridge's visit report, the prissy, fanatically neat interior of the house all seemed to indicate someone in her sixties. But the woman who opened the door was only a little older than herself.

'Yes?'

Walker showed his warrant card. 'We're police officers, Miss Taylor. We are following up the house-to-house inquiries made by our constable yesterday. May we come in?'

North and Walker were escorted into the lounge with a ritual apology. 'Sorry about the mess. If I'd known you were coming . . . You'll have some coffee?'

Walker looked around with raised eyebrows at the incredibly tidy room, cheaply but carefully furnished. 'It's about this washing line. May we see your garden?'

Ann Taylor was surprised. 'The washing line? Oh, yes. I'll show you.'

She took them through the kitchen and out the back door. Walker inspected the posts from which her washing line had once hung. He walked around the perimeter of the lawn and peered in at the windows of the garden shed. A small padlock secured the door.

Back in the lounge, she brought in coffee.

'I thought you were investigating the murder of that poor child.'

'That's right.'

'But I don't see how that's connected to my washing line?'

Walker took a token sip of his coffee and put the cup down.

'We're trying to establish one. Now, Miss Taylor, when you mentioned to our constable that your washing line had been stolen, was that the first time you reported it missing?'

'Yes.'

'So you never reported it stolen – officially I mean?'

'No. I didn't think it was worth it. I'm sorry – should I have?'

'No, no. Don't worry, it's just that there'd be a record if you had, you see. So, when exactly *was* it stolen?'

'One night, just after the fence had been painted. About two weeks ago. Only there wasn't anything on it – washing I mean. Or they would have stolen that as well, wouldn't they? Biscuit?' She offered a plate of custard creams.

Walker shook his head. 'No, thank you. Now, do you know Michael Dunn?'

Ann Taylor's eyes were fixed on the carpet. 'I know who he is, yes. It was in the papers – that he'd been arrested.' She twisted her hands together in her lap, the fingers of one gripping those of the other. 'Er, he used to come round knocking on doors to do odd jobs.'

Walker seemed indifferent to this information. He simply asked, 'When did you last see him?'

'Oh, a long time ago. More than nine months, maybe a year. He looked terrible. Unwashed, filthy dirty. I didn't open my door. Just told him to go away.'

'And?'

'He just walked off.' She looked nervously to Walker then clasped her hands. 'They've been to take tests on the fence. Will they be coming back? I mean it was only a rope.'

Walker got up suddenly, slightly knocking the table on which stood his barely touched coffee. The cup rattled. 'Thank you for your time, Miss Taylor.'

North took a hurried gulp of coffee as Walker moved towards the hall. She got up to follow him. 'Lovely house, you have. You live here alone, Miss Taylor?'

'Yes – since Mummy died.'

The woman hesitated, flicking a glance at North's face, then looking down at her hands. There was something more to this, North was sure of it. But Walker was impatient to be on his way. He was already standing by the front door, his hand groping in his coat pocket for cigarettes.

Miss Taylor smiled wanly. 'I'll show you out.'

On the way to the car, North spoke her mind. 'Bit abrupt, if you don't mind my saying so, sir.'

But Walker was having none of it. 'In case you've forgotten, Inspector North, we have a meeting with the Crown Prosecution Service tomorrow. And I can tell you exactly what they're going to say – we don't have a case. So I don't have time for small talk, OK?'

North decided not to push her luck.

Within five minutes of their arrival back at Southampton Street, Arnold Mallory was on the line. His voice was triumphant. 'We've got what I believe you would call a result from the shoes.'

'I know,' said Walker. 'You said four matching samples. But, as you also pointed out, as Dunn lived there he was likely to walk across the building site.'

'Four matching samples would be good, Walker. But five is very hard indeed to get out of.'

'Five? You're talking about Dunn's shoes?' Walker was taking the call in the Incident Room. As members of the team picked up on the conversation, the area fell into an expectant silence.

'Dunn's shoes – yes. I said we had soil, clay, brick dust and cement, right? All from the area around the pipes. But now I'm also talking about the victim's shoes too.'

'Yes?'

'And your suspect and the little lady walked in the same dog shit. Do you understand what I am saying to you, Walker? Traces of the same turd are on both shoes!' Mallory guffawed, 'You found the post for the washing line, all you've got to do now is find the dog that dropped the load!'

Walker attempted to join in with Mallory's frivolity, and to everyone gathered in the room it sounded like a bark, but no one laughed. Walker's eyes were like chipped ice. Deliberately Walker replaced the receiver. He remained still for a moment, then started walking jerkily around the room in a kind of muted dance of celebration. He was clicking his fingers.

'Yes! Yes-yes-yes! We've got him. We've bloody *got* him!'

There was a low cheer from members of the team. It

died away as Meg Richards, of Family Liaison, came hurrying in looking for Walker.

'Sir, I've got a Mrs Gillingham in my office. I think you'd better come and see her. She says she fostered Michael Dunn.'

Walker was enjoying the moment. His eyes were shining, the crows' feet laughter-lines etched into his temples. He rubbed his hands together.

'Better and better. Lead me to her!'

Mrs Gillingham was dressed in sweater and jeans under a brown car coat. Walker immediately had her down as a middle class liberal, a teenager in the sixties who now got by on charitable work and reading the *Guardian*. She also happened to be very tense, sitting bolt upright in the chair with her hands laced so tightly there was no blood in the knuckles.

Walker positioned himself on the edge of Richards' desk. 'Now, Mrs Gillingham, I believe you know Michael Dunn.'

'Yes – I read you had arrested him so I—'

'I'd appreciate anything you can tell us about him. Anything at all. He doesn't communicate much with us, you understand?'

'All right, well, let me see. Michael was an orphan, Superintendent. He was shuffled round various foster homes, adopted once but returned to an orphanage. He was too much of a handful apparently. But at the home he was subjected to, well, sexual and emotional abuse. Over a period of years. He made no less than three suicide attempts and . . . Well, we didn't know all the facts about

159

his past when we – my husband and I – agreed to foster him. We only found out afterwards . . .'

She stopped, but she had a lot more to tell. Richards looked at Walker warningly and he took the point. This was a witness you didn't push too hard. He simply nodded encouragingly and waited for the woman to go on.

'He was fourteen when he came to us, a very quiet, unassuming boy, and we felt he was really benefiting from being in a stable family environment.' She paused and cleared her throat.

Coming to the difficult bit, thought Walker.

'My daughters were then aged five and seven . . . We trusted him, you see. We did.' She swallowed. Her voice had gone shaky. 'And we left him to babysit one time and he, well, he abused both my daughters, you see.'

Walker blinked. He couldn't quite believe his luck. 'Did you report this?'

'No. No, I didn't.'

'Why not?'

Mrs Gillingham looked pathetic now. Guilt leaked out of her like battery acid.

'I – we – didn't want to subject the girls to any further distress. We just had him taken away – the social workers agreed at the time that nobody's interest would be served by a prosecution or anything like that.'

Richards leaned forward and said, quietly, 'Did he *sexually* abuse them?'

The woman had controlled herself now. Her voice was a little shaky, the emotions discernible but contained. She would make a good witness.

'He did not actually have sex with either of them. But he . . . touched them, you know. Fondled them. According to the presumption of the doctor, and the counsellors

160

we spoke to subsequently, his own sexual abuse could have made him impotent.'

Richards had brought her visitor a glass of water and now she gulped three quick mouthfuls before placing the cup carefully on the desk.

'I wanted to tell you this because I was feeling guilty. Perhaps if we had taken this matter further, not simply returned him to care, then this tragedy – this murder – would never have happened.'

'Mrs Gillingham,' asked Walker, 'would you be prepared to make a statement?'

'Yes. Yes, I would.'

'And would your daughters?'

'Superintendent, I can't speak for my daughters. They are now eighteen and twenty years old. You must ask them.'

'I shall have to do that, Mrs Gillingham. I hope you understand. Do they both still live at home?'

'Yes.'

'Then may I make an appointment to come and see them?'

Michael Dunn's head had not stopped pounding all day. Now it felt cold as well, because those bastards had shaved off his hair. Said he was lousy, the pillocks. They'd spent ages taking his particulars, giving him bedding and such-like. Now he was being marched through the prison and it was unbelievable how the inmates already knew about him – who he was, why he was here.

As he walked past the locked doors of cells, he could hear catcalls and wolf howls and the snarling of imaginary animals. He was called nonce and child killer and he was

161

threatened at every step with the particular names of the bits of him these men wanted to cut off and make him eat. Michael Dunn was terrified.

The screws marched him into an empty cell, where there was a bed with the mattress folded.

'Make up that bed, Dunn. Wing governor'll be along to see you shortly. Behave yourself.'

The steel door closed with a horrible finality and the prisoner looked at the door with its spyhole. He sat down on the bare bedsprings.

'I'm innocent.'

His voice was a whimper in this bare box, where there was no one to hear him. He covered his face with his hands.

'I didn't do it. I didn't do it.'

CHAPTER 14

WITH HIS decision to prefer a charge of murder against Michael Dunn, Walker kissed goodbye to his control of the case. From now on the Special Casework Lawyer of the Crown Prosecution Service, and not Det. Supt. Walker, would call the shots.

But Walker's team couldn't pack up and go home just yet. The job of collecting evidence and processing paperwork went on uninterrupted, but now more sedately. The first few days had been a race against time, Walker driving his team like the devil in pursuit of the damned. Now, under this new driver, the wheels of investigation slowed to walking pace.

A murder trial is a demanding taskmaster. Everything taken from Dunn's flat had to be processed by Mallory's staff. The doll was followed up – its manufacturer in China established, its importer traced, the shops that stocked it itemized. Dunn's past was raked over with archaeological thoroughness and the key witnesses in the case were re-interviewed, their remarks double- and triple-checked against the statements they'd already made. For the Crown there must be no unnecessary weakness in the chain of proof. And above all there must be no surprises at the trial.

The man who now controlled the case was Clive Griffith – the Special Casework Lawyer. His word actually was the law in relation to the prosecution of Michael Dunn. He was a bureaucrat-lawyer, always with one eye on the bottom line. It made him, in a joke he liked to make to his golfing chums, a conviction lawyer: to him, every acquittal was a threat; the only word he wanted to hear was 'guilty'.

Griffith's obsession with convictions made his weekly casework conference a form of Chinese water torture for Walker, as the details of his case were examined drip by pessimistic drip.

'Ah, Superintendent Walker, Inspector North,' said Griffith, hurrying in to the conference room. He was followed by the stick-thin figure of his caseworker, a tall, black stunner called Jennifer Abantu, who carried two thick files. Whenever the atmosphere became too rancid, Walker would secretly refresh his eyes by glancing at Miss Abantu's fabulous body and flawless, sphinx-like face.

'I'm sorry to be a little late. Now, where are we? Ah, thank you, Jennifer.'

Miss Abantu had dumped her files on the table. She slid one of them towards her boss. Griffith reached for the file.

'Look, Superintendent, I have to tell you I'm really afraid the Dunn case is running out of petrol. I'm seriously thinking about pulling the plug, before we get in too deep.'

Walker was staggered. All that bloody work down the toilet! The plug had been pulled on him before, of course – several times in fact. And every time he had been staggered.

'We're in deep already, aren't we? And we haven't had

164

the final forensic report yet. I'm due over there later. So you're not telling me we won't go to trial?'

'Well, I am under a statutory duty to enter a discontinuance if there is no reasonable prospect of securing a conviction. I do feel these circumstance come close to falling into that category.

'Are you serious? Are you really saying—?'

'The fact is, you haven't established he harmed her in any way. The rope to, er, coin a phrase is pretty ropey.'

Walker shot a glance at North and deliberately drew his chair nearer to the conference table. He cleared his throat. 'Mr Griffith, Michael Dunn is a known drunk. He hadn't washed either himself or his clothes for months. Do you think any jury is going to believe that he went to the trouble of stealing a washing line because he had a lot of laundry to hang up?'

'You can't prove he stole the rope. And there is no mechanical fit between the end of the two bits you're offering in evidence.'

DI North interrupted. She had never thought much of Mallory's dismissal of the rope found in Dunn's rubbish bin. 'Mr Griffith, what if he cut the rope twice?' she said. 'that would explain why the ends don't fit.'

Griffith licked his thumb and finger and began leafing through the file. Walker watched him for a moment, then said, 'I wouldn't be pushing this so much if the type of rope wasn't the same. Not similar – identical!'

Griffith was perusing a page. He got out his pen and jotted a note in the margin. 'Hmm. Tell you what – we'll solicit an opinion on the rope from Treasury Counsel.'

'It's not just the rope. There's Mrs Gillingham's statement.'

'What page is that on?'

Walker's own file was tagged with post-it notes. He found the right place. 'Twenty-four.'

'Ah, yes – the foster carer.' Griffith scanned the statement, tapping his teeth with the Biro. 'Well, it's hearsay from the mother, this. You'll have to get statements from the Gillingham girls that Dunn molested them.'

Walker and North exchanged another glance. They'd been trying to get statements from the two Gillingham daughters for the past month. At last it looked as if this might happen tomorrow, but there was no way Walker was going to tell Griffith that now. He'd be told when those statements were in the can.

Griffith had finished reading Mrs Gillingham's statement.

'The only way we'll get this allegation into evidence is under the similar facts rule. It's going to have to be very close to what was done to Julie Anne – same age bracket and the use of some sort of instrument.'

North smiled emolliently. 'Well, we don't know what they're going to say until they say it, do we, sir?'

'No, Detective Inspector, we do not. So let's not waste any more time, shall we?' He turned another few pages. 'Now, another matter that is concerning me is your identifying witness. Mrs Enid Marsh.'

Walker's eyes narrowed. 'Why? She picked him out first time. She was in no doubt.'

'Yes, but number one, she says she'd never previously met Dunn. That weakens her position, though I admit it doesn't demolish her. Number two, and worse, she's old, her sighting of Dunn was brief and it was from high above his head. The judge will have to give the Turnbull Direction, no question.'

Walker scowled. The Turnbull Direction – the warning that judges issue to juries whenever they think a particular piece of identification evidence is not absolutely straight-forward – is detested by the police. Defence counsel, of course, adore it.

Walker made a fist of his right hand and hammered it into the palm of his left. 'She picked him out in the parade!' he cried. 'She was alpha-bloody-positive it was him!'

Griffith smiled in that superior way of his. 'What? A forgetful old lady who lives alone and doesn't get enough attention from the big wide world? Dunn's counsel won't just make mincemeat of her – he'll be going for the whole mince pie, Superintendent.'

For some reason North thought Griffith's smile made him look like a duck as Griffith added, 'Look, we're on course for the committal hearing next week, yes? We won't make a final decision until we cross that hurdle.'

Walker stood up and tucked the file under his arm. He tapped the file. 'And bear in mind, please, we still have more forensic to come, with any luck. I'll be in touch about that – oh, and the Gillingham girls also.'

Defending a client doesn't have to be a crusade. Belinda Sinclair may have been a rookie, but she had her task in proportion. It shouldn't really matter to her if Michael Dunn was innocent or guilty – under the so-called adversarial system of British justice there could be no trial without a defence and, win or lose, Belinda knew she could do herself a lot of good if she didn't mess things up.

Filthy, lousy and with his faculties corroded by drink, Dunn had certainly not been a pretty prospect when she'd met him at Southampton Street. But later, at Wormwood Scrubs, Belinda was pleasantly surprised by his changed appearance and now, making her third call, she'd grown used to the new Michael. His hair was cropped short. He was polite, more or less alert and, above all, clean. He had a winning smile when he felt like showing it and Belinda was even beginning to believe that her young man was incapable of doing this dreadful crime. If only he could be persuaded to make more use of that shy Welsh charm, the jury would surely be brought round to the same way of thinking.

The purpose of today's visit was to go through his proof of evidence.

'Mrs Enid Marsh says she doesn't know you, Michael. Is that true?'

Dunn didn't answer. He was standing casually, half turned away from Belinda, his hands sunk in his overall pockets. Although he'd come through alcoholic withdrawal after three days, he still found it hard to concentrate for long. Belinda tapped her notepad.

'Michael, you must pay attention. I am trying to take your proof of evidence.'

Dunn collected himself. He spoke quietly. 'She saw me when I did the paper round.'

'When exactly did you do the paper round, Michael?'

'Can't remember. Summer, I think. Not last year, the one before.'

'And how many times did she see you?'

'Well, a good few times – just on her doorstep, you know. In the mornings.'

'Did you talk to her at all? Did you say good morning?'

Dunn screwed up his face, trying to visualize the scene on Mrs Marsh's doorstep. He shook his head. 'No.'

Belinda Sinclair scribbled a note and murmured to herself, 'Good.'

'Oh, and I remembered something else!'

'Yes?'

Dunn pulled out a chair and sat down.

'Terry Smith, the bloke, you know, that was with me. Well, he may have gone home.'

'Home, Michael?'

'Yeah, Wales. Where I come from.'

The lawyer was writing in rapid shorthand. 'Seems to be all coming back to you today, Michael.'

And then that smile broke on his face. Belinda thought, bit of a heart-throb this boy could have been, if the breaks had been different. It was a cold and purely analytical thought – not what she herself felt, but what a jury could be made to feel.

She said, 'It makes it so much easier for me to do the absolutely best job I can.'

Dunn opened his eyes wide. 'Doing all right, then, am I?'

She nodded, looking at her watch. 'Yes. Yes, you are. But I have to leave it there, I'm afraid. Got to go. But I'll see you again on Wednesday.'

He watched her as she gathered her papers, making no movement. Then she stood up and extended her hand for him to shake.

'Goodbye for now, Michael.'

The hold he took on her hand was light, shy and – well, she thought, the only word for it was innocent. Then he said, out of nowhere, 'You've got lovely eyes. You're a very pretty woman.'

169

Belinda gave a tiny lift of her head. 'Well, thank you, Michael. Is there anything you need?'

'No, thank you very much. I'm fine here. Like to get out, but really I'm fine.'

'What about your treatment? Prison officers, other inmates?'

Dunn suddenly, and for the first time today, became tense and wary. But he shook his head. 'Fine, nothing. Really I'm OK. It's no problem.'

Like hell it is, thought Belinda. But she didn't pursue it.

Outside the CPS, Walker and North separated. She returned to Southampton Street, from where she would telephone to confirm tomorrow's appointment with the Gillingham sisters. He went on to Lambeth and the Forensic Laboratory. He knew that Mallory's team had come to the end of their tests but Arnold Mallory had kept him in the dark as to their progress and given not a hint about what he might have found.

The scientist was sitting at his desk and contemplating with evident satisfaction a sizeable patisserie carton which sat on his blotter.

'I've got excellent news for you, Walker,' he said without looking up. 'Excellent *epithelial* news.'

He picked up a laboratory scalpel and, after a moment's further thought, sliced delicately through the tape which secured the lid of the box. He then heaved his bulk backwards to allow space for the drawer of his desk to open.

'Shall I spell that for you? E-P-I-T—'

Walker cut him short. 'I've seen the word, yes. Epithelial.'

Mallory's habit of treating all policemen like they were missing a chunk of their brains was infuriating and Walker's nerves were in knots already after spending half an hour with Griffith. He didn't know exactly what epithelial meant, but sure as hell he'd rather look it up in *Black's Medical Dictionary* than be patronized by Mallory.

The scientist gestured at a sheaf of stapled A4. The top sheet had Walker's name highlighted on a circulation list.

'It's written in the report. Epithelial cells from the little lady's mouth, found in samples taken from the lolly sticks.' He was rummaging through his desk drawer.

Walker said, 'Are those the lolly sticks found in Dunn's flat?'

'Exactly. That's just bullet point number one. Point number two: one of her hairs recovered from suspect's carpet.'

'Just one?'

'Just the one. It's enough. And no question it's hers. Point number three: fibres. Blue and red cotton/poly-ester mix, recovered from the couch. These are consistent with the child's anorak.'

'No better than consistent?'

'No – they're common as muck.'

Mallory shut his drawer and stood up. Going across to a four-drawer filing cabinet, he started delving into it, coming out at last with a plastic spoon. 'Some bugger's always pinching the forks. But we also have bottle-green acrylic, consistent with the skirt. This is also a common type – but the combination of the two fibres, that's your evidence.'

Mallory shut the drawer, returned to his desk, tipping open the lid of the cake box. Walker, on the other side of the desk, couldn't see what it contained until Mallory had plunged his spoon in and come out with an overbalancing hunk of chocolate *ganache*. He hurriedly plugged his mouth before the cake could plop on to the desktop.

'No blood transfer?' asked Walker.

Mallory shook his head. 'Nnnh.'

'What about Dunn's clothes? Anything on them at all?'

Mallory's jaws worked over the mouthful of cake for another ten seconds and then, with a convulsion of his throat, he swallowed. 'His own blood. That's all. Now, what else?' He fingered the report, flipping over three of four pages. 'Ah, yes, the doll. Sorry, but the finger-print boys have found nothing on it that belongs to the kiddie. A few smudges only – so it could have been wiped.'

'And the bottles? Nothing on them?'

'His prints, that's all. If he did use a bottle to abuse our girl, we don't have the item.'

'Well, that was a waste of money!' Walker lit his cigarette and sucked the smoke in hard.

'You'll have to learn to be more selective. Do you want some cake? Home-made – at least, local bakery-made. No charge to you.'

Walker exhaled, shaking his head impatiently.

'But to get back to Dunn's clothes,' said Mallory, spooning another dollop of cake between his teeth. He didn't so much chew as pump with his mouth on the food. 'No fibres,' he said at last. 'But if there had been, you'd have lost them. He'd been shedding for over twenty-four hours when you finally collared him.'

'Shedding?'

With his finger, Mallory shifted a crumb of cake from the side of his mouth to his tongue, then sucked the fingertip clean. 'Like an Angora rabbit. His cloth coat was shiny – not a very adhesive substrate. And that, my dear Superintendent, is your lot.' He shut the lid of the cake box and rapped it with his fingers. 'That's all you're going to get out of this office. And don't look so down in the mouth, man. It's all in the report. Tests, double-checked by different operatives, prove beyond peradventure that the child was in Dunn's flat, guzzling his lollies. What more could you want?'

Walker got up, snatched up Mallory's report and strode to the door. 'That's easy. I want proof that he killed her. Goodbye and thanks. I'll keep you in touch with developments about the trial.'

At the offices of Clarence Clough, Solicitors, Belinda was greeted by her two colleagues, Jeremy Oxley and Stephen Cookham, with a familiar patter of jokes and badinage. Beneath, and partly because of, the high spirits of these two young men in her presence she discerned their unspoken fascination for her. The fact that it was a shared, but competitive, infatuation made it easy to keep them both at an equidistance from her.

She sat down at her desk, placing her shorthand notebook in front of her. Stephen came and stood behind her chair.

'And is the notorious Beastman of Beckton keeping well?'

She switched on her desktop computer.

'As a matter of act, Mr Dunn is not as brain-dead as I thought he was.'

Stephen leaned forward, his nose near her spun-gold hair. He inhaled ostentatiously.

'I bet he likes your perfume. It must make such a change from the persistent stench of urine that pervades each and every one of Her Majesty's establishments.'

He suddenly straightened as the door swung open and Derek Waugh walked in, his glasses glinting menacingly. Without missing a beat, Stephen snatched a memo from Belinda's desk.

'And I'll have *this* right back to you!'

'Hey!' she said, trying to grab it back. 'You can't take that!'

The senior partner stood surveying the room suspiciously as Stephen returned to his seat, suddenly all eagerness and efficiency. Waugh crooked a finger at Belinda.

'Belinda – a word, please. And Stephen – affidavits drafted yet?'

'Almost done, Derek.'

'Good. Bring them in when they are. Let's go to my office, shall we, Belinda? There's some fresh coffee.'

They left and Stephen and Jeremy looked at each other.

'Guess what?' said Stephen.

'I think she just lost her Beastman,' said Jeremy.

Waugh looked Belinda up and down as she sipped her coffee. She was certainly decorative. He regarded himself as a bit of a connoisseur of beauty – he personally bought all the original paintings that adorned the office walls. Hiring Belinda, as against the two or three ambitious young chaps who were in competition with her, had been a decision made in the same way as he made a bid at an auction at Phillips. She wasn't expensive, she was more than competent and she'd brighten the place up.

'As you know,' he was saying, 'we've been wanting to get more high-profile criminal work, to complement our extremely successful chancery and commercial divisions. So the Dunn case will have great significance for the firm. But we must also consider what is fair to you Belinda. There will be considerable – con*sid*erable – professional interest and the media is always ready to seize on any irregularity, any pitfall into which inexperience may lead you.'

Belinda put down her cup and straightened her skirt across her thighs.

'I had thought I was managing reasonably well, Derek. I mean, especially with your support, and, er, supervision.'

She wasn't going to give Dunn up without a fight. But she knew that to confront Waugh with anger or weakness would be fatal.

'Was there anything in particular that I've not done right?'

Waugh smiled thinly. 'No, no, Belinda, assuredly not. You've done very creditably. We would be horrified – *horrified* – to think that you might read any hint of criticism in the decision. But that decision has been made – and it is that a partner should now act for Michael Dunn.'

Oh *shit*, thought Belinda. That's it. I'm off the case.

'Now,' Waugh was continuing unctuously, 'if you could just bring in the file, we'll go through it together – all right?'

*

175

The Incident Room at Southampton Street had kept going and now, after a quiet lull towards the end of September, it was busy again. The committal hearing was almost upon them.

Walker strode in and took a cigarette from Dave Satchell. He snapped off the filter and lit it in almost a single movement.

'What's the story?' asked Satchell.

'Short and sweet,' said Walker. 'Nothing for us on the doll. DNA on the lolly sticks all right – the victim's on some of them. But sweet FA on his clothes.'

Cranham came forward. He felt the disappointment on the governor's face as keenly as everyone else.

'But isn't it true we got her hair and fibres on the couch and the floor?'

'They're not denying she's been in the flat. They know she was. But it could have been three weeks or even three months before.'

'What fibres did he get?' asked North.

Walker shook his head. 'Possible anorak and skirt. Bloody useless.'

Dave Satchell said. 'Well, it should do us some good. She's not likely to have gone around three months later wearing exactly the same clothes.'

'I wouldn't bet on it,' Walker growled. 'Doubt there's a lot of money for clothes in that house.'

North, by the noticeboard, knocked on one of the snapshots of Julie Anne. 'She's wearing the same skirt in this photograph.'

Walker had whipped out his notebook and was scribbling something. 'Well, let's check with her mother – find out how new that anorak was. I'm away home now. Goodnight.'

He left a pall of depression over the room.

Satchell went and stood by North in front of the board. He stared at the picture of the golden-haired little girl, riding a bike with stabilizers.

'We don't have a case, do we?'

North turned to him.

'Don't let him hear you say that, Dave. He may be wondering – but there's no plus points for us if he's right. And it's the committal hearing next week.'

CHAPTER 15

As HE strode into Wormwood Scrubs, a pleasant, unaccustomed trickle of excitement told Derek Waugh he was alive and ready for a challenge. In his youth he'd done a fair amount of criminal work, though nothing very world-shaking. And then, during all those years of contracts, patents and other lucrative, boring spokes in the wheel of commerce, he'd often wondered how he would perform behind a top QC in a high-profile murder trial. Someone like Robert Rylands, he thought to himself.

This made it all the more disappointing that the client was fool enough to cling to the skirts of Belinda.

'Look, who are you? What is this?' Dunn was demanding. He wouldn't even sit at the interview table with Waugh. 'I'm very satisfied with Miss Sinclair. I don't want anyone else.'

Waugh cleared his throat. He must have put it too baldly. He'd assumed the lout would jump at the chance of getting a senior partner on his team.

'Naturally, there is no intention of excluding Miss Sinclair completely, Michael,' he lied. 'We were merely concerned to secure for her the benefit of a more seasoned—'

The empty chair clattered and skidded across the floor as Dunn kicked at it, his face contorted.

'Is it *my* fault? I don't want anyone else. I don't want anyone but Miss Sinclair.'

He pointed at Waugh. The attendant Prison Officer looked on, his mouth a slight twist of amusement as Dunn's spittle flew in Waugh's direction.

'I don't want *you*, anyway! I don't like you! I want Miss Sinclair, get it? Understand? Miss Sinclair or nobody!'

As Waugh left the Scrubs the feeling in his stomach had changed to the slight nausea of an adrenalin hangover.

Of course, when he told her back at the office, he made it sound like his own decision.

'I was on my way down there on the tube,' he told Belinda, 'when suddenly I thought to myself Lady Preece's estate is almost as much of a bitch as the woman herself, and then there's the Greenways-Benton thing and the Alphastrom litigation, so personally I'm going to have my hands pretty full over the next few months. Anyway, in the end I managed to persuade Dunn that his best interest would be served if you continued to handle the case.'

'Oh, well, thank you, Derek. Thank you very much.'

'Of course, we'll support you fully from the wings. There's absolutely no question, obviously, of your being exposed to any risks of a professional kind.'

Belinda thought, what on earth could the pompous prick mean? But she didn't dwell on it. She was filled instead with exultation and would have kissed Michael Dunn if he'd been in the room.

'Who's going to be leading counsel on it?' she asked, winking at Jeremy Oxley as he came in with a sandwich from Pret A Manger.

'I'd like Robert Rylands, if we can get him.'

'Rylands? He's the best there is! It'd be fantastic to work with him.'

Waugh was moving towards the door now. He said, sourly, 'I'm sure. So I think it would be politic to find a junior out of the same chambers and get him on board asap – OK?'

Waugh made his exit and Jeremy Oxley could hardly believe what he'd heard.

'Belinda! You've still got the case?'

'Yes, Jeremy, I have. But sadly I don't think we shall need the impressive Mr Rylands.'

'Oh? Why not?'

'Because I'm going to get it thrown out at committal – I think Michael Dunn's innocent. Now tell me, who's the clerk at Ryland's chambers?'

A quartet of builders working next to the Howarth Estate wandered out of the site-hut with mugs of tea. Sitting on breeze blocks, they set about unwrapping their sandwiches. After looking around, Jackie Brown nodded towards the stack of sewage pipes, about fifty yards away.

'Another of them prats having a gander.'

A dark-coated man was standing motionless near the pipes. Ron Corrigan, the site foreman, bit deep into his fried egg bap and chewed noisily.

'Police ought to put a stop to this. Nosy, sick bastards.'

Ron had tried to persuade his bosses to let him take the pipes away, or at least move them. His men thought the child's death would prove a hoodoo and all these sightseers, buzzing like blowflies around the place, seemed to confirm their fear. The employer told him to leave the pipes where they were.

'Perverts,' agreed Jackie. 'Nothing better to do than gawp.'

Ron put down his bap and stood.

'Yeah, and nick stuff too. They've no right to be down here at all – it's a hard-hat site.'

He stumped across to speak to the lone pilgrim. Jackie and the others watched the brief exchange without comment.

'It's all right,' said Ron, returning to the circle and picking up his bap and his steaming mug. 'It's that young copper was here when they were out looking for her. Police are keeping a watch, like.'

The four men resumed their lunch, staring without further comment at the unmoving, solitary figure of PC Colin Barridge, standing like a sentry over the killing ground.

Anita, too, had seen the gawpers from her bedroom window and she too wished the builder would move his pipes. It was just another reminder of the disaster that had carried away her happiness. With Helen gone, she'd hoped Peter would at least make some effort, but he was hardly ever in. And when he did come back he was drunk and foul-mouthed, lashing out at her and the children on any provocation, breaking ornaments.

She asked herself who was now – today – the worst victim of this crime? Not Julie – she was beyond all that now. Was it poor uncomprehending little Tony, whose father hit him when he spilled his food and shook him when he cried? Young Jason, wetting his bed at night, sullen and withdrawn in the day, hardly going near his school? Or Peter, drinking most of the night, sleeping in his clothes on the sofa, unable to communicate, unable to be tender? Anita looked at their lives and thought: how could she have imagined there was anything binding them all together? Why had it taken the death of little Julie to make her see that everything about their so-called family life was a sham – cheap, hopeless and meaningless?

She went shopping and saw people begging on the street, and she thought: we're not homeless. So why do I feel I haven't got a home any more?

She wouldn't say any of these things out loud, not to her mum and certainly not to Peter. A few days before, the vicar of the nearby church had come round. Thank God, Peter hadn't been there. She gave the vicar tea, though he tried to protest.

'No, no, Mrs Harris. I didn't come here to put you to any trouble!'

Then why did you come? she thought.

'I'm not a . . . I mean, I don't go to church or anything, I'm afraid,' she had said.

'Oh, it isn't going to church that counts, is it?' he told her, his bald pate gleaming. The voice was painfully earnest. 'I always feel it's a matter of values, really. And when a tragedy like this strikes, well, it's hard not to feel those values have let you down.'

When he said 'values' he'd accidentally found just the right word. But she never told the vicar this. What could he do to help her? She hadn't believed in God since her father was killed and she certainly wasn't going to start now. But Anita *did* feel let down by the values she'd based her life on – not God and religion, but home, family, decency and prosperity.

When she looked out from the flat and saw that grey heap of sewage pipes, she thought automatically of her dead daughter, lying in the cold morgue, her body cruelly opened and roughly stitched up by the people who owned her now, who wanted to use her for their evidence. Looking down like this, twenty, thirty times a day, Anita wanted her daughter's body back. More than justice, more than revenge, she longed to take Julie, lay her to rest, say goodbye.

It was the last value left, her grief.

CHAPTER 16

TUESDAY 8 OCTOBER. 4 P.M.

BELINDA RETURNED to Wormwood Scrubs feeling like a winning athlete on her lap of honour. Her adversary had been swept away and the field was hers.

'Good news – great news, Michael. We've got your junior counsel on board, Mr Sampara, from Robert Rylands's chambers. That means we might well get Rylands himself if we have to go to trial. He's a top-flight silk.'

Dunn blinked. Why's he called a silk anyway? he thought idly. Something to do with his underwear, probably. At such moments, listening to her voice, he would forget he was a client. He just let the legal terminology wash over him as if he didn't care, as if he was only a detached observer. Being in Belinda's hands felt good, as long as it lasted. But, in his experience, nothing nice ever did last.

'What about that other man then? Mr Waugh? I didn't like him, he tried to get rid of you.'

'Well, thanks to you he didn't.'

Dunn watched the creamy skin of her throat ripple as she laughed. He felt something abrupt ripple through him, too, like an electric shock. She appeared to him like the promise of a new existence, a life in the public eye where fame and money were the means and pleasure the end. She made him unearth those deeply buried fantasies of glamour and fame, the Hollywood dreams that survive even the worst of poverty and human degradation.

'Michael, I think there's a good possibility we can have this dismissed at committal,' she continued, brisk and businesslike again. 'That'll be the next hearing, Michael. The next time you're in court.'

She had told him about committal, although she wasn't sure if he'd retained the explanation. 'It's when they decide whether they have a sufficient case against you and whether your case will be taken to court and a full trial. I don't think they have.'

'You think they'll throw it out?'

She noticed how his mouth puckered, the lower lip trembling. Was he about to burst into tears?

'Well, I don't want to raise your hopes too high, but that's our initial opinion.'

'So there'll be no court, no . . . trial?'

'If all goes well. We're waiting for their papers now.'

Dunn was staring at her. Not at her face or her tits, but at her throat. Suddenly his face broke into a smile and transformed itself. Not the lost and lonely child, but the personable young man. He said, 'That's wonderful.'

And it was.

The papers Belinda had referred to were the contents of a large ring file which now lay on the table at the offices of the Crown Prosecution Service. The solid, outspread hand of Senior Treasury Counsel Willis Fletcher rested on them. Griffith and Walker sat anxiously awaiting his conclusion.

The fingers of Fletcher's other hand idly stroked his beard. 'Well, Superintendent,' he said, 'I've been through the committal papers.'

Fletcher's baritone voice was low-key but convincing and Walker found himself warming to the man. He spoke to you as an equal. His self-assurance was earned, not borrowed. Griffith was sitting bolt upright, eager to get to the question-time of this discussion.

'And what's your view of this rope in his bin? It's just a piece of rope. I don't think it's evidence against him.'

Fletcher opened the file and turned to a yellow-tagged page. 'Can't see why not. It's an identical type to the one that was round the girl's neck. And what else was he doing with it – hanging up his smalls?'

Walker felt the tension in his body ease a fraction. Fletcher was OK. He might even be prepared to take a few risks, stick his neck out. He looked at Griffith, whose mouth was slightly open, ready to pounce with another interjection. But Fletcher was having none of it. He held up his hand.

'The forensic evidence can place the child in Michael Dunn's flat all right. But its value is reduced by the fact that Dunn doesn't deny she visited the flat at other times. That's a card in the defence's hand. But – a major card in ours is that he didn't say so in his first interview. According to the transcript, let's see . . . Yes, Dunn didn't reply when asked if he knew her, then said he didn't know whether he did or not.'

Griffith got in as Fletcher paused for breath. 'Of course, *a fortiori*, the doll proves that she was, in fact—'

But Fletcher shut him firmly down. 'Yes, first he lied about where he found it, then became agitated and admitted the lie in his second statement. But his solicitor had got it all tuned up and running sweetly the second time out, hadn't she?'

'What about the Gillinghams?' asked Walker.

'Mmm, well, it's difficult. This evidence is of indecent assault on two girls thirteen years ago, never reported and it's only hearsay in the form we have it at the moment, the mother's statement ... unless you have a development there?'

'The young women are being interviewed now.' Walker hoped to God it was true. The Gillinghams had been giving them the run-around for weeks.

Fletcher nodded. 'Good.'

'Well, look,' Griffith put in. 'Can I ask you for an overall view at this stage, Mr Fletcher?'

Fletcher raised his large frame slightly from the seat and then resettled himself comfortably. 'Yes, all right. The forensic evidence may not be direct, Mr Griffith, but the *cumulative* weight of the evidence is strong. I think it'll get past half-time all right.'

Derek Waugh discovered the committal bundle on Belinda's desk during her lunch hour. It had been delivered in her absence by the CPS. When she came in, she found the senior partner sitting on the side of her desk leafing as if casually through Mallory's forensic reports.

'Is that the committal bundle?' she asked. She was miffed that Waugh was wrapped round the prosecution's case before she'd even had a chance to read it. Bloody cheek.

'Yes, you don't mind? I've had a look through. I understand you've been having some discussions about getting Dunn's case dismissed at committal.'

He didn't like the idea – Belinda could hear it in his voice. What was the bloody man playing at?

'That's right, Derek,' she said icily. 'I think we could argue that there's no case to answer.'

Waugh turned a page of Mallory's findings and read a paragraph or two before answering.

'Mmm. But all they've got to do at committal is show there *is* a case to answer. And I think they'll succeed. You won't get it thrown out – and you will have very helpfully alerted the Crown to the weak points of their case.'

'But if we put a bit of effort into the committal, we might—'

'Work *smarter*, Belinda. Not harder.' He wafted the air with his hand. 'Let it go through. We don't contest anything.'

He wants the trial, thought Belinda. He doesn't give a shit about the outcome. He just wants the glory of an Old Bailey appearance. How pathetic. But then, a little bit of her wanted that too – quite a lot of her, if she was honest.

'Who's prosecuting?' She couldn't help letting her interest show.

Waugh smiled in a sickly way. 'Looks like Willis Fletcher. He's only cruiser-class as regards my personal naval estimates. Robert Rylands is in a different league.'

'Have we got Rylands then?'

By a few thin millimetres, Waugh's smile widened. 'He can't commit till we've got a trial date. But my informants tell me he's very interested.'

Pat North had driven down to the Gillingham's home in Kent with a single image in her mind. As she was getting ready to leave, the Incident Room fax had started spewing and Meg Richards had ripped it.

'What is it?' Pat asked whilst putting on her coat.

'One of Anita's catalogue shopping accounts. Julie Anne's anorak came from here.'

Richards was frowning as she ran through the rows of figures. North looked over her shoulder and found the coat's purchase date.

'Twenty-second of August. That's two weeks before the murder – too long. No good to us.'

'Yes, but, oh, God, look at this, Pat,' said Richards, running her finger under a payment made only the previous week. 'That little girl's been dead over a month, and they're still paying for her anorak.'

The Gillinghams lived in a tidy piece of Tudabethan suburbia, a place of black-and-white half-timbering and trim evergreen hedges. The hum of garden vacuum machines sucking away the fallen leaves could be heard as she threaded her way through the Acorn Drives and Beech Avenues looking for the address. There was money here but, more important, there was respectability, a way of life that regarded itself as traditional, a sense of self-belief.

Mrs Gillingham opened the door and took her into the living room. North asked to see the sisters separately and it was Madeleine, the elder, who was offered up first. At twenty, she was a slim, fair girl in a print dress. Her manner was tentative and nervous.

'I know this is difficult for you, Madeleine,' North began, 'but we need to know about Michael Dunn. Can you tell me what happened when you were seven and he was living here?'

'What happened?' Madeleine's voice was trembly and

soft, almost a whisper. 'Yes, I'll tell you. He frightened me. He used to touch me, you know . . .'

The voice trailed away. Pat gave it ten seconds before she prompted.

'Touch you? How do you mean? In a sexual way?'

Madeleine thought for a moment, then swallowed. She closed her eyes and clenched her fists together in her lap. 'Yes. Yes, that's what I mean. He touched me in a sexual way. And I didn't like it.'

By the time she had finished her story she was crying. The mother came in, all concern, and stood at the door while Catherine, the younger sister, pushed past into the room.

'Thank you, Madeleine,' said North. 'Thanks very much. You can go now.'

She smiled at the other girl. 'You must be Catherine?'

Catherine sat down. She was wearing denim Levis and an open-necked shirt. Her manner and movements were not like her sister's – they were decisive and confident.

'Would you like me to stay, dear?' asked her mother.

'No thanks. I'm perfectly capable of handling this, mother.'

Mrs Gillingham followed Madeleine out and shut the door.

'Can you tell me about Michael Dunn, Catherine? And what happened?'

Catherine lay back in the plump cushions of the comfortably upholstered armchair. 'I think it's been blown out of all proportion.'

'Oh? How do you mean?'

'With Michael. It was just affection, you know? I was never scared of him. He was so funny, always playing games.'

'Games?' asked North. 'What games, Catherine?'

The girl was completely still for a moment, staring at the ceiling, remembering. Then suddenly, she sat up, leaned forward and put her hand up to conceal her eyes for a moment, then jerked it away. 'Hide-and-seek!' she said.

CHAPTER 17

MICHAEL DUNN was duly committed for trial and, talking to her client on the phone, Belinda sensed his heavy depression, close to some crisis. The rope found in his bin was a grave problem and she went to the Scrubs specially to discuss it.

'I never put any rope in the bin, or anywhere else,' Dunn moaned. 'It wasn't in my flat, not before I left it, I'm telling you.'

'There's no doubt in your mind – maybe one of your friends brought it in?'

'I never saw it or touched it.' He sprang to his feet and walked in an odd, jerky manner around the room.

'All right,' she said. 'Calm down.'

Dunn came back to the table. 'I'm sorry, but one minute you're telling me my case is going to be dismissed and the next I'm going up for one hearing after another and now the police are planting stuff on me. That rope in my bin. I never had a rope in the bin.'

'You are to stand trial, Michael.'

He put his face in his hands, shaking his head.

'Do you know Ann Taylor?' she asked.

'Yes, I know her,' Dunn snapped. 'I did some work for her too. I've said this before.'

'I know, Michael. Just be patient. Go on.'

Dunn sighed. 'She paid me to do a few odd jobs. That's it.' He was slowly moving his head from side to side.

'Just how well did you know her, Michael? . . . Michael!'

Dunn traced the edge of the table with his finger. He frowned. 'She wouldn't like this to get out. It just happened, see?'

'What happened?'

'I was clearing stuff out of her mother's bedroom. She'd died, you see, and Ann was . . . she was very upset. We had a few drinks. She was crying. I put my arms around her and . . . it just led to us being, you know . . .'

Belinda had to stop herself from gasping. She was having a hard time grasping this. She said, very slowly, 'You had a sexual relationship with Ann Taylor?'

He nodded. 'I promised I'd never tell anyone.'

Belinda's head cleared. What were the implications of this? Probably nothing. Ann Taylor had undoubtedly kept quiet about it and they would too.

As she left him, she said, 'We've got Robert Rylands for your defence.'

'He's good, is he?' asked Dunn.

She had smiled broadly at the understatement. 'Very good, Michael. In fact he's the best. And I'm bringing him to see you in two weeks time.'

THURSDAY 31 OCTOBER. 4 P.M.

In thirty years at the bar, Robert Rylands QC had made a considerable name as an anti-establishment barrister of principle, but these days he rarely had time to think deeply about right and wrong. Years ago he'd formulated a personal code that he applied to his practice with a degree of pragmatic flexibility. He wouldn't defend capitalists accused of fraud (he hated big fraud trials anyway: they were 'quagmires'). He would only represent celebrities in libel if he thought they'd been targeted by the puritan establishment. He'd steer clear of organized gangsters and drug cartels – at least, he wouldn't appear for them in open court. (Written opinions, outside the public domain, were perhaps another matter.)

What Rylands liked, and thrived on, were cases involving the little man – legal-aid cases, miscarriage of justice appeals, frame-ups. He enjoyed standing up for lone defendants, the weak, the deprived, anyone easily crushed by the juggernaut of the law. Cynics said that, for a man of Ryland's skill, such briefs were the perfect vehicle. If he won, his reputation soared; if he lost, few found the issue serious enough for comment. These days Rylands rarely lost a case he could have won, but nor did a loss cause him to lose sleep. He could turn in a stunning emotional act in court but no case ever touched his own emotional core.

He had read the solicitor's summary of the Michael Dunn case, and he'd talked about it to young Sampara. Child murder as such had obvious drawbacks for Rylands, in particular the public's revulsion. Some of it could always rub off on the accused man's barrister. On the other hand, it did sound as if the CPS and police were in a bit of bother over Dunn. A pathetic drunk with no serious form, he looked an all-too-easy collar. Rylands decided to take the case. He smelt a scapegoat.

Today, a fortnight after Dunn had been committed for

trial, the instructing solicitor, Miss Sinclair, was taking Rylands to a conference. So he'd got up early in the morning to read the brief. Now, with the papers in his hand, he wandered into the room that he shared with Willis Fletcher, finding the prosecutor at his wide mahogany desk hunched over *Halsey*.

'Are you prosecuting me for this little girl in the pipe?'

Fletcher straightened up. 'I have that honour.'

'Pleasant family party then.'

Rylands eased the door shut with his heel and strolled across to the mantelpiece. He leaned against it, studying the grim police photographs of Julie Anne Harris's body. He flashed them at Fletcher.

'Do you see any *particular* need for these to go in? There's nothing to see that isn't in the pathologist's report.'

Fletcher had returned to his research and was running his finger along a line of closely printed text. 'No, I suppose there isn't.'

'I don't suppose there's any question of keeping the mother out of things, too?'

Fletcher's finger stopped moving across the page. What was Robert up to? With his thoughts full of an entirely different case, he had to think for a moment to recall Anita Harris's testimony. Then he shook his head.

'Absolutely not, Robert. Unless you're prepared to admit the daughter left the doll in your flat.'

Rylands smiled. 'There's no question of agreeing the doll. In fact, I'll be objecting to the identification. The woman was distressed, emotional. They dumped it down in front of her first thing in the morning – it's like a leading question to my mind.'

Fletcher sighed. 'All right, I won't open it.'

'And the Gillingham girls – they're no good to you either, Will.'

Fletcher took off his half-moon glasses and looked warningly at his colleague, who was grinning at him wolfishly. 'Now look, Robert—'

'One says he touched her, the other – and *younger* – thinks it was good clean fun. The facts aren't similar enough, so you won't get it in on that count, will you?'

Fletcher closed *Halsey* with a sound like a distant explosion. 'So be it. Let's talk about you. You've got a drink problem, haven't you?'

Rylands smiled, motioning with the brief. 'Apparently.'

'There's no question of a sudden medical expert popping up to say you did it all in a daze?'

Rylands shook his head. 'No, absolutely not. I'm temperance now and I remember everything. I am quite certain I was having a long talk with my friend—'

There was a rap on the heavy oak door and it opened. A secretary showed Belinda Sinclair inside. Rylands instantly changed his demeanour, stepping forward with a hand extended. 'Ah! You must be Belinda Sinclair. I'm Robert Rylands. It's very nice to put a face to the name.'

They shook hands and Rylands indicated Fletcher. 'You've caught me fraternizing with the enemy. Do you know Willis Fletcher?'

Fletcher rose and Belinda shook his rather fleshier hand in turn. She was surprised.

'I didn't know you two actually shared a room here.'

Rylands laughed. He looked the sumptuous Miss Sinclair up and down.

Fletcher said, 'Oh, we huddle together for warmth, you know . . .' He picked up *Halsey* and replaced it on the shelf. 'Need the room? I can clear off now, Robert.'

'Don't bother. We're going.' He flashed a look at an expensive watch. 'We are taking tea with Mr Dunn.'

The wind gusted, making their unbuttoned coats fly as they waited for a taxi. Unsure whether it was the appropriate question, Belinda asked Rylands what he thought about their prospects, about the brief.

'Crown's on shaky ground with the doll.'

'Well, the mother's identified it very firmly, hasn't she?'

'I know. But it might be worth seeing if she can do so again.'

Belinda looked at him, puzzled. 'I'm sorry? I don't get it.'

Rylands showed no irritation. 'I feel that the dolly may have to appear in an identity parade all of her own. Can you get me a few similar dolls?'

Belinda nodded, smiling. 'I'll have a look in my toy cupboard.'

'Taxi!' shouted Rylands, jerking out his arm.

They settled into the back seat of the taxi.

'Wormwood Scrubs prison,' called Rylands, snapping open his briefcase.

'I have to say,' he went on, after he had perused some of the statements. 'I am a little concerned about the length of washing line in Dunn's rubbish bin. Has he anything to say about it?'

'*Has* he? When I saw him after committal, he got very exercised about that. Vehemently denied it had anything to do with him.'

'All right – but the washing line used on the child was from this Miss Taylor's garden – am I right?'

Belinda nodded.

'And also we know that Dunn knew Miss Taylor. But more than that, he knew her intimately, he had been in her house, in short, he had *slept* with her.'

'Well, actually, the way he tells it, it's quite a sweet story . . .'

Rylands looked out of the window – the Strand, Charing Cross, Trafalgar Square, the Mall – as she told him Dunn's version of his relationship with Miss Taylor. The barrister wasn't particularly impressed.

'Fletcher won't touch any of that, even if she's admitted it. Just – did she know him? – had he been in her house? – did he know there was a washing line?'

'Oh, yes,' said Belinda, 'that reminds me. There's something else you should know about it.'

'What? The washing line?'

'Yes. He didn't just *know* she had it, you see. He actually put it up for her.'

Rylands rubbed his chin. 'Hmm. Does he maintain they parted as friends?'

'He says their relationship ended on good terms, yes.'

'Did he? That's at variance with what she says. We'd better clear one or two of these things up, hadn't we?'

Dunn had been given a jam doughnut with his tea – a perk for the occasion of a QC's visit. He hadn't had anything like it for more than a month and he was putting off the moment when he would bite into it, tormenting himself a little. Meanwhile he listened to Mr Rylands, nodding. Nice guy, Mr Rylands, for a toff . . .

He was especially keen to know about Dunn's friendship with the kids off the estate. All seemed pretty straightforward to Michael. The kids came around. They treated him like a normal human being, unlike the rest of the estate.

'So would it, in fact, be true,' asked Rylands, 'that your flat was a sort of open house, where many people, including children, came and went?'

'Yes. My mates, you know, who I drank with, and the kids like.'

'And you said in interview that Julie Anne Harris had been to your flat. So when was the last time?'

Dunn picked up the doughnut. He lowered his nose to it and sniffed.

Rylands persisted. 'I mean before she went missing, Michael – roughly?'

Dunn put the doughnut down. 'Oh, I don't know. It's hard to say.'

'Would it have been a week, a month? Two months?'

Dunn brightened. He said, 'Tell you one thing, though. Her brother was always with her. He used to bring her with him.'

'That would be Jason Harris, yes?'

Dunn picked up the doughnut again. 'Yes, Jason. It was him wanted to come, see? Watch videos.'

Rylands seized on the point energetically. He looked down the schedule of video titles. 'But you *did* say that your video had been stolen some months previously. Right?'

Dunn nodded and replaced the still untasted doughnut on his plate.

'Do you know how old Jason Harris is?'

'I don't know. Nine, maybe. But he's well ahead of himself in years, that one.'

Rylands tapped his lower lip with a bent forefinger. 'In what way?'

The doughnut was back between Dunn's fingers now. 'Because he didn't come round to watch the Disney cartoons.'

As if to let the implication of young Jason's taste in videos sink in, Dunn now bit into the doughnut. As his teeth plunged gratefully into its mushy innards, he seemed not to notice that a large blob of strawberry jam had squirted out and stuck to his cheek.

In the Incident Room at Southampton Street, Satchell, Cranham, Harrold and Soames were dispersing after a briefing from Pat North when Mike Walker came in.

Walker was tired. He'd been sidetracked by Area into helping out with some new training films for the Met, and he'd spent the day sitting through a series of filmed interviews, on which he was expected to deliver his considered judgement. A waste of bloody time, but someone had to do it.

North approached him warily. 'They've got Robert Rylands – did you know?'

'Yes, bloody did,' growled Walker. 'He'll have his filleting knife out, going through our unused material.'

North spoke quietly, carefully. 'Guv, I've been going through the files myself—'

'You got your knife out too?'

'Not exactly . . .' She glanced at Satchell who was grinning and making knife-sharpening gestures. 'The point is, we still haven't pinned Peter James down for those missing twenty minutes on the day of the murder.'

Walker shut his eyes. 'Peter James, Peter James! We can't seem to knock that one on the head, can we?'

'I think it would be better to have another go over these times before we get to court.'

'Before Rylands makes bloody hay with them, you mean?' He considered. Then made up his mind. 'OK, we'll do it. We'll start from scratch on the timetable for the murder day. I'll see Mrs Harris – Meg! Where is that Liaison Officer? Family visit, please!'

He went off to find the file containing the Harris family statements. Returning through the Incident Room, he seemed to have renewed his springs of energy.

'You're getting to be a persistent woman, DI North.'

'Just keeping you on your toes, guv.'

'Oh, don't worry. I'll be a bloody ballet dancer before this one pans out. What is it, Dave?'

Satchell was at his elbow. 'Guv, it's the meals on wheels woman from the Howarth – Mrs Wald?'

'Wald?' Walker's mind took a moment to retrieve the detail. 'Oh, yes, I remember.'

'She's in reception. Something about Peter James.'

Jason opened the door to Walker and Richards but his mother came drifting along behind him. Her hair looked like a ball of straw and her eyes were half shut. The stomach beneath her dressing gown swelled unambiguously now.

'Oh! It's you!' she said half dreamily. 'I'm sorry, I was lying down. The doctor told me – you know . . .'

She placed a palm on her bulge. Richards smiled her sweetest smile. She wondered what tranquillizers the doctor had been shelling out.

'Sorry to bother you, Anita. We wanted a word with Peter.'

'He's not here. I don't know where he is.'

Richards swapped a look with Walker and looked over Anita's shoulder at Jason, who was still hanging around in the hall.

'Jason still off school, Anita?'

Anita was clawing at her son's shoulder, trying to get him behind her. 'Oh, school!' she said. 'He's got a rash on his legs. It's nothing, just a rash.'

Jason was wearing shorts. Meg and Walker looked at his legs, covered with red marks. They were beginning to turn blue in patches.

'Any idea when Mr James will be back, Mrs Harris?'

'No, I don't really . . . There's nothing wrong, is there?'

Walker said, 'No, no. We won't keep you out of bed.'

He started to leave, but turned at the last minute. 'Oh, Mrs Harris. Just the one thing. What time did you say Mr James left the flat – that lunchtime?'

Anita didn't understand. She looked in panic from Walker to Meg and back again.

Meg said, gently, 'The day Julie Anne went missing, Anita.'

'Oh! I think . . . around twelve-thirty, I think. Yes. Is that all right?'

'Yes, thank you, Mrs Harris,' said Superintendent Walker, jerking his head for Meg Richards to follow him.

North and Satchell's second interview of Mrs Wald was brief but informative.

'You see,' the meals on wheel lady told them, 'I just

phoned my husband and he thinks I should come back to you – he's an Inspector on the buses, you know.'

'I see,' said North. 'What have you come back about, exactly?'

'Well, the murder of that little girl of course. I gave a statement—'

'Yes, I have it here.' North picked up the statement and showed it to the witness. 'Was there anything you wanted to add?'

'Well, I think I should. You remember I said I couldn't remember the face of the young man I saw on the stairs that day? The long-haired man with the dark overcoat? Well, I was doing my rounds today, lunchtime, when I actually met him. It was on the stairs again – he was carrying a tin of beer and he looked dreadful. Anyway, this time I asked him. Are you the little girl's stepfather? I said. You see I'd been up just after it happened with a bunch of flowers. So I just said something about that and he said yes, he was the stepfather and he said thanks and went on his way. It was then I heard the chimes of the ice-cream van and that made me think . . .'

'So now you would like to amend your statement giving a positive identification.'

'Yes. On the day of the murder, I saw him coming out of the flats about quarter past one. Then I delivered the lunch and left Enid's at about half-past one. Then I saw him again at the ice-cream van.'

'The same man you had seen earlier on?'

'Yes. You see, I didn't really get a good look at his face. But now that I've talked to him . . . I mean, it was definitely him, the stepfather. Half-past one.'

*

'Mrs Wald has strengthened her statement,' Satchell told Walker when he got back from seeing Anita Harris. 'Made a positive ID of Peter James coming down the stairs at one-fifteen on 5 September.'

'Well, I've just been to the Harris's,' said Walker, sharply. 'Mrs Harris says she sent Peter James out at half-past twelve. And Poole says he parked his ice-cream van around the same time.'

North and Satchell shook their heads.

'The meals on wheels woman said *she* saw Peter James again at half-past one.'

'At the ice-cream van,' added Satchell.

Walker considered. 'So either she's got it wrong or the ice-cream man has.'

He started to pace – up to the window, then back to the noticeboard, where the timetable of the murder was written up.

'We know the little girl was taken at five past one. So, if Mrs Wald is right about the times, Peter James is in the clear – right?'

'But if Poole is telling the truth, he could still be our man,' added Satchell.

'And Anita bears Poole out, doesn't she? Why would she give a time that puts her boyfriend in the frame?'

A thought struck Walker, as he pictured Anita standing in her hallway, with young Jason hovering behind her.

'Could she just have been confused?' he speculated. 'Or could she . . .' He studied the photo of Julie on the board. 'Julie Anne had all these bruises on her body. And Meg says the marks we saw on Jason's legs today looked like strap marks.'

He turned and glanced round his team. His face was

hard set. 'Bring in Peter James, first thing in the morning. Pat, take Meg, talk to the mother again. Make it nice and easy, nothing confrontational – yet. We've got to get to the bottom of whatever makes that family tick.'

'You've been talking to the *police*!'

Peter's voice was hoarse from all the alcohol and smokes he was consuming these days. But he could still make the ornamental plates on the kitchen shelf rattle with his shouts.

Anita continued peeling a carrot. In the lounge, Tony started to cry. 'They came round here. I never said a word to them. I wasn't well.'

Peter walked to the window and looked out into the dark as Jason wandered in. 'Well, there's one of them bloody watching us. He's on the building site. He's been watching us for weeks, the brickies told me. Watching what we do and whether *he* goes to school.'

Anita gave Jason the carrot and started shaving another. 'I swear to you – I never said nothing. They want to talk to *you*.'

Peter swung round menacingly. 'What about?'

'I don't know. They just asked what time you went out looking for Julie.'

'Oh yes?' His voice faltered, the bluster leaving him. 'So what time did you say?'

Anita told him. Peter looked at her in disbelief, then started hammering on the window pane.

'No, no, no!' he shouted. 'That's wrong. That's bloody *wrong*, you stupid, stupid cow!'

*

Down below the flats a car nosed into the estate, moving at walking speed past the playground before drawing up opposite the now deserted building site. The engine and lights were killed. After a few seconds the driver emerged and walked past the site office towards the pile of sewage pipes. Some wire fencing had been erected around them, but he pushed his way through.

For more than an hour, Colin Barridge stood beside the pipes. He wasn't thinking of anything, he was as blank as a sentry. Inspector North had seen that his mind wasn't on the job so she'd told him to take a couple of days leave. But what she couldn't tell him was how to fill the time. Coming here seemed the only thing to do, a compulsion. He didn't know why.

Perhaps it was because it was the only place he could feel any kind of peace.

CHAPTER 18

'H E'S THERE again – see him?'

Richards and North were back on the Howarth, meaning to invite Peter James to Southampton Street to help them with their inquiries or to speak with Anita Harris if James wasn't there. But DI North was deflected by the sight of a lone figure standing at the place where the body of Julie Anne Harris had been found.

'Come on,' she said. 'Let's get this sorted once and for all.'

'He's no better then?' asked Richards as they started across the muddy, rubble-strewn ground.

'No, he's not. As you know, he found the body. Now he's suffered some kind of reaction. Flashbacks. Says he keep feeling her in his arms. Can't sleep.'

'What about occupational health?'

'Says he's tried that. Doesn't help. I told him to take a day or two off – Barridge!'

They had reached the young constable, who was standing ramrod straight like a guardsman. He was wearing his uniform.

'What the hell are you doing here?'

Barridge had been oblivious to their approach. He gave a start.

'Nothing, ma'am.'

His nose was red and he was trembling with cold.

'What d'you mean, nothing? You were here yesterday as well, so I heard.'

Barridge looked at his feet. 'I'm not on duty, ma'am,' he mumbled. 'I did as you suggested, got some time off.'

North opened her mouth. She was going to tell him she didn't do it so he could feed his morbid state by making sick pilgrimages to the site of his trauma.

But Barridge wasn't listening anyway. He was pointing at the ground. 'That's where I found her shoe. Just there.'

Pat touched his sleeve and said, gently but with a touch of exasperation. 'Go home, Barridge. Take off your uniform. Rest and stay at home.'

They watched as he began to walk back to his car, then set off towards the Harris's block. Trudging up the stairs, they heard a click and a mechanical whirr.

'Lift's working today,' said Pat.

'Stairs are better,' said Richards. 'Calves and thighs!'

Before they reached the Harris's floor and sounded the bell, Peter James had exited the lift three floors below and headed off into the grey morning.

Half an hour later, Satchell found Det. Supt. Walker splashing cold water on his face in the Southampton Street gents.

'Guv – Peter James. He's here. Walked in of his own accord.'

Walker roller-towelled his face then beat Satchell to the door. 'Come on then – let's get at him.'

*

'Anita told me you wanted to see me.'

They were back in the interview room – the eternal, unchanging interview room. Peter James spoke in flat, cautious tones.

'Yes, we did,' said Walker. 'Did she tell you why? We've been a little concerned about marks which the pathologist found on Julie Anne's body – bruises consistent with being struck, several days before the day she died.

Peter shifted in his seat. 'Well, yeah. She was quite a naughty little kid underneath them blonde curls.'

'You hit her?'

'Like I said, her mother and me found her a handful, sometimes.'

'Perhaps you and Mrs Harris have had a talk about this?'

Peter looked straight into the Superintendent's newly washed face, clenching his teeth. He felt rising anger. 'No, but I tell you what we *have* talked about. The fact that we can't even bury her.'

'I am deeply sorry about that, but it's completely out of my control. Detective Inspector North has gone over to yours today. She'll be explaining to Mrs Harris.'

'So how come no one's explaining to me?' He thumbed himself in the chest. 'You think it doesn't affect me? I bathed her, I told her bedtime stories, I took her to school. You sons of bitches are trying to twist everything round to make something sick out of it.'

'But you admit that you've had to discipline the children—?'

'Look – what *is* this?'

'In your role as stepfather, Peter? Are you denying that you've disciplined them physically?'

'No – because I have.'

209

'That's good,' said Walker, jabbing the air with his finger. 'Because you have hit the kids more than once, in fact?'

'Yeah, I have. We both have. That doesn't mean . . . *Look!* You charging me or what? I came here, nobody had to bring me in. So what are you trying on? I never – I swear before God – I never done nothing wrong!'

'OK, take me through it again. What time did you go out looking for Julie Anne on September the fifth?'

Peter James was shaking his head. 'I don't believe this. It was *after* one o'clock! Before that I was in the flat fixing the sink. Anita asked me to get the kids in. But she turned the tap on by accident and soaked me – I had to go and change my clothes. So I didn't go downstairs for fifteen or twenty minutes.'

Walker showed him a statement form. 'That's not what Mrs Harris says in her statement.'

'She doesn't *know* does she? She's confused. She had it wrong. She remembers things a lot more clearly now that she's calmed down. Listen to me – it was well after one o'clock. *Well* after.'

Walker stood up stiffly and sighed. 'OK. Thank you, Mr James.' He moved towards the door.

'Just wanted to get things straight,' said Peter in a soft, conciliatory tone.

'That is exactly what I'm trying to do, Mr James.' He waved Peter away. 'You can go.'

The corridor was busy with officers going about the normal business of the police station. Walker cannoned through them like a dodgem car towards the Incident Room. He urgently wanted to hear what the Harris woman had had to say.

North and Richards weren't back yet. Exasperated, Walker decided to kill some time by juggling a few figures on his budget sheet.

By the time the Inspector and Sergeant came in he was in a terrible mess, with debit and credit figures wandering into the wrong columns as if they had lives of their own. He hurled his pencil into a corner.

'You know something?' he said darkly to North. 'If I'd wanted to run a sodding corner shop, why would I have joined the job? It's a fucking joke!'

North put a handwritten statement, typed and signed, on his desk. 'Guv, this is Mrs Harris's new version. I also double-checked with some of the other residents – not that any of them can remember that Thursday. But they do say the ice-cream van is *always* parked just at the time Poole says it was then – twelve-thirty.'

'And we've had Peter James here – and he says he left the flat at just—'

'After one o'clock,' interrupted North.

Walker nodded. 'Fixing the sink, right? Had to change his clothes?'

'Yes,' confirmed Pat, nodding at Anita Harris's latest statement. 'Word for word.'

Walker shook his head. 'She's covering for him, isn't she? Christ!'

'There's something else, guv. She seemed a different woman this morning, there was something about her – much more together. She was cleaning the place up. Doing the washing. And she seems more clear-headed.'

Walker covered his ears with his hands. 'Give me some good news, for God's sake! Because if there isn't a case against Michael bloody Dunn, where are we going to go?'

On the way back, Peter stopped at the post office to cash his benefit cheque, then decided to treat everyone to a kebab. When he reached home, the flat looked neater than it had for weeks. The windows were open and there was a smell of furniture polish.

'Hi!' he called. 'Got you a shish kebab.'

He went through to the lounge. On the sideboard, flowers and cards were arranged neatly, as round a shrine, in front of the framed photographs of Julie. *Good-bye, sweet Julie. We missed you, darling . . .*

Anita was sitting on the sofa. Nearby, Tony rolled on the floor in a T-shirt and nappy but she was taking no notice. She looked pale and stunned.

Peter crouched beside her. 'You all right, girl?'

Jason appeared. He was sniffing like a dog, smelling the kebabs.

Anita said, weakly, 'Jason – go to your room.'

'Mum, I'm hungry.'

'Go on – do as I tell you.'

Peter looked at Jason, who seemed to flinch from the glance, but Peter handed Jason the take-away bag.

'Here, take it with you.'

Jason grabbed the food and disappeared. Tony went on rolling and mumbling.

Anita said, almost in a whisper, 'I found the doll.'

Peter froze. 'You *what*?'

She stood up. 'I swapped their mattresses over, Jason's with Julie's. And I found her Barbie doll.'

Peter said nothing for several seconds. He got up

and walked to the window. 'Did you give it to the police?'

She shook her head. 'No, I—'

'Where is it? Anita! I'm warning you, I've had all the hassle I'm prepared to take this morning.'

He advanced on her, his fist raised. 'Anita, if that bastard Dunn gets off, it's me they're going to charge, you know that, don't you? They're after *me* for it, I can tell. And I never touched a hair of her head.'

Anita's hands were clenched together, white with the tension. She had begun to weep.

He grabbed her arms, shaking her, pushing her backwards. 'Anita! I never touched her! *I never touched her!*'

He let her go. She simply stood there, weeping, her arms raised from her sides. She made no attempt to defend herself.

Peter was snarling. 'I *loved* her, *listen* to me . . . I *couldn't* have harmed her.'

In his bedroom, Jason was sitting on the floor with the kebab bag spread open in front of him. Slowly he was eating the food, stuffing chips and chunks of meat into his mouth in continuous succession. And as he chewed he counted every slap of Peter's hand against his mum's face.

CHAPTER 19

A T CLARENCE Clough, Derek Waugh was sniffing around the Dunn case again, in spite of the complexities of Lady Preece's will and the horrific breach of contract liabilities faced by his client, Alphastrom Management Systems.

'Not found the alibi witness yet, I see,' he said, waving Belinda's report commissioned from a South Wales private investigator. 'If you don't track him down pretty soon, we're looking at a blank on the alibi, Belinda.'

He dropped the report back in her pending tray, where he'd found it.

She kept her eyes on the computer screen, controlling an urge to snap. 'There has been a *possible* sighting of Terry Smith at the Simon Community in Cardiff, Tiger Bay. And I'm just drafting an ad in the *Big Issue* in London.'

Waugh snorted. 'Last people who read that thing are the homeless. Now, I was thinking about something else. Aren't you going to need independent forensic confirmation that the little girl frequented Dunn's flat, so that those fibres could have been left there any time? All we've got at the moment is his word.'

'Well, Dunn did mention that Jason Harris, the brother, was always—'

'Keep away from the family, it's a public relations hornets' nest.'

Waugh strode to the door but stopped as he gripped the handle, as if seized by a further thought. 'Has Rylands been over any likely cross-examination yet with Dunn?'

'No, we're doing that today. We thought it would be better to get a bit of rapport going between them first.'

The senior partner twisted the doorknob and stiff-armed the door open. From the corridor he called back, 'Well, don't feather-bed him. The Crown aren't going to.'

The door slammed and Belinda made a snarling face.

At the CPS, Walker and North were winding up a progress report to Griffith. It was basically a 'no-progress' report.

'So,' said Griffith, 'there's nothing more on the forensic front?'

Walker frowned. He wished to God there was.

'No,' he said. 'And I think what we've got is all there is. Also there's a lot of pressure to release the body for burial and I think we should do that now.'

'Agreed?' Griffith looked from Fletcher to North. 'Agreed,' he confirmed when they both nodded.

Walker continued, very subdued, 'There's really nothing to add to the scientific evidence and I'm afraid we didn't get quite what we'd hoped from the Gillingham interviews.'

Almost distastefully, Griffith flicked through the pages of the evidence bundle, now bulkier than ever. 'I have a responsibility not to waste public money on a case which is going to fold up. And I have to tell you . . .' He stared at the two police officers over his half-moon glasses. 'I *have* to tell you, I am coming to the view that we should offer no evidence.'

Willis Fletcher sat beside Griffith, his eyes fixed on an open page of his own copy of the file. The barrister's face was grave but with a suggestion of humour somewhere in the corner of his eyes. Walker found some encouragement in that. At the other end of the table Jennifer Abantu's face was as impassive as ever – Walker had no idea if her opinion counted for anything with Griffith. But then, he had no idea what her opinion was.

'Dunn still hasn't come up with his alibi witness,' he said. 'I think there's a very good chance we'll be able to show he's served a false notice of alibi.'

Fletcher stirred in his seat. 'Well, that *would* be a help,' he remarked.

Griffith looked at him without appreciation and closed the file decisively. 'I shall take that into consideration when making my decision.'

'Hang on,' said Walker desperately. 'There's something else you should take into consideration. I'm sure the Director of Public Prosecutions doesn't want any *more* sensitive, national cases dropped for lack of evidence, leaving *more* grieving families to drag their private prosecutions through the courts.'

He was going out on a limb here, and he knew it. But he ground on. 'Sometimes it's important to try a case. Sometimes it should be *seen* to be tried.'

Griffith stood up, capped his pen and clipped it into his breast pocket. 'I execute policy,' he said darkly, 'I don't play politics. I'll let you know what I decide.'

In the car, Walker pounded the dash with his fist,

working out his pent-up aggression. 'Fletcher wants to proceed – I can feel it. Griffith doesn't, but surely he won't have the balls to drop it?'

'You're going to need yours, I reckon.'

Walker looked at her.

She smiled, braking sharply. 'That crack about the DPP,' she went on, 'it didn't go down at all well.'

Walker banged the dash again. 'I *still* put money on Dunn.'

'What about Peter James, though?'

He shook his head as she put the car into gear. 'No. I don't like him, but I don't think he's a killer.'

As they pulled away from the lights, Walker shook off the sense of despair. 'Tell you what – get Satchell to have another go at the ice-cream seller. Speak to his boss this time. If he's lying . . .'

North nodded. 'Peter James would be in the clear – yes?'

'He'd be laughing and so would we. If I'm reading Griffith right, the reason for why he doesn't want to go on against Dunn is he's afraid the real killer's Peter James.'

Robert Rylands, the inveterate defence brief, had a favourite performance in prison conference rooms – acting the prosecutor. It was part of his job to play the game of putting a client through his witness box paces, to test him with the difficult questions the Crown would ask and gauge his readiness and credibility. And Rylands played the game hard, turning the small prison interview room into a court, circling the client like an attack helicopter, pouncing on his uncertainties and inconsistencies.

At Wormwood Scrubs, with Michael Dunn in his

sights, he wondered, not for the first time, why he found this task so satisfying. Perhaps, after all, he should have been a prosecutor himself. He'd have been a bloody good one.

'Now you admit you let young children into your flat unchaperoned?'

'I'm sorry?' asked Dunn. 'Unwhat?'

'Unsupervised. Without any adult with them.'

'Yes, I suppose so.'

'And you showed them videos. Why?'

'Because they like them.'

'But why did you want them to come to your place?'

'Because . . . because . . . I enjoyed their company.'

Dunn looked nervously at Belinda. He couldn't understand the change that had come over Mr Rylands. He'd gone so hard. She nodded encouragement at him, gave him a smile.

'And what sort of videos were these?'

'Well, cartoons and—'

'And some quite unsuitable material – am I right?'

'I don't know.'

'*Child's Play 3, The Terminator*?'

'Yes, I had them. But my video was nicked and I couldn't show them films any more, see.'

'But children came to your flat after the video disappeared, didn't they?'

'Yes.'

'When was the last time there were children at your flat?'

Dunn shook his head, bewildered. 'I don't know, I can't remember.'

'Can you remember a specific day when Julie Anne was at your flat?'

'No. No, I can't.'

Rylands rubbed his hands, a gesture which seemed to show he was pleased, though neither Dunn nor Belinda could see why.

'All right, Michael, let's turn to your alibi for 5th September. You know what an alibi is, don't you?'

''Course I do.'

Rylands paced to the window and swung around, leaning with his elbows on the sill. He pitched his voice a few semitones higher, his most sceptical courtroom voice.

'You've named two men and a woman as alibi witnesses. Of the men, one won't cooperate and the other can't be found. The woman's never heard of you. How did that happen, Mr Dunn?'

'I don't know, I was confused. I couldn't remember exactly—'

'Because if you were *not* with those people, then it is possible that it was you whom Mrs Marsh saw from her window, you who took a little girl by the hand and led her back to your flat. Isn't it?'

Dunn was shaking his head pathetically. 'No, really. There was never any little girl in my flat that day.'

Rylands thought for a moment, looking at the ceiling. 'If you can't recall any specific day or date that Julie Anne was at your flat – how can you be so sure she wasn't there on 5th September?'

Dunn was frightened now. His eyes were wide with anxiety as he looked for support to Belinda, then back to Rylands. He said, 'She used to come all the time. All the time. Just ask her brother. Ask Jason.'

Rylands held his gaze for a moment, then relaxed, smiling, coming forward to the table. He began assembling his papers.

'That's all right, Michael. Just remember it's in their interest to try to make you lose control of yourself. Just answer the questions and keep cool.' He tapped a stack of papers against the table to straighten them. 'We'll leave it for today, OK? I will see you again before trial.'

On the way back to town, Rylands was whistling to himself.

'You seem pleased,' Belinda said.

'Moderately, moderately. I wouldn't put it higher than that. You?'

'I don't know. There's something Michael said that's bugging me. Ask Jason, he said. Do you think we could?'

Rylands shook his head. 'Tricky. Young child witnesses? Very, very tricky . . .'

Two hours later Peter and Anita's door opened and Helen let herself in. She carried a suitcase.

'Didn't know you had a set of keys,' Peter told her when he met her in the hall. He glowered at her.

'I've come for the funeral.'

'Well, you're not staying here.'

Hearing voices, Anita came through. She gave her mother a hug. 'I want you to stay, Mum.'

Peter simply swore.

CHAPTER 20

KENNETH POOLE lay naked across a sturdy refectory-style kitchen table of Norwegian pine. A young woman was walking her fingernails up and down the length of his spine while he licked a few last vestiges of the strawberry yoghurt that he'd spooned into her navel a few minutes earlier. And then the telephone was ringing.

Most of Poole's Sunday mornings were like this. Around nine o'clock, after a look through the *News of the World* and a breakfast at his Bethnal Green flat of two fried eggs, a fried slice and grilled bacon, he'd catch a bus out to Romford. It was from there, at a quarter to ten sharp, that his boss would leave his comfortable home for the office and keep reliably busy all morning completing the previous week's accounts. Poole found it intensely exciting to lurk in the bus shelter opposite the house, waiting for Frank Petrie's exit.

It was always the same pantomime, starting with Petrie's jaunty appearance on the path, buttoning his camel coat. Kenneth watched as the electronic key beeped open the Merc's doors, the door opened and closed with a soft cough and Petrie settled in the driver's seat, lighting his first Cuban panatella of the day and stroking the

221

engine into life. Then, at last, as the growl of the Merc's radials died away, Poole nipped across the road, slipped through the side door of the house and slid into the willing arms of the young and lovely Mrs Petrie.

Kenneth knew he would never have that expensive coat, that Merc – or even that panatella. But what he did have, by the gift of nature, was the equipment to make Michelle Petrie, from time to time, a very happy woman. So, between ten and midday, before he himself had to clock on at the depot to start his Sunday shift, he and Michelle would cavort around the house like a pair of bonobo chimps. They did it on the World of Leather four-seat sofa in the lounge. They did it on the hairy astrakhan rug in front of the ingle-nook fireplace ('ingle-nookie' as Michelle called it with a delicious giggle). They did it rolling around the smoked-oak parquet in the hall, on the Cumberland slate worktop in the kitchen, in the dusty intimacy of the broom-cupboard, in the bubbling cauldron of the huge Jacuzzi bath. They even, if they felt lazy, did it in the emperor-size bed with its five-speed vibrating mattress.

And so, for a couple of hours each week, Kenneth Poole thought he'd died and gone to heaven. It couldn't last, of course.

As the phone warbled, he paused in mid-lick but Michelle didn't miss a finger-step. Nonchalantly she raised the portable handset that was never out of her reach.

'Yeah?'

Kenneth strained to listen. He recognized Petrie's nasal twang coming fuzzily through the earpiece. Michelle was drumming her fingers on his shoulder blade.

'What they want then?' she asked.

Judging by his tone of voice, Petrie seemed upset. It was even more squawkingly petulant than usual.

'Oh, OK,' his wife said at last. 'See ya later, sugar.'

Michelle laid the phone down and began to writhe her limbs, those limbs whose God-given shapeliness could make Kenneth break out in a sweat just thinking about them. She was evidently manoeuvring to force Poole's mouth to make a lower contact on her body. But, for the moment, he declined the gambit.

'What did he want?'

Michelle went on wriggling. Then she brought one of her nicely shaped feet up to the tabletop to give herself purchase.

'Oh, nothing.'

'What did Frank *want*?'

'Just, the police are down at the depot, asking a lot of questions about some murder, so he's going to be late.'

'A *murder*?'

Michelle sighed and lay still a moment. 'Yeah, but it's nothing to do with Frank, it's nothing important. So come on big boy, forget about it and just—'

'Wait a *minute*, Michelle. I want to know. What murder?'

'That little kid over docklands, it was in the news. A while ago. One of our vans was nearby when it happened or something.'

'Holy buckets of shit!' said Ken, rolling off the table and scrabbling for his jockey shorts. 'I got to go.'

Satchell hated funerals. He sometimes had an inexplicable impulse to laugh, so he tried to stay away. Now, with the

Guv and Pat North in attendance at the Harris burial, he felt it was OK to miss it.

Checking on Poole's story, he'd been down to the depot at eleven to interview Frank Petrie, the ice-cream van king. According to Petrie the vans went out at twelve every day.

'We got a roster of calls for every unit,' Petrie told him as they stood in his office. He walked and knocked on a chart on the wall. 'I got eight vans at the moment – goes up to a dozen in summer. And this chart plots every site visited by every van, how long they stay and so on. That way, nobody doubles up and we don't get into no turf wars with the opposition. Used to be anarchy out there at one time.'

Satchell said, 'So you know exactly when Mr Poole arrived at the Howarth Estate on 5th September?'

Petrie's face took on a crafty expression. 'I know when Poole *should* have been on the estate. He should have been there at half-past twelve. But I don't know if he actually was. I've had trouble with that young man before. Wouldn't put it past him if he was getting into the knickers of some tart on my time.'

'What – *Confessions of an Ice-Cream Seller* type of thing?'

Petrie lowered his voice and said contemptuously. 'I wouldn't put it past him.'

Satchell glanced at his watch. 'Is he working today?'

'Poole? Yes – due on at twelve, as usual.'

'Would you ask him to come down to the station when he knocks off? I just want to take him through his statement again.'

Now Satchell was back in the Incident Room cross-checking through the door-to-door inquiries for references to the visit of the ice-cream van. A call came through from the front desk.

'Got a Kenneth Poole here for you, Dave.'

Poole was early – it was only half one.

'OK,' he said. 'Be right down.'

'I was scared, you know? Thought I'd lose my job because he's a right bastard and I'd had one warning anyway . . .'

Poole was gabbling through nervousness. And from his breath, Satchell could tell he'd been in the pub for a few stiffeners.

'I mean, I never thought it would matter – half an hour, like.'

'What did you think wouldn't matter, Mr Poole? Just spell it out, easy like.'

Poole swallowed. 'I didn't get to the Howarth Estate until gone one on the day the little girl was murdered.'

He was rubbing his hand through his hair.

'Oh, shit! I knew it'd all come out.'

'What? What would come out?'

'I was shagging his wife, see? She'd give me a few quid, you know, to cover for the ices I might have sold and . . . well, he knows now because I told him. I got the boot – said he suspected I was with a tart, so I told him exactly who the tart was!'

Dave Satchell's mouth was open. This was absolutely bloody choice. He couldn't wait till he told the lads. Leaning meaningfully forward, he tried to keep a straight face.

'Well, this is potentially serious—'

'Serious? You're not joking. I lost my job!'

'I mean we could have you for making a false statement. You know that?'

'Yeah, of course. Look, I'm sorry. Me and Michelle, well, we stopped meeting in working time after that. We thought of another time.'

'I'm glad to hear it, Mr Poole, but let's not get sidetracked. Now, I want you to make out a new statement about your true movements on 5th September, OK?'

Half an hour later, DS Satchell was standing inside the door of the church where the funeral of Julie Anne Harris was just beginning. If you'd paid him he couldn't have waited with this news.

'He who dies and believes in me shall live,' intoned the vicar. 'And he who lives and believes in me shall never die . . .'

Satchell spotted Walker, North and Richards sitting near the back so he slid into the pew immediately behind and leaned into Walker's ear.

'Guv, the ice-cream seller lied about the times. He didn't get to the Howarth Estate till gone one.'

Walker looked round. 'Did you—'

'Yeah, I just took a new statement. This puts Peter James in the clear, right?'

Walker couldn't suppress a smile. He hammered once with his fist on his right knee. If he'd had a Marlboro between his fingers he'd have snapped off the filter.

He whispered to Pat North. 'Hear that? Griffith can't pull the case now – can he?'

'And', whispered Dave, 'Michael Dunn still has no alibi.'

Pat kept her face to the front, but she too was smiling faintly. They were back on track. Meanwhile the vicar's voice echoed over their heads.

'. . . and in the midst of life, we are in death.'

Belinda knew it was the funeral today and had even considered attending but dismissed the idea, remembering her violent reception at the Harris's front door. So she'd come to work instead.

Working on a Sunday was nothing new to Belinda. The offices of Clarence Clough usually had a few lawyers in over the weekend and security there was round the clock. Not that she thought much of the security presence – a bunch of dozy old men.

She had been re-reading the forensic reports on Julie Anne's clothes when one of the security men confirmed her worst opinions. He rang her from the front desk.

'Er, Miss Sinclair? Man's just come in for you.'

'Who?'

'A man.'

'And this man's name?'

'Oh, I see. Sorry, miss. There's only me on the desk, see? I must've forgot to ask him.'

'Well, ask him now.'

'You'll have to ask him yourself, miss. I've sent him up.'

'Did he say what it was about?'

'No, miss. Just that it's important.'

'Well, really! I've already had threats against me working on this case. And now you've let some strange man walk straight past you and up the stairs.'

227

'Well, like I say, miss, there's only me on the desk, it being Sunday.'

She hung up and called out to see if there was anyone in the next office. 'Stephen! Jeremy!'

There was no one and, as she heard the tread on the stair outside, she realized she was on her own.

In the church they were singing one of those funeral hymns that make you feel like crying even if you didn't know the deceased. At the front of the church, Helen was weeping copiously, but silently. Anita was bent forward in her pew, trembling and heaving as she breathed. Peter grasped her hand, his face taut with strain. Jason sat in the pew behind, the only impassive figure in the church. He was sitting next to his dad.

> *Gentle Jesus, meek and mild*
> *Look upon a little child*
> *Pity my simplicity*
> *Suffer me to come to Thee.*

Thomas Harris, in his dress uniform, sat rigidly to attention, his eyes brimming with tears that he just managed not to shed. And, at the very back of the church, in newly pressed uniform, was Colin Barridge. He stood, equally to attention, but for him there was no will to suppress the grief. Fat, frank teardrops coursed down his cheeks while rivers of dilute mucous poured from his nostrils. And when at last it was time to leave the church for the graveside, Barridge found himself stumbling around blindly among the cohorts of press and camera crews. He couldn't see his colleagues, until Meg Richards came up and gently walked him over to the rest of the funeral group.

The man was burly with a boxer's face. He was wearing a well-worn leather overcoat, blue jeans and red neck-scarf and Belinda was considerably taken aback by the way he looked around at the comfortable furniture and fittings of the office. He did this with undisguised contempt.

'Huh,' said the man in a marked Cardiff accent. 'Lawyers! Fat felines. Pampered pussycats.'

'Excuse me,' she squeaked, 'would you please state your business?'

She felt somehow that a show of extreme formality might protect her and certainly the man's manner did change. He had a rolled-up newspaper, somewhat battered and torn, in his hand and he pointed it at her in the same way, it occurred to Belinda, that you aim a gun.

'You Belinda Sinclair?'

'Yes, I am. What do you want?'

Then he changed suddenly, became business-like, unrolling the paper, which he opened and spread out on the desk between them. His movements were quick and precise but his breathing was laboured, with an intermittent smoker's crackle. The clothes smelt musty but somewhere there was an underlying scent of soap.

He said, 'It's just that I understand you're looking for me.'

She glanced down at the paper and up at him. She had recognized the title but anxiety made her slow-witted and she didn't see the clear connection. He stabbed one of the small ads with a nicotine-stained finger.

'It says in here that you want to see me. My name's Terry Smith.'

Her coffin was white and so small that Thomas Harris had picked it up and carried it by himself, across his arms like an offering, to the graveside. Now the vicar was reciting the ancient formula about ashes and dust.

Helen did not hear it. She was attending to Anita, because something bad was happening even worse than this terrible grief that she felt, Thomas felt, and which, she knew, was tearing at Anita's guts.

Anita had pulled free of Peter's hand. She was clinging on to her mother's arm, bending and swaying as she stood there, her breath coming in gasps.

'Mum,' she whispered, 'promise me you won't leave Peter alone with the kids.'

'What do you mean? What is it love?'

Anita looked up at her mother, her face white and pleading. And then it clenched, every muscle seizing up as a blaze of pain raked through her. Anita dropped her hand from her mum's arm and bent over her swollen belly. Her hands were braced now against her thighs and she was making sharp hiccuping sounds. Then Helen understood.

'Oh, my God, no! Anita, no!'

The vicar was still praying when Peter set off, hurdling across the graveyard as he yelled desperately for a car. They got Anita inside it but by this time she was bleeding. The press were running after them, clustering around the car, their questions muffled and distant but the flash of their cameras harsh and piercing, like the pain itself.

*

'So, Mr Smith, how can you be so sure of what you are saying?'

Belinda had made a pot of tea and she poured for them both.

'I mean, you did a lot of drinking that day, and—'

'I did a lot of drinking *every* day, miss. I'm an alcoholic, I admit that. But it doesn't mean I'm completely ga-ga. And anyway, now I'm off the booze completely – one day at a time, of course – my head's clear as crystal.'

He sipped from his mug and mildly smacked his lips. 'I didn't know which was more important to me, drink or politics. But, now I've got my head straightened out, I know.'

'So which is it?'

'Politics, miss. The Revolution – that's my only stimulant now. Better to die on your feet than live on your knees – a great Spanish revolutionary said that.'

Belinda nodded wisely, wondering how she was going to get Smith back on track. But she needn't have worried.

'Anyway, I can remember it all. We got together in the Scrubbery – you know, that little park place near the benefit office – after the office opened, about eleven o'clock. We started off there, then went to the chippie, then back to the park—'

He was interrupted by the door swinging open and the entrance of the senior partner in Sunday mufti, beige cardigan and Hush Puppies. He looked at Smith in surprise.

'Ah, Derek,' said Belinda. 'Do come in, join us.'

Feeling a sudden rush of triumph over Waugh, she didn't bother with introductions but carried straight on talking to the witness.

'So, Mr *Smith*' – she shot a quick glance at Waugh to

clock his astonishment – 'you read our advertisement in the *Big Issue* and you remember spending the whole day with Michael Dunn – right?'

Smith nodded.

'But how can you be certain it was that particular Thursday, the 5th September?'

Smith snapped his fingers. 'Easy. The Berringham by-election, fifth of September. Bloody Spartacist knocked our fellow out.'

Belinda scribbled a note. The by-election certainly rang a bell, and the date was easy enough to check.

'Good,' she said, 'very, very good.'

After Smith had left Waugh paid her a gruff compliment.

'Well done, Belinda. Fellow seems a good witness, though a bit of a Trot which we shall have to watch. That surprised me, actually. I thought Terry Smith was supposed to be a wino.'

'He was,' said Belinda. 'He's reformed. So you see, Derek, there's hope for us all.'

She was enjoying herself enormously. She would enjoy even more telling her client that his alibi had been confirmed.

CHAPTER 21

THE MOOD of elation amongst Michael Dunn's defence team could not be too publicly celebrated. There was a need for secrecy. As Waugh told Belinda – and for once he was right – there was no requirement for the defence immediately to tell the CPS that Terry Smith had been found. In the interests of their client – of his more effective defence – they would keep their alibi witness under wraps until just before the off.

So it was that, only four days before Dunn was due to appear at the Crown Court to answer the charge of murder against him, Belinda Sinclair picked Terry Smith up from the hostel where he was living and brought him east to Southampton Street to make a sworn statement.

The scenes in the Incident Room were of consternation.

'Why the bloody hell couldn't *we* find him?' stormed Satchell. 'Bunch of incompetents are we, or what? Bunch of dozy bastards fit for nothing but touchline duty at Leyton Orient? Christ!'

'How did they find him, then?' asked Phelps. 'I can't believe their luck!'

'They advertised, didn't they?' said Satchell. 'Bloody

advertised! Well, of course, that's the difference, isn't it? We got no bastard advertising budget.'

'He was living in a hostel drying out,' put in Henshaw. 'Apparently he's obsessed with Lenin.'

'What – the Beatles?' asked Marik.

'Pillock!' said Henshaw, swiping Marik round the head with his copy of the *Daily Mail*. 'Len-*in*. He's political. A leftie.'

'Didn't know there was any of those no more,' retorted Marik. 'Could be good for us, though. Expose him as a Trot, a troublemaker. Discredited witness.'

Pat North heard this as she came in.

'I'm sorry, Marik, but it's more likely to harm us. Lefty's not much of a bogeyman any more. My guess is he'd come over as bright and serious, and a little bit of a romantic, you know? One of a dying breed.'

'Yes, but he might start mouthing off in court, have a go at the judge or the legal system,' said PC Brown hopefully. 'That would be good, wouldn't it?'

'I don't think, somehow, Rylands is going to allow that to happen,' said Satchell. 'But if he does, we'll know he's losing his grip big time. Is Smith here now, guv?'

Pat North was removing papers from a filing cabinet.

'Yes. Mike and I are about to take his sworn statement. Wouldn't it be nice if we could just make him disappear instead?'

She smiled all round and swung smartly out of the room to meet the man who might just extract Michael Dunn from a life sentence.

Walker smoked his amputated Marlboros more or less continuously during the interview and he let Terry Smith have free access to the packet as well. It wasn't generosity. Walker was so angry he was having a hard time concentrating so he just didn't notice the witness helping himself. Sitting beside Smith, Belinda, though she hated the smoke, saw it as a fair sign of how rattled the police were.

Walker had Smith's printed-out statement in front of him. He'd been over the statement again and again, but there was nothing he could prise from it, nothing of any use to his side. All that was left was for Smith to sign it.

'So, Mr Smith, you and Michael Dunn started talking about politics at eleven o'clock on that Thursday did you? Until when?'

'All day, like it says,' said Smith.

'What on earth was there to talk about *all day*?' said Walker incredulously.

There was a tap on the door and Satchell put his head in to beckon to Pat North. She left the room while Smith expanded.

'We were talking about whether the desire for property is natural to mankind. You see the Russian peasants before the revolution used to have little plots of land . . .'

Walker flicked a glance at Belinda who was clearly having to suppress a smile. He scowled but Smith was just getting into his stride.

'These guys were called kulaks, you see, and when it came to dealing with them, Lenin formulated a plan about which there has been considerable controversy over the years—'

'Yes, yes, yes. I get the gist,' said Walker. 'This isn't the Evening Institute. And you say this all-day drinking session didn't affect your memory to any material extent?'

Terry Smith smiled. Everything about him was so open and honest it made Walker cringe.

'No, I had a tolerance for it, you see. I'm telling you, I'll stand up in court and say it: Michael Dunn was with me all day on September the fifth. All day long, until six, seven at night.'

'He didn't leave at any time?'

'No. He didn't leave.'

Again Walker looked hopelessly at the statement, his eyes going this way and that over it as if casting about for comfort and finding none. His expression was bleak. He slid the statement on to the table, face up in front of the witness.

'Right, Mr Smith, I thank you for your co-operation in this matter. Would you like to read and sign the statement?'

Pat North returned to the room and stood near the door while Smith read rapidly through the text and, taking a pen from Belinda, scribbled his signature at the bottom. He handed the paper back to Walker like a bailiff serving a writ.

Belinda said, sweetly, 'There you are, Superintendent. All right if we go now?'

Walker couldn't bring himself to speak. He nodded.

After they'd left, he almost spat. 'Like the cat who got the cream, isn't she? What did Dave want?'

'Anita Harris has been released from hospital, guv,' said Pat.

'In time for the trial. Poor woman.'

'Yes. Buries one, miscarries another. Hard even to contemplate what she must be feeling right now.'

'I tell you one thing I'm feeling. More bloody determined than ever that Michael Dunn killed that child. And

I want to nail him. I want to hammer in those nails personally.'

'There's a bloke down there in the playground,' observed Karen Hyam, looking idly out of the staircase window in the early afternoon, as she and her friend Ivy Green hoisted the black bin bag down the stairs. 'He's going round on the kiddies' roundabout.'

She had caught a glimpse of the play area, deserted during the lunchtime of a school day. The man was sitting on one of the tubular bars which divided the revolving platform into four sections.

'Some men never grow up,' said Ivy Green drily, forging ahead of her friend up the stairs.

Ivy and Karen had volunteered to help get Enid Marsh to court on the Tuesday, properly dressed and in good shape to give her evidence. As a preparation for the big day on Tuesday, they'd decided to go down to her with some possible clothes for her outfit. The poor old dear had nothing much of her own, so they'd been round their friends – and their friends' mothers – on the scrounge.

When they arrived they saw that Mrs Wald, the meals on wheels, had been in half an hour earlier and the remains of Enid's lunch were still on the table.

'Come on, dear,' the practical Ivy had said, picking up the plates and bustling through into the kitchen. 'We've got you in some things to try on. For the trial.'

'Oh!' shrilled Enid. 'But there's no need for that. I've got plenty of things to choose from in my bedroom, I have.'

'No, you've not, petal. I've looked. It's all too old.' She caught the look of dismay on Enid's face. 'I'm not saying they didn't look brilliant in their day, but the moths have got at them. Now me and Karen have searched out a few pieces for you to choose from. Make you look exactly like a super model. It's only right – with you the star witness. Go on, Karen, back me up.'

'Oh yes, Enid, we've found some lovely things,' said Karen encouragingly. 'Near enough Paris fashions, some of it.'

As she watched the two neighbours, younger than her by decades, pulling skirts and blouses out of the bin bag, Enid Marsh started to get used to the idea. It was true she hadn't had on any of her really good clothes for a long time – not since the Silver Jubilee, probably. Spent most of her time in her old cardigan and jumper – never had the occasion to dress up. Moths – yes, it was very likely the good stuff was full of holes. She brightened. New clothes to try on. Come to think of it, that *did* sound nice.

Half an hour later she was sitting on her sofa with clothing strewn around her. She was wearing a powder blue sunray pleated skirt which looked like something Dame Vera Lynn might have worn. It *was* a tiny bit too big for her, but Ivy and Karen thought they could tuck it in at the waist and make it look very smart. The effect was topped off by the white nylon blouse with a frilled jabot, found at the bottom of the bin bag by Karen.

'Everybody's been so kind,' Enid was saying, looking at a portion of herself in the small portable mirror propped up on the table. 'Before all this happened, I never saw a soul.'

She twitched the skirt to arrange the pleats closer to the vertical. 'You don't think it's a bit bright?'

Ivy came over and considered for a moment. She had

her hand to her mouth and was pinching her lower lip between finger and thumb. 'Looks lovely, Enid, dear. But Mrs Kingsley says she's got a Jaeger suit if you want it.'

Karen, standing by the window, was pulling Enid's net curtains aside. 'Here, that man's still down there. I reckon he's staring up at this window. Bit of a toff.'

Enid shuffled across to join her, peering down. He was a well-dressed, well-preserved man in his mid-fifties, wearing a dark-grey woollen overcoat. The three women watched as, seeing their heads looking down, he turned away and bent to pick up his briefcase.

'I think I'll try the jacket now,' said Enid without further comment. 'And that mauve skirt – I haven't had that on yet. And what was you saying about a suit, Ivy, love?'

That afternoon Anita was also trying on clothes. Ten days after the miscarriage and she still had a fat stomach. She had even thought of going to court wearing the black maternity dress she'd bought for the funeral, but Helen told her no: it wouldn't look right.

'But nothing fits me,' Anita complained. 'I still look as if I'm pregnant.'

I still *feel* pregnant too, she thought. Three times before in her life she'd given birth and each time, once the baby was out and feeding, Anita had felt feather-light. Never had a day of post-natal depression either. This was her fourth, except it wasn't. Birth is all about life, that's why it's called *giving* birth. So she went on feeling heavy and burdened because she had given nothing, nothing had happened. The baby was dead.

In hospital she couldn't cry. Until they'd found her a

private room the second night she'd been stuck in a post-natal ward, full of other mums sitting up in bed nursing their little bundles, a cot next to every bed except hers. Anita was simply withdrawn. She hardly responded when anyone spoke to her. She stared straight ahead and talked silently to herself. The baby was dead; giving birth's about giving life . . .

'You should go out and buy something, love,' said Helen now, flicking through the dresses and jackets that hung in the wardrobe on their wire coat hangers. Truth be told, there was little enough here. 'You've got all those donations and I don't suppose anybody'd begrudge you.'

'It's too late now. I haven't got time. I can't go out and buy something, just like that.'

'Well, be warned. Peter's dipping into them all the time. Taking himself off to I don't know where.' She sniffed. 'I've hardly seen him – sober, that is.'

Anita touched her mother on the arm. 'Hey! Don't, Mum. Just don't get into that. Anyway I'm better off without him around.'

Helen took down a dark-blue jacket that looked OK, though it needed taking to the cleaners.

'A white blouse under that'll look nice in court, eh, my girl.'

Anita pushed her arms out behind to let Helen slip the jacket on for her. Turning this way and that in front of the mirror, she was trying to remember when she'd last worn it.

Darkness had fallen but the figure of a man in white shirtsleeves could be seen crossing the road and making for the sewage pipes. He carried a bundle in his arms.

It had been wet the last few days and the trench dug for the pipes was flooded. He stood on the edge of the trench, watching the reflections from the site security lighting wobble as the water was troubled by the wind. He was thinking of another flooded area not many yards away, where a dead cat had floated and he had fallen in. Put off doing a proper search because he swallowed some water. Stupid and unprofessional.

Barridge felt a heavy weight in the pit of his stomach. It was the weight of responsibility, the weight of guilt. For a long time during the investigation he had believed that finger was on him – like that lottery advert, it could be *you*. It was a pleasant feeling, a light feeling. He had trodden on air for a while, a man specially chosen who could do no wrong.

But doing *that* – well, he shouldn't have. That was wrong and Colin Barridge knew it. He'd have to come clean, he'd have to tell. And then they'd kick him out.

With a groaning sigh he raised the bundle in his arms and tossed it into the water of the trench. His uniform tunic gradually soaked up the water, then opened out, arms spreading, the chrome buttons catching the light.

CHAPTER 22

ROBERT RYLANDS was studying the list to see which judge had been allotted to the case. Barristers, solicitors, witnesses, police and officers of the court bustled through the lobby behind him as the Crown Court's working day began to unroll.

'Good morning, Robert. Alone and palely loitering?'

He turned. It was the solid figure of Willis Fletcher who, like him, had yet to robe. Behind Fletcher, in a little knot, were the Crown team – Griffith, Jennifer Abantu and Rylands's junior, Tom Jolowicz. They all hefted large tagged bundles, deep ring-files and thick law books.

'It's Winfield,' said Rylands, tipping his head back towards the list on the board behind him. 'Did you know?'

'Yes, I've seen the list. He's decent enough.'

'Babbles like the bloody brook, though. I'd have thought—' He broke off as the figure of Derek Waugh pushed eagerly through the crowd.

'Robert – it's delightful to see you again.'

Fletcher winked at his chambers room-mate and, stepping back, rejoined his team. Rylands looked down on the shorter man as if inspecting a dead fish.

'Very nice to see you, too, Derek. Show of solidarity by the firm?'

'Yes – ah, I thought I might just pop down. Belinda's with our friend downstairs.'

Rylands was only half listening – he was scanning over Waugh's head at the crowd. At last he saw Noah Sampara, his junior, struggling towards him laden with papers and carrying a plastic bag, out of which straggled several locks of beautifully permed nylon hair.

'Ah, Noah!' said Rylands heartily. He nodded at the carrier bag. 'Brought your friends with you? Good!' He glanced at his watch. 'Look, I'd better go and get clobbered up. See you both shortly.'

He turned to leave, then checked and tapped Sampara on the arm. 'It's Winfield, by the way. Neutral choice, I would think.'

Then he left them and walked smartly to the Queen's Counsel's robing rooms where he dressed carefully in his silk jacket and gown.

In the holding cells below the court, Belinda was doing a rapid repair job on her client's face.

'Dear God, Michael. How did this happen?'

'I just, bumped into something.'

'Oh, yeah?'

He had a large bump near his right eye, to the right, and another on the cheek, where it had also bled. She had a pot of pancake make-up and was smearing it over the damaged tissue.

'It's all right,' he said, wincing.

'No, it isn't. I told you to keep out of trouble.'

'Sorry.'

She screwed the lid back on the pot. 'Now, don't be frightened to look at the judge and the jury. But don't, whatever you do, stare at them. Just don't look as if you are avoiding their eyes. You're innocent, remember?'

'That's right. I got nothing to hide.'

'And don't smile, Michael. I want you to look serious – all right?'

He nodded. There was a rap on the door. It was time.

'Right,' she said. 'We're on. Ready?'

In the hierarchical and clearly mapped space of the courtroom, everyone has an allotted position. In some ways it is like an old-fashioned church, with the Judge sitting at his massive desk, as if planted in a great High Altar. Above him, suspended from the wall, is a resplendent royal coat of arms; below him is the Clerk of the Court at his desk with the stenographer and then the bar of the court like a communion rail, separating the officers of justice from those who have come in search of it.

The wood-panelled court is an easygoing place full of quiet conversation until the judge takes his seat. Like wedding guests, divided according to their allegiance and waiting for the arrival of the bride, the prosecution sits on one side and the defence on the other. They occupy ranks, the barristers to the fore and solicitors behind. Here, awaiting the arrival of Mr Justice Winfield, were Rylands, Fletcher and the other briefs in their gowns, bands and wigs. Rylands signalled with his finger to Fletcher and shifted a few seats towards the Prosecution side.

'You up for a game of tennis? Thursday night?'

'What time?'

'Court's booked for seven-thirty. I've got Roly and Bill on-side. Think you can make it?'

Fletcher flipped open a pocket diary and jotted a note. 'Certainly. Already looking forward to it, Robert.'

'Good. Should be a good game.'

He slid back to his place, next to which Sampara was checking the post-it notes he'd placed in their deposition bundle. Waugh was glancing at the crossword. Behind the lawyers were benches for the police and any other interested officials connected to the case. Even further back, and to the side, was a cramped area reserved for the press and media. And along the side wall, bridging the fore-and-aft division of the court, was the enclosure for the jury of twelve ordinary men and women, chosen at random from the electoral roll. At this stage of Regina vs. Michael Dunn the jury box was empty.

The public, too, were set apart, confined on a gallery perched above the court, as if in a kind of purdah and policed in officious style by ushers. They were present strictly on sufferance. And at the very back of the court, slightly raised, stood the dock, which would soon be offering up its prisoner for judgement.

At ten o'clock, before the clock on the tower had finished striking, the elaborate formality of the murder trial began.

'Be upstanding in court.'

Having arrived just ahead of the judge, Belinda hardly had time to take stock of Winfield before he started speaking. She had asked around about him and been told he was dry but decent. With judges it is always difficult at first sight to see the man under the wig, but he seemed a shrewd individual of about sixty, hurrying into his seat as if wanting to have the trial done and dusted with efficiency and speed. He nodded to the Clerk whose job it was to dock the prisoner.

'Put up Michael Dunn,' called the Clerk.

Dunn appeared at the back of the court flanked by two security guards. There was a palpable hush as the court registered his presence, followed by a rustle of whispered comment. Belinda turned to look at him, trying to catch his eye. Leaving him a few minutes earlier, she had felt sick with anxiety, but Dunn was calm and seemed almost at ease. So did he now. In suit, shirt and tie – bought by arrangement with social services – he looked nothing like the dirty, drink-ravaged social misfit that the police had arrested back in September. Searching the array of faces that had turned towards him, he found Belinda's. She smiled encouragingly and his mouth gave the merest twitch.

'Are you Michael Frederick Dunn?' asked the Clerk severely once the accused was standing in the dock.

'Yes.'

His voice came over as quiet, unassuming. It would lilt pleasantly when he gave evidence. Quite illogically, given that proceedings had not even begun yet, Belinda felt a surge of optimism. He was innocent and they would beat this.

'Please be seated,' said the Clerk. 'Jury panel, please.'

There was a renewal of the murmuring in the well of the court as fifteen men and women filed in, shuffling self-consciously until they all stood in a knot at the back of the court. Winfield, who had been writing and paying little heed to events so far, suddenly looked up, quelling all conversation. He turned without further ado to the jurors and cleared his throat.

'Ladies and gentlemen, this case involves events which took place on the Howarth Estate in East London. Without wishing to impugn the ability of any of you to apply your minds objectively to the evidence in the case, rather than to, er, any extraneous consideration, out of excess of caution I am sure you will agree that – if there *is* anyone here who has a close connection with the Howarth Estate, it would be better if you did not serve. Is there in fact anyone who falls into that category?'

The jurors looked sidelong at each other but no one spoke. Winfield nodded to the Clerk who turned to the accused and began to intone.

'The names you are about to hear are the names of the jurors who are to try you. If you have an objection to any of them you must say so before they come to book to be sworn, and your objection shall be heard.'

The Clerk turned to the panel of jurors. 'As your name is called,' said the Clerk, 'would you please answer and go and sit in the jury box.'

He had in his hand a pack of filecards. He shuffled the pack and picked up the top card.

'Sheree Granger?'

One of the jurors, a young woman, started slightly and said, 'Er – present!'

As the jury were being empanelled and sworn, Walker fidgeted. It wasn't the physical space of the courtroom that bothered him on these occasions, it was the way these trials inhabited the dimension of time – so leisurely, as if ritualized tedium was the essence of it all. It was like cricket – another of those English rituals that he, as a Scot, was baffled by. Five days to play a game that could be settled just as easily in an afternoon!

He looked at his watch then leaned towards Pat North's ear. 'Just going out for a smoke.'

Then he tiptoed out of the court.

*

Barridge had been anticipating the trial in a state of mounting distress. It was as if he was waiting for his own trial.

His uniform had been returned to him eventually. A building worker fished it out of the trench and they'd phoned Southampton Street from the site hut. The Super had called him in for a bollocking. Not a rap on the wrist: a right what's-got-into-you, it's-bloody-irresponsible, are-you-trying-to-make-a-laughing-stock-out-of-me type of bollocking.

Having been told, if he did it again, his size twelves wouldn't touch, he was fired into Mr Awad at Occupational Health. Awad meant well but Barridge had struggled from the off to communicate with him. The man had a habit of nodding and saying 'yes, yes, yes', as if hurrying him, when Barridge spoke about the flashbacks and the guilt and feelings about being chosen. It was so irritating that Barridge had never confided the most important and most secret details of all – the thing he had done. The unforgivable thing. After three appointments he had not felt like making a fourth.

At home, his dad never noticed a bloody thing, but his mum knew there was something very wrong.

'It's still that kid you found, isn't it? It's bugging you something terrible.'

'Don't know.'

'It is, Colin, I know you. And you're not sleeping. Well, if you won't go and see the doctor, what about that man at work, that Awad? You should go back to him again. Have another try.'

'Don't want to.'

'He might help, son. You got to do something. You can't just mope around here.'

Eventually he seemed to let himself be persuaded to go back to Awad. Privately he knew he would have to face him again anyway, and tell the truth. Today was the last possible day – the trial began this morning. Before it was too late he had to tell someone what he'd done – the thing they would call a perversion.

Fletcher opened for the Crown and from the first he showed his determination not to spare the jury.

'There are a number of things, members of the jury, which will not be in dispute: that Julie Anne was first strangled into unconsciousness by means of a rope ligated around her neck. That she was sexually assaulted and was then placed – alive – in one of the sewage pipes on a nearby building site. There are some photographs which I would like you to look at in the bundle.'

The jury turned to their copies of the site where the child's body had been found.

'As you can see,' said Fletcher, 'this is a pipe of narrow diameter and the position in which Julie Anne was placed forced her head down into her knees, restricting her breathing with the result that she died – some time later – of asphyxia or suffocation. There is no doubt, then, that Julie Anne was murdered.'

Walker had returned to his place before Fletcher got to his feet. Now he glanced at the public gallery – the grandmother was there and one or two of the Howarth Estate residents, dressed up as if for a charabanc-ride to Southend. Then he saw the stepfather come in, looking angry and unkempt, his eyes staring. Walker saw him favour Helen with a look of vicious hatred as he found a place in the row behind her.

'Now, members of the jury,' continued Fletcher, 'I would like you to view the evidence in this case as you would the pieces of a jigsaw. It may be that one or two of the pieces are missing – that there are some questions that will not be answered or details that will not be filled in. But enough of the overall picture will emerge for you to be certain that the person who murdered Julie Anne Harris in the way I have described is the defendant, Michael Dunn.'

Now Fletcher's glance met Dunn's eyes, which were fixed steadily on him. In Fletcher's experience, guilty men nearly always looked away first. Innocent men did too, sometimes. But it was a rule of thumb for Fletcher that guilty men never took him on in a courtroom staring duel. Dunn, it seemed, was going to be the exception.

'Michael Dunn did not deny in interview that he liked children – and, on the face of it, of course, there's nothing wrong with that. Children often visited Dunn's flat and he says that he used to watch videotapes, of various kinds, with them. He also kept toys there for the children's use. And he admitted in interview that he knew Julie Anne Harris.'

Fletcher stopped and drank from his water glass, still maintaining eye-contact with the jury over the rim of his glass.

'You will hear evidence,' he went on, replacing his glass on the desk in front of him, 'from a neighbour who says she saw a man, whom she later identified as being Michael Dunn, approach Julie Anne in the playground on the fifth of September, the day of her death. The Crown maintains that he took her from there to his flat. You will hear that genetic material of Julie Anne's, DNA contained in saliva, was recovered from a wrapper and

250

stick of an ice-cream bar which was found in Michael Dunn's kitchen. The Crown says that this is no coincidence.'

Fletcher remained still for a couple of seconds then brandished his index finger.

'Nor, the Crown says, is it any coincidence that fibres recovered from Michael Dunn's furniture are consistent with those taken from the clothes Julie Anne was wearing on the fifth of September. You must also consider if it is a coincidence – or something more significant – that the same sample of dog faeces was found on the footwear of both Julie Anne and Michael Dunn, as worn on that same day. You must consider what construction to put on these facts.

'One construction, and the Crown says it is the correct one, is that, on the fifth of September, Julie Anne Harris went out wearing the clothing from which the fibres would later be recovered, and there she trod in some dog mess; that Michael Dunn approached Julie Anne and, in so doing, trod on the same ground. He then took Julie Anne by the hand and led her to his flat, where she was indeed in contact with the furniture and the carpets. It may well be that she was encouraged there with the offer of an ice-cream, which she ate, leaving the wrapper and stick to be recovered later by police.

'It is possible that hair from Julie Anne's head, found on Michael Dunn's floor, was dislodged during the attack and sexual assault on her. We know that a rope was then used to strangle her until she lost consciousness – and it may not surprise you to learn that this rope, which was found around her neck by the police, was the same as one which Michael Dunn put up as a washing line for a neighbour – and which subsequently disappeared. Finally, on that day, Julie Anne was placed in the sewage pipe in which she died. Her clothing was found discarded in a nearby cellar. Significantly, a length of washing line of an identical type was discovered by the police in Michael Dunn's bin. The Crown cannot say how it got there, but if you come to the conclusion that Michael Dunn stole that washing line from his neighbour, you must ask yourself why? What did he want with it? What did he have in mind?'

With a piece of gentle, low-intensity mime, Fletcher held his hands out in front of him, as if lightly grasping some object, and drew them slightly apart.

'Was he experimenting in some way? The rope or line may well suggest to you, as it does to the Crown, that this was not an offence committed on impulse but that it was quite carefully pre-planned.'

Rylands had listened to Fletcher with his eyes half-closed, his face expressionless. But Belinda was worried. This was a highly confident start by the Prosecution. The jury were sitting up in their seats – marking every word, some of them nodding their heads or scribbling notes. By the time Fletcher was ready to call his first witness, Belinda found that her initial confidence was rapidly draining away.

CHAPTER 23

BARRIDGE WAS well aware that some of his colleagues were inclined to deride the Metropolitan Police's Occupational Health Service, and to scoff equally at those who became its clients. It was known as the Funny Farm or, more succinctly, Barking.

The idea behind the scheme is to offer counselling to officers traumatized in the course of their duties, either because of what they've seen or done in the line of duty or because they have been physically injured and need help in coming to terms with that.

The staff are professional counsellors, specialists in post-traumatic stress, marriage breakdown, alcohol problems and other hazards of the job. Barridge had no idea where his own counsellor, Awad, was coming from, but he was highly reminiscent of a man who had taught chemistry at Barridge's comprehensive school. Whenever he sat opposite him, watching him nodding his head, he couldn't help thinking about potassium sulphide.

The entrance to Area's Occupational Health Unit is discreetly placed in a side street – a small anonymous office with total discretion assured. Barridge pushed his way in and approached the reception desk, behind which a young woman with brightly painted nails was talking on the phone.

253

'Yeah, I know,' she was saying, 'spent all that money at the hairdresser and all. Shame on him . . . That's what I say, serve him right. He'll never know what he missed . . .'

Barridge was trying to control the shakes. He looked around. Various posters about stress were pinned up.

Stress avoidance – a checklist of dos and don'ts: DO take plenty of physical exercise such as aerobics. DO set aside a period of time each day for silent relaxation. DON'T rely on alcohol, sex or drugs for relaxation. DON'T privilege your work at the expense of family and friends.

There was nothing about going swimming with putrefying cats. There was nothing about finding what he'd found.

'Well, look, I got to go now,' the receptionist was saying into her phone. 'Yeah, same here. OK. Bye.'

She hung up.

'How can I help you?'

Barridge gripped the edge of her desk. There was a feeling of fatalism about him now.

'I'd like to see Mr Awad, please.'

'Oh! I'm afraid he's not in today.'

'Is there anyone else I can speak to? I've got to speak to someone.'

He was hyperventilating as the receptionist flipped through the appointments book in front of her. He pulled at the collar of his shirt.

'We-ell – there's Mrs Cheshire. But I'll have to ask her and she's busy right now.'

Barridge was sweating and his legs felt tingly, as if he were about to get an attack of pins and needles.

'I have to speak to someone.'

She gave him an odd, questioning look.

'All right, why don't you sit down in the waiting area and I'll have a word with her when I can. What did you say your name was?'

Barridge gave his name then wandered back to the door.

'I'll . . . I need some air. I'll come back in . . . ten minutes.'

The receptionist stared curiously at the swinging door then picked up her phone. 'Mrs Cheshire? I've had an officer in here, a PC Barridge. Seems in a very bad way. You couldn't see him, could you?'

Mrs Cheshire had a gap between appointments at ten-thirty. She had planned to nip out to the chemists but agreed to see Barridge instead. She was fortyish and far more like a school nurse than a science teacher, which Barridge found a little encouraging.

'So, how can I help you, PC Barridge – Colin?'

'Well, it's something I want to get off of my chest, see? It's hard. I don't know if I can come right out with it, like.'

'Uh-huh. Let me have a bit of background first, why don't you?'

This was one disadvantage of Awad's absence. He would have to go back over ground he'd already covered, otherwise Mrs Cheshire wouldn't understand. And he desperately wanted her to understand. So he started to tell her about the Howarth Estate case, and the missing child and the search in the rain and him falling in the water in that cellar and then finding the body and the terrible sadness and sense of waste and emptiness he'd had inside him every since the suspect had been arrested.

'Julie Anne, that's the little girl I found, I kept on seeing her face and I couldn't sleep.'

He was almost crying. He could feel the raw mass growing in his throat and the tears welling up. His voice wobbled and he had to struggle to control it.

'It was as if she was reaching out to me. They knew it was him ... everybody knew. We knew it was him. I mean, we were certain, so certain. And the trial's started today. He's in the dock, and it's got to be stopped ...'

The counsellor got up and went to where a water jug and some glasses stood on a shelf. She poured water, brought it back to her desk and placed it in front of Barridge. He was shivering, tipping over the edge into tears.

'You say it's got to be stopped? Do you mean you now think that this man might not have committed the murder?'

Barridge shook his head. 'I don't *know*,' he wailed. 'Maybe. It looks like him. But . . . it might not be.'

'Well, isn't that the purpose of the trial? I mean, surely the police officers have done their work – including you, Colin – and now it's up to the jury to decide—'

'That's it! Our work! That's what I have to tell you. It was my work, it was me wanting to be sure he'd be found guilty.'

The room felt very hot. Barridge's face was a deep red.

Mrs Chesire spoke very quietly. 'What did you do, Colin?'

'Do? I – I – well, I tampered with the evidence! I cheated.' He picked up the glass of water and drank.

Mrs Cheshire's eyes narrowed. 'You mean, in order to make it more likely this man would be convicted?'

He put down the glass and nodded his head. There, it was out. He'd admitted it.

'I see,' said Mrs Cheshire. 'And you've told no one about this?'

'No. No, I haven't. That's what I'm trying to tell *you*. That's why I'm here!'

'And what do you want me to do, Colin?'

'Get it *stopped*.'

Barridge felt the pins and needles again in his legs. He was sitting right on the edge of the chair. He reached for the waterglass again.

'He could end up with a life sentence for something he didn't do, if you don't believe what I'm saying.'

Mrs Cheshire was frowning, chewing the end of her Biro. She shook her head. 'I'm still trying to assimilate what you're saying.'

Oh, for Christ's sake!

Barridge hurled the glass down on the desk, scattering water all over Mrs Cheshire's papers. He was yelling openly now.

'*Look! I bought the rope. I cut it in two. And I put it in Michael Dunn's BIN.*'

He was snivelling, his head down again. 'I want the trial stopped because he might not have done it and, oh, *Jesus . . .*'

Mrs Cheshire said, 'Look, Colin, will you be all right?

Just while I pop out for a few moments. But I'll be back very shortly, all right?'

She whisked out of her office and went straight to reception.

'Denise – do you mind getting off the phone so I can use it, please? I think this is a bit of an emergency.'

CHAPTER 24

'ARE YOU Mrs Enid Marsh?' asked Willis Fletcher, when the old lady had completed her tortuous journey from the court corridor and was safely berthed in the witness stand. 'And do you live at number thirty-three, Howarth House?'

'Yes.'

Enid looked around. The stand was placed on the judge's left, across the court room from the jury box. In all her long life she had never entered a court of law. But she had seen Charles Laughton in *Witness for the Prosecution* many years ago and, ever since, she'd had quite a taste for courtroom dramas on television. For a murder trial, this was a smaller room than she had anticipated and less intimidating.

'And what floor is that on?'

'The sixth floor.'

'Please could you look at these photographs, Mrs Marsh?' He passed the photographs to the associate to take to the witness while Fletcher addressed the judge. 'If these could become exhibit one, m'lord?'

Enid looked at the numbered prints then placed them on the edge of the witness box and started fumbling for her glasses.

'Could you look at photograph number three, Mrs Marsh? Does it show what can be seen from your window?'

'Oh, yes,' said Enid as the picture came into focus. 'It does.'

'Just describe to us what you can see.'

'I can see the entrance to the flats and I can see the . . . the right-hand side of the playground.'

'Is there any particular time of day when you are in the habit of looking out of your window, Mrs Marsh?'

'Yes. I look out at lunchtimes. I wait for the meals on wheels every day.'

'Every day?'

'Yes.'

'Are you able to remember the day when Julie Anne Harris went missing? That was the day the police first called at your flat.'

'Yes – I remember it very well.'

The witness seemed to have shrugged off the uncertainty of her first replies. She was sounding positive and eager now.

'Tell the court about it, would you?'

'Well, I looked out at a quarter to one – I looked at the clock because she's usually brought my lunch by then. I mean, Mrs Wald, the lady who brings my lunch . . . And she – I . . .'

Enid had seized up again, unsure where her train of thought had started from. Gently, Fletcher brought her back on track.

'Yes, and what did you see when you looked out of the window?'

'I saw the little Harris girl playing on her own. I often saw her playing with the other children.'

There was a slight disturbance as the door of the court opened and Satchell came in. He slid along the bench beside where Pat North was sitting and began whispering urgently in her ear.

'Were you able to recognize that it was Julie Anne Harris at that distance?' continued Fletcher.

'Yes, I was. But you see, she was on her own. I thought she shouldn't have been left.'

'What did she do?'

'Well, she was playing and then she started covering her face and peeping out – sort of through her fingers, like this.'

Enid laced her twisted old fingers together and peeped girlishly through them at Fletcher.

'It was as though there was someone else playing with her . . .'

'Weren't you able to see that person?'

'No.'

'And did you see anything else unusual that lunchtime?'

'Yes. Well, I was looking out again at five past one for the meals on wheels, because it still hadn't come you know. And, anyway, I saw a man bend down and take the little girl's hand.'

'What did you see of that man, Mrs Marsh? Did you see his face?'

'Yes, I did. It was sideways on. But yes, I did, I saw his face.'

'Had you seen that man before?'

Enid shook her head. 'No. I didn't know him at all.'

'But did you see him again?'

'Oh, yes, I saw him again in Kilburn.'

Fletcher looked at her, questioningly. 'Kilburn?'

'You *know*, the parade thing – the identification parade. He was the one I picked.'

She made it sound like judging the supreme champion at Crufts Dog Show.

'Just one last thing, Mrs Marsh. I notice you are wearing glasses. Would you mind telling us if you always wear them?'

'Oh no, I only need them to read. I can see as well as anyone over a long distance. It's got better over the years.'

'Thank you very much, Mrs Marsh. Would you please wait there so that my learned friend can ask you a few questions?'

In the gap between Fletcher's examination of Mrs Marsh and Rylands's cross-examination, DI North and DS Satchell left the court. The door was still swinging as Rylands rose majestically to his feet and began to speak.

'Good morning, Mrs Marsh.'

She smiled uncertainly. 'Good morning.'

'It's very nice to see you again.'

She looked at him in his wig and black silk gown, a large and handsome but undeniably forceful figure. She frowned. 'I beg your pardon?'

Rylands propped a hand in the small of his back, looked down at his feet and up again at Enid.

'Don't you remember seeing me before?'

Enid hesitated again. Then shook her head. 'No. No, I don't.'

'Would this help?'

Rylands flipped his wig and his glasses from his head and got an instant reaction from the judge.

'Really, Mr Rylands,' expostulated Winfield.

'Please, m'lord—'

'I hope this is taking us somewhere.'

Pat North had crept back into court and was whispering to Walker. Winfield waved Rylands on.

'You *were* at your flat on Friday of last week at twelve-fifty p.m., were you not? And you were looking out of the window, at the playground.'

Enid did not reply. She scented some trap.

'Mrs Marsh, counsel often do go to the scene of a crime, as part of their preparation.'

'I saw a man in a blue suit,' said Enid hotly. 'He was carrying a briefcase and he was looking up at my flat. Was that you?'

'So you saw this man, carrying a briefcase? You noticed him and he was looking directly at you?'

'Yes.'

'Mrs Marsh,' said Rylands softly now. 'There will be evidence in due course that that man was myself. You saw me, you noticed me, you were able to describe my clothes and my superficial appearance. But, even though I was looking straight at you, you were unable to remember my face.'

'Oh, well, I . . . I mean, I'm sorry.'

'It's all right, Mrs Marsh, I am not offended in the least. Now, you identified a man at an identification parade as being the one you saw with Julie Anne, am I right?'

'Yes.'

There was another waft of air through the court and the sigh of the door as Walker and North left hurriedly. The judge frowned but said nothing, letting Rylands continue.

'Would you be so sure of your identification, if I told you that there was another man with long dark hair on the Howarth Estate around lunchtime on that day? Not the man you picked out but another of similar build?'

Winfield butted in firmly. 'I trust there is going to be an evidential basis for this.'

'There will indeed, m'lord. Would you like me to repeat my question, Mrs Marsh?'

He was as sweet as sugar to her now. He knew when not to crow over a witness's discomfort.

'Oh, no. I don't know . . .'

'You don't know if you *would* be sure?'

Enid shook her head despairingly. 'I don't know.'

Rylands hesitated, letting the import of the witness's confusion sink in. Then he swept back to his place.

'Thank you, Mrs Marsh.'

Winfield looked at Fletcher. Did he want a re-examination? Fletcher shook his head and the judge said to Enid. 'You may leave the witness box now, Mrs Marsh.'

Meg Richards came forward to help Enid down. All the fight had gone out of her, she seemed crumpled suddenly and, worst of all, disbelieved.

Winfield surveyed the court, looked at his watch and cleared his throat. He was hungry.

'I think this might be a convenient moment . . . er, if we come back at five past two.'

He rose and left the bench, scuttling through his private door into his chambers, where rather a fine *boeuf bourguignon* awaited him in the Judges' Dining Room.

During lunch, Belinda visited her client, who was brought up from the cells to one of the conference rooms. He seemed troubled.

'How are you feeling?' she asked.

'Been better.'

She saw the quiet confidence he'd had first thing in the morning was lost. Now he looked hunted; not yet scared but anxious and suspicious.

'Mr Rylands says to tell you that the beginning's always the hardest part, Michael. We've done well with the judge, too. He's the best we could have got.'

Dunn continued to appear doubtful.

'I don't know whether he likes our barrister,' he mumbled.

'What makes you say that?'

'Well, confusing that poor old woman like he did.'

'That poor old woman, as you put it, Michael, is one of the two principal planks of the Prosecution case.'

Dunn brooded for a moment and then suddenly laughed hysterically.

'Planks!' he said. 'That's good!'

By the time Walker and Satchell had driven from the court to Southampton Street, the tyres of the car were all but smouldering. Walker swept into the Incident Room baying for Barridge. All the way Walker had kept up a flow of invective.

'Wait till I see that bloody little pillock. I'll croak him. I'll have his nuts. Planting evidence. It'll probably stop the fucking case in its tracks. Don't these turniptops get any education at all? But I tell you what really turns me over – the stupid shitbag put his hands up. Don't they know Rule Number One about bent behaviour – never, *ever* own up? Jesus! It's unbelievable.'

Now he was sitting in his office with Barridge. The PC was sitting on a wheeled office chair, pushing himself backwards and staring at the floor. With every shuttle of his chair the wheels squeaked. Walker ripped a cigarette from its filter and rammed it in his mouth.

'What the fuck have you got to say for yourself, Barridge?'

The constable was sobbing unconsolably.

'I did it, sir. I'm so sorry.'

Walker lit up with exaggerated deliberation. He had regained control of himself after the fury he'd unleashed in the car.

'I have to tell you that I am suspending you from duty. You will have to surrender your warrant card. There is also the possibility that the defence may ask for you to be tendered as a witness.'

Barridge said nothing. He couldn't meet the Superintendent's eyes. He simply pushed his chair backwards and forwards in a kind of rocking motion.

'Do you understand, Barridge?'

Barridge nodded, streaming tears. When he spoke his voice was hoarse. 'If they want me to give evidence I'll have to tell the truth. I understand that – I've got to tell them the truth. I knew Dunn was the one. I wanted him caught.'

Walker sucked on his cigarette. Suddenly overwhelmed with tiredness he couldn't look at Barridge any more. He shut his eyes.

'So you planted the rope that was discovered at Michael Dunn's flat?'

'*Yes!* Anybody that hurts a little girl . . .'

He was choking on each word now, choking and shouting. 'Anybody who does that should hang. And if they ask me I'll say that too. I'll say it in court. They should *hang*.'

The surge of anger subsided as quickly as it had come and Barridge ran out of words. He shrugged his shoulders hopelessly. Walker watched the storm blow itself out then touched Barridge on the shoulder.

'You'll be all right, son.' He turned sharply to Satchell. 'We'll have to stop the trial,' he said. 'Come on – back to court!'

On the way in the car, Walker was talking into his mobile to the court.

'This is Detective Superintendent Walker speaking . . . Yes. I'm officer in charge of the case against Michael Dunn . . . no, no. Delta, Uniform, November, November. Dunn. Yes . . . It's started today in court one. Something very urgent indeed's come up and I need . . . No, no. I'm asking you: can you get Fletcher to wait for me before he goes into the afternoon session? What? What was that? No, Willis Fletcher, prosecuting counsel. I need to speak to him. Oh. Oh, I see. OK then.'

He disconnected as Satchell looked at his watch.

'It's after two.'

'I know. They've gone back in. Mrs Harris is giving evidence.'

CHAPTER 25

ANITA WORE black in the end. The skirt was maybe a little short, but it wasn't sexy or anything. And she'd been to the hairdresser yesterday for a trim. Helen thought her daughter looked much younger than she really was. A teenager, so you'd think. But she looked sensible, anyway.

Recently Helen had been having flashbacks of Anita as a little girl. It must have been because of Julie, and thinking about how her life had been snuffed out so easily and suddenly at five years old. Anita, too, had been five years old once, not so long ago actually. And now look at her, a grown woman even if she did look as young as she did. She was also, Helen knew, a good woman, a loving woman.

But some of the press had not been too kind to Anita. There'd been plenty of tabloid tears, of course, but Helen always thought they were much the same thing as crocodile tears. There had also been a lot of snide stuff about kids on rough estates being left to play out on their own, a prey to evil paedophiles. Well, what did they know?

Fletcher had given Anita a chance to settle comfortably in the witness stand after she'd been sworn in. His voice was gentle and supportive.

'Mrs Harris, are you Julie Anne's mother?'

'Yes, I am.' Anita frowned and added, 'Well, I was.'

Fletcher looked down at his notes. 'Mrs Harris, there is only one matter I want to ask you about. Did Julie Anne have any toy, or favoured object, to which she was particularly attached?'

'Yes, she had her doll.'

'Can you describe her doll for us?'

'Yes, well it looked like a Barbie, but it wasn't a real one. I bought it in the market for her. She always . . .' Anita took a deep breath to blow away the huskiness in her voice. 'She always carried it with her.'

'And did she have this doll with her on the day she went missing?'

There was a moment's hesitation, then, 'Yes, she did.' Anita's eyes filled.

'I am sorry, Mrs Harris,' said Fletcher caressingly. 'I realize this recalls a very distressing time. But did you see the doll again, after Julie Anne's disappearance?'

'Yes. The day after . . . the police . . .' She dabbed at her tears. It was hard to speak. 'I told them it was hers,' she managed finally.

The judge stopped writing on his pad, looking over his glasses at the witness. 'Mrs Harris, would you like a short adjournment?'

'No, no. I'm all right.'

She sniffed, then blew her nose as Fletcher said, 'Thank you, Mrs Harris. No further questions.'

Now it was Rylands's turn. Anita had not even considered him but, from the public gallery, Helen had. He was dangerous, that one. He was more powerful than Fletcher. Helen sent mental messages over to her distressed daughter. Don't let him trip you up, my darling. Keep cool.

The first thing Rylands did was signal to the usher to lay out the dolls which Sampara had brought in the carrier bag with two dolls found in Dunn's flat. Slowly and meticulously this was done on a table near the witness stand. Rylands waited patiently and then addressed the witness.

'Mrs Harris,' he said in a voice which, by comparison to Fletcher's, seemed dangerous and calculated, 'you last saw this doll that you have mentioned – the one the police found in Mr Dunn's flat, m'lord – first thing on the Sunday morning, which was the day after you learned of your daughter's death. The police came round and woke you up, is that right?'

'Yes.'

There was a minor disturbance at the back of court, where Dunn was muttering to himself.

'I found that doll. *Found* it.'

Belinda swivelled round and frowned at him. He shrugged.

'And do you feel certain,' continued Rylands, 'that you did not make a mistake in confusing one massproduced doll manufactured by the thousand with another?'

'Yes, I do,' said Anita, positively. Yet she had seen the array of dolls on the table waiting for her and she was dreading Rylands's next move.

'Could you perhaps help us, Mrs Harris, by picking out Julie Anne's doll for us now?' He glanced at the bench. 'If the witness could perhaps step down for a moment, m'lord?'

Winfield assented and Anita stepped down to stand in front of the dolls. She remembered that the one the police showed her had one arm – but was it the right or the left?

She looked at these dolls and they were all one-armed. Looking closely at them it was obvious they were not identical, yet it was impossible to pick out any distinguishing characteristics in any of them because, unlike people, these were bland, generalized figures, with their frozen smiles and dazzled eyes.

Why had Anita told the police the Dunn doll was Julie's? Not because she'd particularly wanted it to be the doll. She really thought it *was* the doll. But it was too late to go back now. She looked among the dolls again, each of them with a paper tag tied around its ankle. She would have to make a choice.

'Oh, it's . . . it was such a long time ago, I . . .' she said, and then cursed herself for speaking. She sounded an idiot.

'I appreciate that, Mrs Harris, please take your time.'

'I think it's that one.'

She pointed to one of the dolls which, if truth be told, she'd picked out at random. Rylands stepped forward and seized it.

'M'lord,' he said, 'could the doll which Mrs Harris has just identified become exhibit six?'

He picked up a second doll in his other hand and held it up for Winfield and the court to see.

'It's not exhibit five, the doll found by police in Michael Dunn's flat.'

Pat North was waiting at the entrance to the court when Walker and Satchell arrived.

'What's going on?' asked Walker.

'We've just lost our ID on the doll, guv.'

271

Walker's eyes bulged. '*What*? How come?'

'He tripped her up, the usual Rylands theatricals. What's the story on Barridge?'

North was feeling flat. It had not been a good day so far and it didn't promise to get any better.

'He did it. We'll have to try to get the trial stopped. The wheels are coming off one after the other. What's happening in there now?'

'Fletcher's got the pathologist, Foster, on the stand.'

'There was evidence of sexual assault,' Foster was saying in his carefully studied, neutral courtroom voice. 'The hymen had been ruptured with some blunt instrument, the defect measuring three centimetres.'

'And have you seen similar injuries in other cases, Doctor Foster?'

'Yes, I have. I have seen similar injuries which were established to have been caused by a bottle and I would say this could well have been the case here.'

Fletcher nodded. 'Thank you, Doctor Foster.'

Before Fletcher could hand over to Rylands, Walker and Pat North entered the court and, bowing to the judge, made for Fletcher. Griffith joined them in a huddle as they whispered together. After half a minute Fletcher, looking as if he'd just been mugged, spoke to Rylands and then addressed Winfield.

'M'lord, Could I ask m'lord to rise? A matter has arisen . . .'

Winfield sighed wearily like a schoolteacher dealing with a recalcitrant pupil. 'How long, Mr Fletcher?'

'Twenty minutes, m'lord?'

Winfield considered, glancing at the jury. Counsel

always underestimated the length of time they needed. 'Half an hour,' he said crisply.

In the bar mess Fletcher and Rylands conferred over cups of coffee. The fascinating thing for Willis Fletcher was that his friend didn't want the Crown to throw in the towel. Was he enjoying himself too much?

'OK, I'll tell you what. You'll have to make a clean breast of your rope trick. And live with it, I'm afraid. The jury may take a dim view given that you—'

'Opened with it?'

And so would you have, Fletcher was thinking. But of course the point was that he had presented a circumstance in his opening that was based on tainted evidence. If the trial was to continue the jury would have to put it out of their mind, or else the trial would have to start all over again with twelve new good men and true.

One step, ahead of his opponent, Rylands smiled. Fletcher, furious with the police for putting him in this position, could hardly raise his head, let alone a smile.

'You said practically nothing about it,' said Rylands. 'I'll object if you try to get the jury discharged.'

'Do you want me to tender the boy for cross-examination?'

'The policeman? Poor bastard's lost his marbles, hasn't he? I'm happy to leave him out of it.' He sipped his coffee, smirking mischievously. 'I'll draft a suitably damning admission which you will be happy to make – all right?' He sniggered with laughter as Fletcher winced.

'We'd better go and see Winfield,' Fletcher said gruffly.

But Rylands hadn't quite finished. 'And in the circumstances, I think we'll have woman-with-rope – brackets

NOT manufactured by basket-weaving policeman – down here in the witness stand, don't you?'

Fletcher walked glumly towards the door. 'If you mean, Miss Taylor, I'll call her in the morning. Satisfied?'

As soon as the adjournment was called, Walker had sent Satchell over to Occupational Health to see Mrs Cheshire and get a report on Barridge's mental health. At that stage there was still a chance Barridge might be called as a witness but, in any case, he was going to have to put in a disciplinary report. He might as well have all the facts.

Now, an hour later, Satchell was back. Hustling up the court steps he almost bumped into a nice-looking old bloke carrying a bag of golf clubs.

'Good afternoon,' said the man politely.

Satchell could have sworn he knew him. Three steps further on it clicked: Winfield! Going to the golf course!

He spotted Walker and North standing at the top of the steps, deep in conversation. Satchell joined them, pointing after the retreating golfer.

'That was the judge, wasn't it? So he's stopped the trial?'

North shook her head. She looked mystified. 'No.'

'What? You're kidding me?'

'Wish we were, pal,' said Walker, also shaking his head. The thought of what Rylands could do when proceedings recommenced didn't bear thinking about.

'But what about Barridge and the rope? They can't go on with it now, can they?'

'Yes they can,' said North simply.

'But it means the evidence was contaminated.'

Walker laughed grimly. 'Our man tried. But that

274

bastard Rylands is something else. The judge has adjourned until tomorrow and then it's business as usual.'

'I just don't believe it,' said Satchell.

A mobile phone rang and Walker reacted, patting his pockets. 'Where's my mobile? I couldn't take it into court so I put it down somewhere.'

North pulled the trilling receiver from her briefcase. 'You gave it to me, sir.'

Walker moved to the other side of the steps, switched on the phone and listened.

'Yes? Is this an emergency? . . . This is not an emergency and Daddy's told you never to . . . No, just listen to me! This is *not* an emergency. Put your mother on . . . Look, you'll have to talk to her. I've told her not to play near the conservatory. If she's broken the glass she'll have to pay for it out of her pocket money . . . No, all right – I'll tell her myself, I'm coming home. We've got the afternoon off.'

'So what happens next? Rylands is going to use this to get Dunn off,' said Satchell.

'We may not have a trial here this afternoon,' said Walker grimly, thinking of the glass of his conservatory, 'but I've got one at home.'

'What exactly does Fletcher think he's doing?' asked Satchell.

'He's going to look a fool,' observed North drily.

'We are looking even bigger ones,' Walker said, starting down the steps. 'They're calling Ann Taylor to give evidence tomorrow.'

And he set off to hear the case against his daughter.

CHAPTER 26

IT WAS a late start in court. The judge had required Rylands and Fletcher in his chambers at ten-thirty to go through the text of Fletcher's admission on the planted length of washing line. He had OK'd it and, after an eleven-thirty start, Fletcher was now nearly at the end of his scheduled grovel in front of the jury.

'. . . I must therefore emphasize to you again,' he was saying, 'that there is no question of the defendant being responsible for this piece of washing line. Its presence in the defendant's dustbin was entirely attributable to the actions of Constable Barridge. You must exclude it entirely from your minds.'

The jury had sat through this without showing any apparent reaction. Murder trial juries don't have much experience to draw on – everything is new and more or less unexpected to them. But what they would conclude about the strength of the Crown's case once they'd started to think about Barridge's rush of blood was anybody's guess.

Fletcher had finished. He turned to Rylands and fractionally lifted the sheet of A4 on which the admission had been printed. Rylands gave an almost imperceptible nod of the head and Fletcher placed the statement with his other papers.

'Now, if I may continue with the case for the Crown, m'lord, I should like to call Ann Taylor, please.'

Ann Taylor appeared. She walked very hesitantly into court, looking around like a bird at the ranks of people, lawyers, the court officials, judge. Her head turned nervously in every direction except towards the dock.

She was sworn in and Fletcher began by establishing her address and knowledge of the defendant. Then he went on: 'Did Michael Dunn come to do odd jobs for you in your house?'

'Yes.'

'What sort of things did he do?'

'He did, well, different things. Six or seven times. Once he put up my washing line.'

A ripple of conversation washed around the court at this information and then died, quelled by Winfields' disapproving eye.

'Could you describe that washing line for us, please?'

'It was – it was blue and red. Plastic. I bought it in a local shop.'

'And when was that?'

But now the witness seemed to have frozen. So far Dunn had been looking at the rail of the dock throughout Ann Taylor's evidence. Now he raised his head and looked straight at her.

'When *was* that, Miss Taylor?'

She was flustered. She knew Dunn was staring at her. Suddenly she looked across the room and met his glance.

'Oh, um . . .' she wavered, her mouth trembling. She looked down and took a deep breath. 'It was quite a while ago. A few months. I didn't see him again for

'. . . quite a while. In fact, no, I mean, I didn't see him at all.'

Anyone looking at Pat North as she watched these exchanges with intense concentration might have been surprised to see her sudden grim smile. Ann Taylor was proving an awkward witness for Fletcher. Her embarrassment was palpable – she was blushing uncontrollably – but what was its cause? Not just the shyness of a middle-aged spinster thrust into the limelight, surely.

Then suddenly she saw it. Of course, how could they have missed this when they'd interviewed her?

She nudged Walker, leaned sideways and whispered. 'Guv, you don't suppose she and Dunn . . .?'

But Walker had got there already. Without taking his eyes off the witness, he murmured. ''Course they bloody did.'

'And what happened,' asked Fletcher, 'to this length of line subsequently?'

'It was stolen. Um, towards the end of August, I think.'

'Thank you, Miss Taylor.'

Rylands stood up slowly and regarded the witness steadily without speaking. He went on doing so for slightly longer than was polite, but not long enough for the judge to call him for intimidation. Then he said, 'When did you move into your house, Miss Taylor?'

'Two years ago in April.'

'Have petty thefts of property from your garden been a problem ever since that time?'

She nodded. 'Yes, I've had a lot of things taken.'

'Did you ever find out who took any of them?'

'Only once. The police caught some boys on the estate with – a sort of urn.'

'Some boys. Thank you, Miss Taylor. No more questions.'

'Mr Fletcher?' asked the judge but Fletcher, with no further wish to expose his witness's confusion, shook his head. Winfield glanced at his timepiece. Despite the interest of the evidence, he'd caught himself thinking over the last half hour about the crackling on the loin of pork that was at this moment sizzling and spitting in the Crown Court judges' kitchen.

'Perhaps this would be a suitable time . . . Five past two.'

As the court started packing up for lunch, North watched Ann Taylor as she left the court, then stood up herself and pushed past Walker to get quickly to the exit.

'I'm going to have a word with her.'

North caught up with Ann Taylor in the hall. The witness stand had left her shaken and she was glad to spot someone she recognized. When North suggested they sit down, she accepted North's hand steering her towards a bench beside the wall.

'There was more to your friendship with Michael Dunn than you told us, wasn't there, Miss Taylor?'

'Was it so obvious?' She was calmer now – rueful rather than tearful.

'Yes, I'm afraid it was.'

'I felt so sorry for him when he told me what a terrible life he'd had – what had been done to him. Just a little boy when it first started, six years old. But then you must know that. He said the only kindness he'd ever known was when this family fostered him – but then they sent him back.'

She paused, biting her lip.

'That's why I never reported it. But I knew it was him that took the washing line. He took the sherry too.'

'The sherry? How can you be sure?'

'My mother didn't approve of drinking and I kept some hidden outside. He was the only person who knew where it was.'

Ann Taylor smiled and North caught a glimpse of the pretty woman who was normally masked by the bleak figure cut by this disappointed spinster.

'A pointless little act of rebellion, I suppose. I hardly ever drink myself. Forgot it was there most of the time, but he persuaded me to have one with him when I was grieving for Mother. I think we must have had more than one actually because, well, you know, it went further than it should have . . .'

North touched her on the forearm. 'It's been difficult, all this, hasn't it? You should go home and rest now.'

'Will it all come out, what I told you? Will I have to . . . tell the court?'

North wished she could tell her no. 'I don't know. It may not be necessary. Let's hope not, eh?'

In the Crown Court holding cells, Michael Dunn was as unhappy as Ann Taylor.

'I don't like the way he treats people, that Rylands,' he told Belinda while he waited for his lunch. 'I *told* you I didn't like the way he talked to the old lady. He got her all upset, and don't give me all that "planks" crap either! He shouldn't have asked Ann – Miss Taylor -- all about--'

'Michael, calm down, for goodness' sake.'

'No! You lied to me. You said he would just ask if I worked for Ann. Not that other stuff.'

'It wasn't Mr Rylands who asked those questions, it was Mr Fletcher, the prosecuting counsel. I can't control his line of questioning.'

'She was nice to me, she was . . . She was a friend to me. And I won't have it. You tell him where he can stuff his planks. He shouldn't have upset her. Tell him I don't want any more of it – you hear me?'

Belinda fought to beat down the rising panic she felt. Dunn was verging on the uncontrollable. He might do anything in this mood – try to sack Rylands, make a kamikaze admission, anything. She had to take control back. She spoke as firmly as she knew how.

'Michael – Mrs Rylands is conducting your defence in the way he thinks best to secure your acquittal. You *must* trust him.'

'I did trust him – but he's messing me around.' Dunn thought for a moment, then upped the stakes a little more. 'I'm not going in the witness box to be messed around by him, that's for sure. No way. You tell him that, plank or no plank.'

There was a knock on the door – the defendant's lunch had arrived.

In the bar mess, Sinclair sought out Rylands and Waugh to tell them the bad news.

'We might have a problem here,' she told them. 'Michael's got upset about Ann Taylor. Now he doesn't want to give evidence.'

Ryland's face brightened – it didn't seem to be particularly bad news to him. 'Fine – it's just what I've been saying. We won't call him.'

Waugh frowned. He didn't like this. 'Robert, I think—'

But Rylands hadn't finished. He drew on his cigar and spoke through the gush of exhaled smoke. 'We shouldn't call any evidence for a defence. We don't have to. Their ID's worth virtually nothing. Their doll's gone out the window. We can explain all the forensic as innocent contact. Plus, they've had to admit police shenanigans. No jury's going to convict him on that!'

Derek was shaking his head. He looked like an old horse plagued by flies. 'We'll incur the adverse inference if he doesn't go on.'

'They'll do us just as much damage if he does. They'll be dragging him over the two alibi witnesses he couldn't find. Leave it alone.'

'I don't agree. Since they're trying to show a false alibi, we can show a true one. I honestly think I'd rather carry on according to plan – belt and braces and all that.'

Rylands released another stream of yellow Havana smoke into the atmosphere. Belinda looked at both men, wondering if they were going to ask her opinion. Not a chance.

'Well, you're instructing me, Derek,' said Rylands. 'But I think you're courting a risk here. That's my *considered* view.'

'I can't agree with you, Robert. I think they want to hear Michael Dunn deny it from his own lips.'

'As you wish, Derek.'

Waugh turned to Belinda. She could tell he was excited at having beaten Rylands into submission. She could almost hear him saying it, crowing about it back at the office: not many people could say they'd done *that*.

'Warn our boy, Belinda. Try to get him settled down.'

'Derek, I don't know, he was very upset.'

She looked at Rylands for support, but the silk had already mentally begun to work on how he would tackle Dunn on the stand.

'Nevertheless,' Waugh said firmly, 'he'll be giving evidence tomorrow.'

CHAPTER 27

PETER HAD slept with Anita the previous night. They'd not made love, but at least they'd shared the bed. They began to feel again like a couple who loved one another.

Peter said nothing about Anita's evidence in court until the next morning. He'd come in from the newsagent with the papers and a carton of milk and found her out on the balcony, leaning against the rail, staring down at the playground.

'You got the doll wrong,' he said.

It was just a statement of the fact.

'Yes, I know, I'm sorry Peter.'

'So am I.'

She flicked a glance at him, a fearful glance. She steeled herself. Was this going to be another shouting match, another rough house of bitterness and blame? But Peter's voice was unexpectedly soft.

'I'm sorry about the way I've been. Really. But losing Julie and then the baby, well . . .'

Anita stared at him. She opened her mouth and thought about saying to him: you? How do you think *I* feel – their mother!

She didn't say it because, incredibly, Peter was crying

and for the first time he was revealed to her as being as vulnerable as anyone else. She put her arms around him.

'It's going to be all right,' she whispered, stroking his hair. '*All*, all right. That's right. Better now.'

Later, when he'd cried all his tears and he felt lighter than he had for weeks, he said, 'Hey, 'Nita. Let's not go to court today, eh? I just can't face having to listen to them trying to get that filthy pervert off.'

The Thursday afternoon had not been quite sufficient for Fletcher to wrap his case, so the evidence of Arnold Mallory, his last witness, was heard first thing in the morning. As ever, the scientist put up an impressive performance, taking the jury through the evidence of the fibres and the ice-cream wrappers, showing them DNA profiles and enlarged microscopic prints of various fibres, all of which proved beyond peradventure that Julie Anne had been in Michael Dunn's flat.

There had been one moment of comedy, when Rylands cross-examined on the dogshit.

'Would you say, Professor Mallory, that there is a lot of dog faeces lying about on the Howarth Estate?'

'I wouldn't know. I haven't studied that question.'

'Well, would it surprise you to know that, when I visited the area last Friday, I myself came away with some on my shoe?'

'No, it wouldn't.'

'Why not?'

'Because I would say that stepping in faeces was a hazard of your profession, sir.'

The press gallery had cracked up at this and even the

jury seemed entertained. If Winfield, too, had rather enjoyed the jibe, he concealed it.

Mallory's evidence had concluded Fletcher's case and now, without any interruption, Rylands rose to present his defence.

'I call the defendant,' he boomed. 'Michael Dunn.'

The element of serenity, evident in his appearance on the first day, had deserted Dunn. His face looked sullen as he was sworn in on the Bible and afterwards, awaiting Rylands's questions, he glowered ill-temperedly down at the court. Rylands, whose ability to read a court's atmosphere was legendary, felt the tension and expectation of the entire room feeding back at his client in a loop of anxiety and resentment. He decided to get straight to the meat of the thing.

'Where were you during the day of the fifth of September last year? That's the day before you were arrested by the police.'

'I was drinking in the park with a friend of mine – Terry Smith.'

'Which park was that?'

'The Scrub—, er, Princess Elizabeth Park. It's near the estate.'

'Were you alone there, the two of you, or was there anyone else with you?'

'There was another man there, I ... I can never remember his name.'

'How long were you there, the three of you?'

'All day, from eleven o'clock until early evening.'

'What did you do there?'

'Well, we were drinking, mainly, and talking. We were talking, er, politics like.'

'How much did you have to drink?'

Rylands was keeping it simple, his voice moderated if not exactly gentle or over-sympathetic. He wanted to present his man as a victim of prejudice and circumstance, a factual matter to which he hoped the jury would respond without emotion.

'Oh, quite a lot. Lager and vodka mainly. I wasn't drunk, though. I remember it quite well now.'

'In a pig's arse you do,' thought Pat North when she heard this. But would the jury think that? Dunn was beginning to come around under Rylands's businesslike approach. He was starting to look sympathetic again.

'Did you leave the company of Terry Smith and this other man at any time between eleven and the evening?'

'No, sir, I didn't. We bought some chips and some drink, but we went together to get that.'

Rylands took a drink of water and turned over a sheet of his notes. 'Now, did you know the little girl who was killed, Julie Anne Harris?'

'Yes, I did. That is, I didn't exactly know her. I knew her brother. He brought her round to my flat a few times.'

'Was it a common occurrence for children to play in your flat?'

'Yes, there was kids there all the time. I used to leave the door open. I didn't care who was there when I was drinking.'

'Did you see Julie Anne Harris at any time, even for a few moments, on the fifth of September?'

Dunn looked at the jury. He was innocent. He hadn't done this. He was telling the truth. 'No, I didn't.'

'Are you quite certain about that, notwithstanding the fact that you were drinking on that day?'

'Yes, I am, sir.'

'Did you not, for example, see her in the playground and bend down and speak to her or take her hand?'

Dunn shook his head. 'No, I didn't. I never saw her at all.'

Rylands glanced at his notes and then at the Court Associate. 'Could I ask you to have a look at the child's doll which has been referred to as exhibit five in this case?'

The doll was handed to Dunn, who took it in his hand and turned it over a few times as he looked at it.

'Do you recognize that doll?'

'Yes, I do. I had it in my flat. I found it on the estate . . .'

By the time Rylands sat down, he felt things hadn't gone too badly. He had broken through Dunn's initial resistance to the idea of giving evidence and the brisk, factual approach had played well. Now, after a brisk forty minutes or so, it was Fletcher's turn.

Willis Fletcher was not the Crown Court diva that Rylands could claim to be but, when he turned it on, he could be severe. He decided in advance that, in this cross-examination, he would go for the jugular as soon as it presented itself.

'Is it true, Mr Dunn, that you told police in interview and subsequently instructed your solicitor that you were with three friends, not two – two men and a woman – from eleven o'clock until early evening on the fifth of September?'

'Yes, but . . . I was confused then.'

'Were you confused about the people present, or were you confused about the day?'

'It was the people I got wrong. I got mixed up.'

'Unless of course . . .' Fletcher looked at the jury and then back at Dunn. 'Unless you weren't confused at all but were in fact telling untruths about your movements on that day.'

Dunn's mouth dropped open in surprise at the sudden accusation.

'I never said anything that wasn't true. I was with Terry Smith the whole day.'

'That's not right, is it Mr Dunn? You were *not* with Terry Smith for all of that time. And you *did* see Julie Anne Harris on that day.'

Dunn mustered all his reserves of sincerity. 'I didn't, sir. I never saw her.'

But Fletcher had his prey's neck between his teeth now. He decided to start applying pressure. 'You took Julie Anne Harris from the playground. You took her back to your flat. You then—'

'That's not *true*!'

'You then assaulted her sexually and took a rope which you'd previously stolen from a lady, er, acquaintance of yours and you—'

'No, no, no. Not at all. That's rubbish. I would *never* have stolen anything from Ann—'

He pulled up short, looking around. The court was suspended in silence, its attention riveted by his outburst. He set about trying to repair the damage. 'I mean, from Miss Taylor.'

There was a further moment's silence while Fletcher waited. Sometimes it paid to let distraught witnesses have their outbursts. He cocked his head to one side as he regarded Dunn, inviting him to continue and he did.

'I mean, I worked for her. She trusted me. She knew I was somebody she could . . . you know, trust.'

The last word came out as a mumble. Fletcher cut across it.

'And you then placed that rope around Julie Anne Harris's neck and you strangled her.'

'No, no. I didn't. I never *saw* her.'

'After which you took her unconscious body to a building site and you rammed it – you *rammed* it – into a sewage pipe like a bundle of rags. And you left that little girl to die there . . .'

His mouth turned down in revulsion at the acts he was describing, he stared at Dunn who simply stood before him, drooping.

'Didn't you?'

Stunned by the ferocity of Fletcher's attack. Dunn realized at last that his mouth was open but no word was coming out. He had to reply – but what *could* he say?

'*Didn't* you, Mr Dunn?'

At last, after what seemed an age, Dunn managed to shake his head and whisper the word, the one word that his thick, dry tongue had been groping for. 'No.'

'No more questions,' said Fletcher and sat down. Immediately a rustle of speculation and comment filled the court. Dunn had not cut a convincing figure in the witness box and the public gallery was beginning to wonder if there were to be any further twists in the unfolding of this trial. The buzz died away only as Rylands once more took the stage.

'I call Terry Smith, m'lord,' he said.

Smith walked into court looking dignified and confident. He was wearing a suit, not new exactly but even if it had come from Oxfam it was clean and pressed.

He took the oath with a touch of swagger in his bearing that did not escape Rylands's notice. It was OK, even quite attractive, for a witness to display a hint of independence, but it would have to be watched. Juries hate blatantly arrogant witnesses.

'Now, Mr Smith, you are an acquaintance of the defendant?'

'Yes.'

'A friend, even?'

'We used to drink together, yes.'

'And is it true that you, like Mr Dunn, used to have a problem with alcohol?'

'Yes, I did,' said Smith, loudly. 'I am an alcoholic.'

Rylands almost stopped in his tracks. 'You are—? Do you mean you are still addicted to alcohol?'

'Yes.'

'But you're not . . . not drinking to excess at present?'

'I'm not drinking at all.'

Rylands was rarely at a loss, but at this moment he came close. 'Forgive me, Mr Smith, but if you say you *are* an alcoholic—'

Rylands was floundering when a voice from the bench came to his rescue.

'I think what the witness means,' said Winfield, amused at the chance to air his knowledge of the operating principles of Alcoholics Anonymous, with which Robert Rylands was clearly not familiar, 'is that addiction to alcohol is considered a lifelong condition, which can be managed only by total abstention.'

He looked down at Smith who smiled cheerfully up at him.

'That's right, your Honour.'

Rylands bowed submissively and said, with only the barest suggestion of amusement in his voice, 'I'm *very* much obliged to your Lordship. So, Mr Smith, you now follow a regime of total abstinence from alcohol?'

'I do, sir. I gave up last month, sir. There's no other way.'

'I see. Now, I want to ask you about the fifth of September. Do you remember that day?'

'Yes, I do, sir.'

'And did you have a lot to drink on the fifth of September?'

'Pretty much the usual. I had, um, four cans of lager, then three more. Then half a bottle of vermouth and then some vodka.'

Smith was casting his eye around the court, clocking the jury, the benches for police and lawyers and the public gallery. Finally his eye rested on the dock. He seemed to be looking at Dunn strangely, as if he was trying to remember something.

'But that wasn't an unusual amount for you. You feel your perceptions and recollections of that day were more or less normal?'

'Yes, they were. I had a tolerance for drink then, you understand.'

'And who were you with on the fifth of September?'

'I was with Michael Dunn.'

As he spoke Smith's head turned back to the dock and he pointed at Dunn dramatically. 'And I think *that* bloke was there too. He had long hair then but it was definitely him. He was there.'

Rylands's train of thought jumped out of gear. What the hell was this? Who did Smith imagine Michael Dunn was? Winfield was slow to clamp down on the buzz of talk in court. He was equally mystified.

'Er, Mr Smith,' he said eventually, pausing in his note-taking, 'let us just be clear about your evidence at this point. Did you say that that man there was with you *as well as* Michael Dunn?'

Smith looked puzzled. Had he said something wrong? 'Yes, your Honour.'

'So the man you see here in court is not the man you have referred to up until now as Michael Dunn?'

Smith shook his head. 'No, your Honour. Michael Dunn – he was the other one. At least, that was my understanding.'

The court stirred like a carpet of leaves in a gust of wind. Rylands turned to Belinda Sinclair and whispered to her urgently, '*What the hell is this?*'

She merely shook her head helplessly, the pit of her stomach turning over. She'd never shown Smith a photograph of Dunn. Stupid? No, it was bloody cretinous.

'But that bloke was there as well,' Smith was saying now. 'I remember him. He's Welsh. We were there in the park, just by the gents toilet.'

Rylands turned back to the witness, smiling tautly, and took a deliberate flyer. 'Perhaps it doesn't matter, Mr Smith, by what name the defendant was known to you, if your evidence as to his presence is the same – yes?'

Rylands was decidedly not enjoying this. He'd been forced into breaking rule one in the code that governs the examination of witnesses: never ask a question to which you don't know the forthcoming answer. He wondered if Winfield was going to let him get away with it.

He shouldn't have wondered.

'Yes,' said Winfield impatiently, 'if it *is* the same. Now, Mr Smith. Was that man also with you continuously all day?'

Smith nodded, blinking ingenuously. 'Near enough,

your Honour. He went off I think a couple of times when we ran out of drink. He was the one brought us back the sherry, as I recall. I remember the sherry particularly because the bottle was made of blue glass.'

Walker murmured to North, 'What did Ann Taylor say?'

'Dunn took a bottle of sherry, guv.'

Walker nodded and pulled out his notebook. He was scribbling a note as Winfield was saying, 'Do you have a clear recollection of how long he was absent for?'

Smith pushed out his lips. 'Not long. About . . . half an hour, forty minutes each time. Round lunchtime.'

Walker passed the note he'd written to Fletcher who read it, nodded and conferred with Griffith.

Winfield said, 'Mr Rylands, is there anything else you would like to ask this witness?'

'No, m'lord.' Almost dumbfounded, Rylands sat down.

'Has the Crown any further questions to put to this witness?'

Still holding Walker's note, Fletcher leapt to his feet. 'Mr Smith – that bottle of sherry. Do you recall what became of it?'

'Yes,' said Smith, looking pained, 'as it happens I do. It got bust before we ever touched a drop.'

Before another question was asked, Walker and North were on their way.

CHAPTER 28

THE TYRES squawked in protest at Walker's aggressive braking as he brought the unmarked car to a halt beside Princess Elizabeth Park, also known as the Scrubbery.

'We'll never find it,' said North as they strode towards the bench near the public toilet. 'It's been months.'

'Well, I'm going to have a bloody good try,' said Walker. 'Nobody's cleaned up here for a lot longer than that – years.'

There was rubbish scattered right across the park, but especially among the leafless bushes and shrubs. They started poking around in the bushes. The whole area stank of urine.

'Jesus,' said North, making a face. 'Why can't they go in the loo? It's just over there.'

'Not open all the time. Look at that – we'll have to go through the lot.'

He gestured at the litter of glass, some of the bottles intact but mostly broken, that was scattered around amongst the dead leaves.

They could hear car doors slamming and the running feet of Satchell, followed by Cranham who had been plucked from the quiet of the Incident Room. Satchell called out even before he reached them.

'I spoke to Ann Taylor. The sherry bottle was blue glass all right. She can't remember the make.'

'Right,' said Walker, as Cranham, Phelps and Brown arrived panting from their exertions, 'we are searching this area for a blue bottle or fragments thereof. If we find it, it will need to go to forensic, so handle carefully. Got it everybody?'

In court Rylands had called Mrs Wald to the stand. His performance as he questioned her was downbeat, as if still affected by the stun grenade that had been tossed into court by his previous witness.

'. . . and what did he look like, this man who you saw at five past one in the Howarth Tower – by the way, was he coming in or going out?'

She was giving her evidence with a primness bordering on the fastidious.

'I'm afraid I cannot remember if he was going into the building or coming out. But he was certainly wearing a dark overcoat and he had long hair.'

'And did you on that day see the defendant, Michael Dunn, in or around the playground?'

'No, I did not.'

'Thank you, Mrs Wald. I have no further questions.'

Nor did the Crown have anything to ask Mrs Wald so Rylands rose again and said to Winfield, 'M'lord, that concludes our case.'

Winfield beamed benevolently up and down the court. 'Thank you, Mr Rylands. Shall we adjourn for five minutes before speeches? No, fifteen minutes – to allow the jury time to muster their fullest concentration.'

'I don't understand why Smithy didn't recognize me,' said Dunn to Belinda, fretting. 'He knows me perfectly. Bastard.'

Belinda soothed him as best she could.

'It was a bit of a surprise, I'll admit. But don't forget, you couldn't remember the name of the other man yourself – and *he* probably thinks you're Terry Smith. So it seems everybody's mixed up all round.'

'So what's going to happen now?'

'There'll be closing speeches by Mr Fletcher and Mr Rylands, and then the judge will sum up. That's why you see him writing notes during the evidence: he has to summarize what's been said in court by both sides before he sends the jury out to decide.'

'But they will find me innocent, won't they? I mean it's gone well, hasn't it?'

Belinda considered. Had it gone well? Not half as well as they originally hoped. The alibi had been a near disaster, and it had been her fault. But, self-protectively, she said nothing of this.

'It's gone very well, Michael. And another thing. Mr Fletcher will close tonight but there's every chance our side will be held over till tomorrow. That's good because Mr Rylands's words will be much fresher in everybody's mind than Mr Fletcher's.'

She left him then. Michael Dunn shut his eyes. He didn't think he could bear to sit through another session of blame and denigration from that Fletcher man. Why should he? He was just a scapegoat, a sacrificial victim. The filth had only picked him up because everybody on that estate hated him.

Why should he have to put up with listening to Fletcher's lies and sneers? He was innocent, wasn't he? This whole thing was a nightmare and he couldn't wake up.

'On Tuesday,' Fletcher reminded the jury, 'I asked you to consider this case like a jigsaw puzzle. You are now in possession of the available pieces and I trust you are also in a position to fit them together to form a true picture. It is a picture of a man, Michael Frederick Dunn, living alone, who admits to holding open house for children in his flat. Dunn is a heavy drinker – a very heavy drinker indeed, one might say – and he is also a man who harbours a tendency to anger and violence which, in his pathetic way, he dares to turn only against those very children who come so trustingly to his house.

'But there is another figure in this picture, a very tragic figure. This is a little girl of very appealing appearance, five years old, whom Michael Dunn knows. But even more significantly this little girl, Julie Anne Harris, knows Dunn for she has been to his house and watched cartoon videos there. These are the people in the picture. Now let us turn to what is happening in this picture . . .'

Fletcher went on to spell out the timetable of Julie Anne's death – between her last sighting and her finding the next day, ignominiously stuffed into the sewage pipe. He recalled Enid Marsh's evidence and her positive identification of Dunn at the parade. He ran through the pathologist's evidence of strangulation and sexual assault. Lastly he laid out the forensic evidence – the footprints, the dog faeces, the soil samples, the clothing fibres, the washing line, all of which, he said, compellingly placed Michael Dunn, the rope and Julie Anne together on the day of her death.

'So much for the truth,' he declared. 'Now we must turn to the big lie: the defendant's alibi. He claims he was with Terry Smith throughout the day, and Mr Smith gave evidence that he was indeed drinking – heavily – with Michael Dunn on the fifth of September. But – and here is the crucial piece of our jigsaw ladies and gentlemen – Michael Dunn was *not* continuously with Mr Smith all day. He absented himself for two separate periods.

'When did Mrs Marsh see the defendant? At lunchtime. When did he absent himself from Mr Smith and the other man? At lunchtime. If you accept the evidence of Mrs Marsh and Mr Smith, Michael Dunn has not only *lied* to the police, as was admitted – you will remember what he said when he was first interviewed about the doll – but he has *lied* here today, on oath in front of you. You must ask yourselves what motives Michael Dunn might have for telling these lies. And it is my contention that his only possible one is that he killed Julie Anne.'

Fletcher took a drink of water and approached nearer to the jury for his final flourish.

'A jigsaw puzzle, ladies and gentlemen, often has a few pieces missing but, as I said at the outset, the overall picture can be clearly distinguished. A clear picture has, I believe, emerged from the evidence you have heard in this case, and it is one which points conclusively to Michael's Dunn's guilt.'

He sat down and immediately Winfield, as Belinda had predicted, called a halt for the day.

'We shall resume at ten-thirty tomorrow,' he decreed.

Jason wet the bed earlier than usual that night. He woke up at half past ten in a pool of his own urine and came out of the room crying for his mum.

She gave him fresh sheets and pyjamas while Peter stood with the damp undersheet, trying to dry it out in front of the bar fire in the lounge.

'Don't bother drying it,' said Anita, coming in after tucking the child back in. 'I'll put it in the washbag for tomorrow.'

'Did you get that rubber sheet like I told you?'

Anita shook her head. She took the sodden sheet and wrapped it around the pyjama bottoms. 'I meant to, I—'

Peter came up to her and held her hips. He said, very gently, 'You thought about what I said? This.' He nodded to the wet bundle. 'It's every night now. It would be better for him. They know how to handle this kind of thing.'

Anita looked at him sadly. 'You'd know, would you?' She sighed. 'Well, I spoke to Mum, but she couldn't take him.'

'Look, 'Nita. It would give you some rest. I'm only thinking of you. They've got special homes for kids like Jason. The way things are—'

'I don't want to talk about it.'

Anita suddenly turned away and walked out of the room with the sheet and pyjamas. She felt hot, suffocated. Peter stood there without moving, his fists clenched in frustration. A few seconds later Anita came back and moved over to the sideboard where the shrine to Julie was. She started to rearrange some of the photographs.

'It would only be for a short while?' she said quietly. The fight had all gone out of her. 'I mean – not for ever?'

''Course not,' said Peter. 'Just so you can get yourself back to . . . you know.'

'Normal.'

'Yeah. Normal.'

Anita was drifting out towards the hall.

'I'll call them . . . in the morning.'

In the dark at the Scrubbery the work went on under arc lights. The ground had been carefully squared off in a grid made of string, each grid sifted and any debris bagged. So far there had been no blue glass found.

But Satchell had raised a drain cover that had been hidden under a thick pelt of dead leaves. As the one with the longest arm, he was lying down, trying to search the inside of the drain.

'I can't reach any further. Should we start digging it up?'

'Yes,' said Walker decisively. The rest of the ground had turned up nothing. The drain looked their last hope.

'You sure?' said Satchell grunting with effort. 'We're talking about going into the drains now, guv. It'll be a big job and it's way past midnight . . . Hang on! I've got something. Glass.'

He pulled out a sizeable shard of glass. Eagerly Walker shone his torch on it.

'Shit!' said Satchell.

It was green glass.

'Is there a chance of more in there?' Walker asked.

'Sure, guv.'

Walker nodded grimly at the fragment in Satchell's glove. 'Well, call me colourblind, but in this light I'd swear that this piece of glass is from a blue bottle.'

A quarter of a mile away, a builders' security fence rattled slightly and, with a grating sound, a section of the galvanized mesh was pushed aside. A shadow slipped through and became a silhouette as it crossed a patch of ground lit by security lighting, then a shadow again as it passed into the gloom surrounding a stockpile of building materials.

Anita was wearing leggings, a sweatshirt and strapless sandals. She had come out on impulse, a sudden feeling that the funeral, the trial, were not enough to bring an end to the terrible event that had come along like a careering truck and smashed into her life. Out here in the dark and away from people and the bits and pieces of everyday life, there was one part of it at least that could be finished.

It was not a cold night. A breeze rustled the plane trees near the parade of shops. The remote drone of London's unceasing traffic came from almost every direction. The black rectangles of the two tower blocks, with a few lit windows, could be seen rearing up in the almost clear sky. Looking back, Anita could see her own bedroom window, from where a low light shone. Perhaps Peter was going to bed.

A dog barked and she crouched down. She knew there was a security presence on the building site now and she didn't want a big Doberman leaping at her throat. After the barking stopped she waited for a few seconds then walked rapidly towards her objective, stumbling here and there on broken bricks and chunks of hardcore. Finally she reached the pipes. But which one was it? No one had told her which particular pipe Julie Anne had died in. She hadn't known how to ask.

She fumbled around, a pallet nearly slipping on top of her as she disturbed its precarious balance. She knew only that she was looking for a narrow pipe – couldn't be the larger diameter ones at the outside of the heap. What about this one, tucked away in between? At this moment, high above Anita, a nearly full moon chased clear a bunch of cumuli and a silvery light caught the end of the pipe. Anita saw the remnant of yellow police tape on the narrow pipe and knew this was the one.

She huddled down and felt in her pocket, pulling out the small blue teddy bear that Julie had had in her bed every night of her life. Thomas had bought it at Woolworth's on his way to the hospital on the day she was born. Anita pressed her nose to the cheap artificial fur.

Reaching forward, smelling dampness and earth, she placed Julie's teddy inside the pipe and stayed crouching there, watching over the tiny object as it lay in the near darkness.

'Bye, bye, Julie,' she said. 'Bye, bye, my darling.'

Quite suddenly a wave of pain crashed through her. She may have thought she'd grieved for her daughter but she hadn't, not truly. Now, as grief mowed into her, she started to sob uncontrollably. It was like a racking physical pain crossed with terror – like the sudden cramps of sickness, the contractions of childbirth.

The moon slid behind the clouds once more. The teddy bear could no longer be seen. And Anita's low, mewing, inarticulate voice, like that of some sorely wounded animal, mingled with the sounds of the night.

CHAPTER 29

FRIDAY 22 NOVEMBER. MORNING

WALKER HAD been on to Griffith's home number as soon as he realized there was probably more glass in the drain. It couldn't be investigated at night – they needed daylight and proper equipment to excavate. They needed time.

'So will you get on to Fletcher first thing in the morning and ask him to request an adjournment? New evidence with an important bearing on the case, et cetera.'

'OK, Walker,' said Griffith drowsily. He'd been asleep for an hour. 'I'll ask but don't hold out too much hope.'

When Winfield heard in the morning that there would be a request for adjournment he immediately sent the jury out.

'M'lord,' said Willis Fletcher, 'I wonder if I might ask for a day. Some portions of a blue bottle have been discovered and there is at least the possibility that this might be the bottle mentioned by Mr Smith in his evidence. There is the further possibility that this was the bottle used to assault Julie Anne Harris.'

North, tired and dishevelled after being up all night,

was the only one in court from Southampton Street. Walker had sent her down specifically to get Winfield's reaction when Fletcher made his request. She watched him considering it, turning back a few pages of his notes to refer to some piece of evidence, probably Smith's. North saw Rylands turn to Belinda Sinclair and confer urgently. The judge cleared his throat.

'Mr Fletcher, what exactly are you asking me for?'

'A day's adjournment for the police to carry out further investigation.'

Winfield played with the pages of his notes for a few more seconds. He was no fool. North guessed the judge knew the police would want to fingerprint the glass they'd found and try and prove it was Ann Taylor's sherry bottle. But, even if they came up with Dunn's prints, what more would that prove? Everyone accepted that Dunn had used the Park. North watched closely as Winfield made up his mind. She just wished Fletcher had mentioned DNA in his request for an adjournment, to underline that they hoped to find a trace of Julie Anne on some piece of the bottle. But it was too late now. The judge was thinking in terms of the accused's traces.

'I am sorry, Mr Fletcher,' Winfield said at last. 'I imagine a person addicted to alcohol may handle a great many bottles in any one day, and I can't see any real justification for delaying the trial at this stage. We shall continue with Mr Rylands's closing speech. Ask the jury to come back in please.'

The scene at the park was now one of intense and concerted activity. TSG had been brought in with the intention of opening up the entire underground conduit while other members of Walker's team were searching the open ground and undergrowth of the rest of the park.

'I want this drain opened up. I want the pipe smashed open so we can look inside.'

'Guv, the Borough Surveyor's got to give the go-ahead.'

'Well? Where is he? He should be here.'

'Guy on the phone says he's off sick and—'

But Walker had left him to meet North, who was almost running towards them.

'He won't adjourn,' she gasped. 'They're going on and Rylands is closing now.'

'How long have we got?'

'Till lunchtime, at least. Robert Rylands would listen to himself all day – right?'

Wrong. Rylands had drastically curtailed the closure he had originally planned. He knew that Walker had got on to the scent of something. He also knew that, once Winfield started his summing up, there was not much chance of him allowing whatever that something was to be given in evidence – and none at all once the jury had begun considering their verdict.

'I said when I got up that I would be brief, ladies and gentlemen,' Rylands was now telling them. He had been on his feet all of fifteen minutes and had, to his own satisfaction, if with considerably more abridgement than was ideal, exposed Fletcher's argument on the forensics, identification and alibi to ridicule. 'You may now feel that, far from having been presented with what the Crown would say is a clear evidential picture, you have in fact been presented with a ragbag of unrelated fragments.

'And you may feel, too, that the full truth has not been heard from anyone in this case – juries, I am sorry to tell you, often do. But you must keep in mind that Michael Dunn is not charged with telling untruths. He is charged with *murdering* a little girl.

'Even if you do not believe that everything he has said, every word of the story, is true you must *not* – without more proof – convict him. For Michael Dunn himself need prove nothing. It is for the prosecution to prove their case and to satisfy you so that you are *sure* Michael Dunn murdered Julie Anne Harris.

'The evidence you have heard, you may think, falls far short of that. In fact, it falls short by such a long way that the only verdict which is in good conscience open to you is one of "not guilty". Thank you.'

As he sat down it was apparent that even the judge had been caught on the hop by Rylands's unaccustomed brevity.

'Well,' he said, 'since Counsel have been so particularly succinct, I shall begin my summing-up now, without an adjournment. And I hope I shall follow their admirable example as to clarity and conciseness.'

''Nita, get a bucket. We're going to get rid of this little bastard once and for all.'

Peter was standing in the kitchen, holding Julie's doll in his hand. Anita produced a plastic bucket and showed it to him.

'Not that one – the galvanized one. I'm going to cremate the bloody thing. Burn it.'

He started pulling the limbs off the doll, unpopping the socketed legs, arms and head and yanking until the rubber ligaments snapped. He dropped the parts into the bucket which Anita had placed on the floor and rummaged in a drawer. Somewhere he'd got some fire-lighters left over from that barbecue they'd had last summer.

'When they come for him, it's best we've got rid of it. You know his big mouth.'

Anita was peering into the bucket where the dismembered doll lay in a heap, half covered by its gleaming blonde coiffure. Peter had found a firelighter which he'd broken up and was dropping fragments into the bucket. She struck a match and dropped it on the hair, which began to burn, frizzling as the flame ate it up.

'You – get out of here! Get out!'

It was Peter yelling at Jason, who had smelt the burning nylon and come wandering in.

'Don't you touch him, Peter!' Anita yelled. 'They'll be here any minute. Jason, get your bag. Jason!'

But Jason wasn't listening. Jason had been told he was being taken away and put in a home and he wasn't listening to anything any of them said. He went up to his mum and punched her as hard as he could. His fist bounced off her arm. He struck her again in the stomach, his face distorting with fury. She tried to fend him off, flailing with her arms, but the boy hit his mother two or three times more before Peter yanked him away.

And then the firelighters caught and Julie's little doll, the one she always had with her, the doll she wanted a wardrobe of party dresses for, burned. First the hair caught light, then the pink plastic body began melting and the kitchen began to fill with toxic black smoke.

*

The TSG officers, using sledgehammers and a drill, cracked the side of the drain four feet from the raised access cover and managed to open a jagged aperture a good eighteen inches long. There had been no permission from the Borough Surveyor, the water company, the environmental health or anybody else. Walker had just told them to do it and to blazes with the consequences.

A TSG officer was now lying down, his arm inserted into the pipe up to the armpit. He had already dragged out the remains of a dozen crisp bags, cigarette packets, leaves and other debris, which lay sodden and putrid in a mound by his side. Now he was grasping some polythene waste, a carrier bag perhaps. He drew it out and held it up. Walker saw a large plastic food bag, the sort used in freezers. Its neck had been tied. It was filthy, with decayed leaves and dirt stuck all over it, but everyone could see that the contents included some broken pieces of blue glass.

'Yes! That's it!' yelled Walker. 'That's it, what we're looking for!'

The officer handed up the bag very carefully and its glass contents clinked as the sour, nutty smell of a long-spilt Amontillado sherry met their nostrils.

'The issue is not what sort of a person the defendant is, or whether he is always truthful, but whether he is guilty of the very grave offence with which he is charged.'

Winfield took seriously the injunction that, when summing up, the judge should risk monotony rather than to allow emotion to enter his voice. His own voice, solemn and deep, had little problem complying, for it scarcely fluctuated in pitch.

'It is only if you feel that his reasons for lying tend to show he committed the offence – that he has lied out of guilt and a fear of the truth – that you should consider the fact that he has lied as relevant at all . . .'

While remaining admirably impartial, the style of delivery made the speech a little difficult to concentrate on. There was a lot of coughing and shuffling in court and not a few suppressed yawns.

Walker sent the bag under police escort to Arnold Mallory and, while it was still on its way, phoned the professor with the plea – no, the demand – that he drop everything just for this one day.

'So, what is it you're sending me?' Mallory wanted to know.

'Broken bottle. Found inside a polythene bag in a drain. It just might be the one Dunn used to assault the child. You got to do dabs and DNA.'

'Do try not to tell me what I've *got* to do, Walker. I'll do what I can.'

And by the time Walker, North and Satchell arrived at the lab, Mallory and his team had already done a considerable amount. They had in fact reassembled the broken bottle.

'We're good at jigsaws here and most of the glass survived.'

He showed them the object, clamped to a stand. The fault-lines where it had shattered were traced by the pale adhesive. The only missing piece now was the neck, which Mallory slotted into its place as they watched.

Mallory then took a sheet of filter paper and folded it in four. His face set in a mask of concentration, he moved the bottle aside, then with a fine pair of tweezers he picked up the rim they had removed from the bottle. Holding this in his left hand he used the pointed corner of the folded paper and prodded at a tiny, dark clot of matter that was stuck to the rim. A little of it came off on the paper.

Carefully, Mallory opened the paper and laid it flat on a glass petri dish. He opened a bottle of liquid chemical and, with a dropper, allowed a single drop of the chemical to fall on the sample. A colourless, circular, damp stain spread out around it. Replacing the stopper and returning the phial to its rack, he selected a second phial and repeated the procedure. This time the dampness instantly turned a bright pink.

Mallory released his breath in a wheezing exhalation. He glanced round the circle of expectant police officers.

'It's blood,' he declared.

Walker took a moment to register. Then he was patting his pockets as if for a cigarette but, in fact, for his mobile phone.

'I can't tell you yet,' continued Mallory, 'whether it's the girl's blood or not. The next step is to establish a blood group . . .'

Walker looked at North. He must have left his mobile in the car.

'Get me through to the Crown Court – quick! They'll have to adjourn now. We can't try him twice. We got just the one shot at him.'

At about the time that the pink stain appeared on the filter paper in Mallory's lab, Winfield wrapped up his speech and invited the jury to retire. As North's message came through for an urgent word with Clive Griffith, one of the ushers was being sworn in as jury bailiff.

'. . . I shall not myself speak to them, nor suffer any other person to speak to them, save to ask them if they have reached their verdict.'

Griffith read the note and slipped out of court. But by the time he had used his phone, he knew it would be too late.

North snapped her mobile shut and returned to the lab bench. Mallory had just completed a test on a second sample from the bottle.

'Look – same blood group,' he said. 'AB negative. We're getting there!'

'Too slowly, I'm afraid,' said North grimly. 'I've just spoken to Griffith. Jury have retired. We're too late.'

'Shit!' Walker clenched his fists. 'What's been going on down there? Rylands must have been going for the fastest fucking closing speech on record.'

He was patting his pockets again and this time pulled out a packet of Marlboro. He said to Mallory, 'You will finish the tests, won't you? Whatever happens, you will do the DNA?'

Mallory smiled. He was a selfish man but towards this impassioned policeman he felt as near as he ever would to kindliness.

'Yes,' he said, 'I'll finish them. We all want to close the book on this, don't we?'

At the Howarth Estate, Enid Marsh's curtains twitched. She had no idea what was happening today at the trial. Television had an item on the news at dinner time, all about closing speeches, summing up. But for all she knew it was finished by now.

On the back of Enid's door, the outfit she'd worn hung waiting for Ivy or Karen to come and claim it. When they did, Enid had planned a little tea party. There were some ginger nuts she could put out. It'd be nice to have a cuppa and a chat. But nobody had been near Enid since Wednesday except Mrs Wald and she didn't know any more than Enid about the trial. All the rest of them had stayed away.

She looked out across the estate. There were some people making their way out of the tower block below and going away towards the car park. One of them was that boy Jason, little Goldilocks's naughty brother. He was being almost dragged along by his fast-walking stepfather, Peter James. Enid knew him, she'd seen him in court.

Looking back she saw the boy's mother coming along behind them, accompanied by a stranger. This was a woman with short grey hair, a pale mac and a shoulder bag. She had social worker written all over her. The mother carried a suitcase. Where were they going?

Enid watched on. At the edge of the playground, the mother handed the suitcase to the social worker, who nodded her head and set off after Peter James and the boy, catching them up just before they reached the corner. She must have said something because Enid saw the kid twisting round, turning and trying to catch a glimpse of his mother. He called out, 'I want my dad! I want my dad!'

Enid could see Anita standing there, watching the departing group with her arms folded. What Enid could not see was that Anita was weeping. 'Taking the little bugger away,' Enid thought. 'Good riddance, he'd always been trouble.'

Anita didn't call out. She just watched as Jason was helped into a car. At length a car engine started and Enid saw the young woman, the mother, give a solitary wave. Peter James came back, took Anita in his arms, and walked her back to the tower block and out of Enid's sight. She never heard the mother, who had lost not one, but two of her babies, but was now sending a third away. Never heard the plaintive cry, 'I love them.'

CHAPTER 30

FRIDAY 22 SEPTEMBER. AFTERNOON

COLIN BARRIDGE sat on the bench in the Dockland Light Railway station, impervious to the trains going by. An hour ago, when he had walked out of Southampton Street in his civilian clothes, he had ceased to be the bearer of Her Majesty's warrant. He no longer stood – or sat – in the office of a constable. He was no longer, even, in possession of the uniform of the Metropolitan Police.

This was what suspension meant. It also meant hanging, didn't it? If this was the old days, it could be Michael Dunn who was going to be hanged, not him.

The jury were out on Dunn. He knew that. They would probably decide the guy's fate before the day was out. His own fate would take weeks to resolve. There would be a disciplinary hearing, evidence, admissions, severe words, tears. His dad would tell him I told you so. His mum would cry and cry and not be able to face the neighbours.

Barridge didn't want to go home to his mum and dad. He wanted to stay here. He was drained of all desire, all need, all ambition. Once he wanted to be a Detective Inspector in the Flying Squad. Now he watched train after train go by without feeling the need to move at all.

Belinda Sinclair went down to sit with her client in the holding cell. She didn't actually have to do this but, then again, there was no one else to do it.

There wasn't much conversation. Dunn was staring at the wall, humming to himself and smoking a roll up.

'How long's it been?'

'Fifty minutes.'

'Oh.'

He went on humming tunelessly.

Looking back on the trial, Belinda saw that her original faith in Dunn's innocence had been rather dented by Smith's failure to recognize Dunn in court. But this damage to her belief in the case had been mitigated by her own sense of responsibility for the cock-up. If only she had shown Smith a photograph of Dunn . . .

Michael had been terrible in the witness box yesterday. She couldn't understand it. He seemed so bright and personable, now that he'd got the booze completely out of his system. But as soon as Fletcher started to question him about things that happened on the day of the murder he'd fallen to pieces. Started looking shifty and, then, guilty.

Fletcher had been bloody good, better than flash-Harry Rylands, if truth be told. Their brief had been a little *too* brief in his closure, to her way of thinking. Then she remembered that Rylands's advice had been not to call Dunn at all. God, how she wished they'd taken it.

'How long now?'

'An hour.'

'Christ! How long's it going to take them to realize the police case is a load of shit?'

'An hour is nothing, Michael. Sometimes the longer they stay out the better.'

Was that true? In an apparently cut-and-dried case a long jury deliberation would be interesting. But was this such a case? Once she had thought it was.

'But you do think they'll acquit?' asked Dunn. He sounded pathetic now, forlorn, but that was hardly surprising in view of the fact that the sword of Damocles hung about an inch from his cranium. She remembered the last thing Rylands had said to her outside the court.

'We've got him off, Belinda, never fear.'

She replied, 'Or you'll eat your wig, Robert?'

But Rylands had just smiled enigmatically before waltzing off to the bar mess. Instead of telling Dunn about this exchange, she just said weakly, 'I sincerely hope so.'

He was kicking the leg of the table now, swinging his foot against it rhythmically. She wondered what would happen if she asked him to stop, but he stopped of his own accord anyway. There was something he wanted to ask her.

'Could I . . . well, let you know how I get on . . . afterwards?'

She looked sharply at him. What was he asking?

'Yes, of course,' she said guardedly. 'You have the office address.'

'Yes, I know. But you might leave, get married or something. So I thought . . .'

Jesus, she thought. He's asking if we can meet.

Before Belinda could cut him short or devise a reply, there was a sharp rap on the door. A voice called, 'Jury's back!'

She looked at Dunn, wishing he would hurry. His eyes were saucers but she was oddly unmoved.

He said, 'I'm ready now.'

'Come on, then.'

It was a long wait for the jury and all the time a long, long private prayer by Helen that they would find him guilty. She wanted it over and it wouldn't be, for any of them, until then.

Helen was the only member of the family who'd been at the trial every day. Some of the estate people had come in for the first and last days but, out of the relatives, even Thomas hadn't showed up for the verdict. Surely they'd have given him compassionate leave if he'd wanted it?

Helen understood why Anita stayed away, but she was adamant about her own presence. There had to be someone the same flesh and blood as little Julie present at the— She nearly thought the phrase 'at the death'. The end.

What had been hard, especially, was listening to the pathologist and then that fat scientist telling what happened to Julie. They used that clinical, soulless language. From time to time, in the middle of it all, Helen had been flooded with memories of Julie alive. Sitting alongside her on the bus, bouncing on the cushion and talking away to herself, or to complete strangers.

'My dad's a soldier,' she'd tell them, 'but he hasn't got a gun.'

And at Helen's house after television: 'I'm going to be a dancer on *Top of the Pops*, I am. I can do disco, granny, look.'

And at bedtime, when Helen babysat one time: 'I love you best, granny.'

In court she'd had to listen to how her granddaughter's tongue had protruded in death through clenched teeth. How her neck had been injured, the ligature indenting the neck tissues. How she had been bruised, how she'd been penetrated . . .

'I love you best, granny.'

Helen studied the members of the jury as they filed in. They knew the verdict but you couldn't read anything in their faces, just seriousness. Michael Dunn never glanced at them. He stood in the dock, staring at the floor. Everyone in court could see how he was shaking.

'Would the foreman please stand?' asked the Clerk.

The woman who had led the jury into court rose to her feet. She was middle-aged and seemed to Helen educated, intelligent.

'Madam foreman, answer this question – yes or no. Members of the jury, have you reached a verdict upon which you are all agreed?'

The woman glanced at the judge then back at the Clerk. She nodded her head. 'Yes.'

A perceptible thrill of anticipation flickered through the court then died to a profound silence. The Associate gave a slight cough.

'Do you find the defendant guilty or not guilty of murder?'

There was a second's pause in which nobody breathed. Then the jury foreman herself took an intake of air so that she could speak up.

Helen continued to hold her breath.

*

Peter and Anita sat in their living room. Tony, his nappy a little sodden and its adhesive tabs coming adrift, was crawling around the floor with a long string of drool dangling from his mouth. Anita was impervious. She stared at her fingernails.

'Come on, love, we talked it through. I know it's hard but it's best for Jason, it really is. *They* even said so.'

He lapsed into silence when she didn't reply or react. He sat watching Tony, who was trying to stuff a plastic block into his mouth. There would be a time to talk about Jason but this wasn't it.

The phone rang. Peter looked at his watch and then at Anita and she was looking at him now with eyes wide. They both knew.

'This is it,' he said.

He went out to the hall and picked up the phone. Anita heard his responses, very quiet and short. She bit into a fingernail and it gave way with a loud snap. She heard Peter ring off.

He didn't come back instantly but lingered in the hall. She waited, holding the fragment of nail between her tongue and teeth. What was he doing?

Then Peter was standing at the door. His pose was easy, casual, leaning on the door frame. He was smiling when he gave her the news.

'It's guilty.'

Anita covered her face with her open hands and leaned forward to rest her head on her knees.

Belinda was shocked and Rylands too, perhaps, though he didn't show it. There was no one in court to boo or hiss the verdict. In the public gallery they celebrated.

Rylands was on his feet. Winfield raised an eyebrow.

'There is nothing I wish to say, m'lord.'

Rylands knew there was no point in mitigation, as Winfield was about to underline. The judge nodded to the associate who told Dunn to stand.

'Michael Dunn,' intoned Winfield, 'as I am sure you know, you have been convicted of an offence for which the sentence is fixed by law. There is only one sentence I can pass and I sentence you accordingly to life imprisonment. In this case, I recommend that the minimum term to be served should be no less than twenty years. Take him down.'

In the bustle and disturbance of the courtroom that followed the verdict. Belinda Sinclair had the odd feeling that she was in a kind of bubble of silence. It wasn't shock or disbelief – she'd always known this reverse could happen – but a sense of detachment. She'd done her best but it hadn't been enough and the jury had gone against her. Who was she, even silently, to criticize them?

She felt a tap on her arm and it was Detective Superintendent Walker. She looked at him without warmth.

'Miss Sinclair, I would like you to know this. We found something, a blue glass bottle. Tests carried out today have shown that traces around the neck of that bottle are blood – the same group as that of Julie Ann Harris – AB negative. It's a rare group. The bottle was found in a drain in Princess Elizabeth Park.'

She listened to what the policeman had to say. And as soon as she heard it she realized that she already knew this. At some point, in the last twenty-four hours, she had unconsciously changed her mind about Dunn. And she realized that, if she had been a member of the jury, she would have found him guilty too.

It was her duty to go down and see her client now. She made her way into the basement and was shown into Dunn's cell, where she was told she had a couple of minutes. The transport was about to leave.

He was sitting slumped at the table. Belinda took a packet of Silk Cut out of her bag and lit a cigarette, dropping the almost full packet on the table in front of him. He raised his head and looked at her. There were traces on his face of very recent tears.

'What happens now?' he asked. He looked more lonely, more pathetic than ever, but it didn't touch Belinda even remotely. Not any more.

'New evidence has apparently been found by the police, Michael.'

She looked steadily at him. She accused him with her eyes and he shrank away.

'But I didn't do it. I didn't. I *swear*. I'm innocent. I didn't do it!'

A security Guard hammered on the door – the transport was ready to take him. Belinda stood by the door as it swung open, then swivelled just for a moment.

'Yes, you did, Michael,' she said. 'Oh, yes, you did.'

And she went out to look for some fresh air to breathe.

Walker was not a man to go fishing. He liked an occasional day at the races or a football match with his boy. But even then he never truly relaxed. On the day after the trial was over he'd managed to get some tickets at Spurs for the Newcastle match, but the whole ninety minutes he was thinking about Mallory and what the DNA would turn up next week.

Dunn was safely banged up but Walker knew in his

heart that they'd been lucky. There had been as many defensive mistakes as he was watching out there on the White Hart Lane park. Barridge's own-goal should have finished them completely but then Rylands put Dunn in the witness box and the Crown got one back. Fletcher was brilliant. Terry Smith's failure to recognize Dunn was important too, but in the end it probably came down to the jury's intuition.

Which is why he still needed that DNA. The very last thing Walker wanted was a rematch at the Appeal Court with Rylands. Or a book exposing a so-called miscarriage of justice. Or – God forbid – a *Rough Justice* TV documentary.

He'd told everybody to take a long weekend but he himself was back at Southampton Street on the Monday, trying to disentangle the chaos that was the budget for this investigation. The station Super wanted the Incident Room packed up by the end of the week, before which he had to make sure all the reports, statements, notes and audio tapes were tagged, docketed and filed along with car logs, overtime sheets and all the other paper palaver that had to be placed these days in long-term storage. Then there was the Barridge disciplinary to deal with. He'd spent all Sunday morning writing his report.

Now Soames, Harrold, Macklin, Grimes and the others were humping files out to the AMIP van in the loading bay, while he furiously double-checked Mallory's invoices. He was cursing forensic's meticulous paperwork, with every procedure, even the most minute, timed and charged for, when the phone at his elbow sounded. It was the man himself on the phone.

'I thought you'd like to be the first to know, Detective Superintendent,' boomed Mallory.

'You've got the DNA tests?'

Walker signalled to North, Satchell and anyone else within earshot. They instantly stopped what they were doing and gathered round. The room fell silent.

'I have indeed,' said Mallory. 'I have carried out the tests you requested on the blood deposits found on the bottleneck from Princess Elizabeth Park.'

'And?'

'They prove without doubt that it was Julie Anne's blood on the bottle. Congratulations, Mr Walker. You got the right man. There'll be no books by leftie journalists trying to make a name for themselves. There'll be no shouting about a miscarriage of justice. You'll have my full report in the morning. Goodbye.'

Walker hung up and told his team. The cheer rattled the Venetian blinds and somebody's cap crossed the room like a frisbee. Walker went up to Pat North – he knew Satchell too well to say anything to him. He shook Pat's hand.

'Congratulations, Detective Inspector,' Walker said. 'I look forward to working with you again.'

Pat North smiled. Yes, she thought, it's been a hell of an experience, and some of it was just plain hell. But she was glad she'd done it.

CHAPTER 31

DUNN KICKED at the hard-backed solitary chair, then he picked it up and threw it against the wall. He tore the mattress off the bunk-bed. He tried to rip it apart, then he couldn't get his breath. He kept on clawing at his shirt where the tie they had given him had been. Even the open collar felt as if it was throttling him. It was the terrible rage of his own guilt slowly surfacing, and he began punching himself, slapping his face, ramming and hitting his head against the wall as the rage consumed him in agony. It was the same rage that had swept over him when she, Julie Ann, had begun screaming, she'd almost bitten his fingers as he closed her mouth. No one had heard his screams, so she had to be silenced, just as his abusers had silenced him. A rope round her neck, not too tight, only to frighten her, then he would carry her some place, hide her, as they had hidden him. There was nothing wrong. He hadn't done anything wrong. He had done nothing that hadn't been done to him. He was innocent. He didn't do it. His voice screeched into a howl. Spittle formed in globules at the edge of his mouth as he repeated over and over again: 'I didn't do it. *I didn't do it.*'

His own voice sounded hollow and empty, as empty as Belinda Sinclair's beautiful eyes when she had left his cell.

325

'I didn't do it. *I didn't do it.*'

There had been such pain, such disgust in her soft, musical voice. It had cut through his brain like a jagged knife.

'Yes you did, Michael. Yes you did.'

Michael Frederick Dunn was guilty but he was also a wretched, tragic young man who had learned as a child that if he did cry out no one would listen. No one had ever been punished for their crimes against him. He had never understood that what had been done to him was wrong . . . until it was too late.

All Pan Books are available at your local bookshop or newsagent, or can be ordered direct from the publisher. Indicate the number of copies required and fill in the form below.

Send to: Macmillan General Books C.S.
               Book Service By Post
               PO Box 29, Douglas I-O-M
               IM99 1BQ

or phone: 01624 675137, quoting title, author and credit card number.

or fax: 01624 670923, quoting title, author, and credit card number.

or Internet: http://www.bookpost.co.uk

Please enclose a remittance* to the value of the cover price plus 75 pence per book for post and packing. Overseas customers please allow £1.00 per copy for post and packing.

*Payment may be made in sterling by UK personal cheque, Eurocheque, postal order, sterling draft or international money order, made payable to Book Service By Post.

Alternatively by Access/Visa/MasterCard

Card No.   ☐☐☐☐☐☐☐☐☐☐☐☐☐☐☐☐☐☐☐☐☐☐

Expiry Date   ☐☐☐☐☐☐☐☐☐☐☐☐☐☐☐☐☐☐☐☐☐☐

Signature   _____

Applicable only in the UK and BFPO addresses.

While every effort is made to keep prices low, it is sometimes necessary to increase prices at short notice. Pan Books reserve the right to show on covers and charge new retail prices which may differ from those advertised in the text or elsewhere.

NAME AND ADDRESS IN BLOCK CAPITAL LETTERS PLEASE

Name _____

Address _____

_____

_____

_____

8/95

Please allow 28 days for delivery.
Please tick box if you do not wish to receive any additional information. ☐